Henchmen

by
Eric Lahti

Dedicated to my wife and son.
And everyone who ever wanted to do the wrong thing for all the right reasons.

Also by Eric Lahti

Arise

Steven was having a pretty good time for a guy who helped release a captured god. He had a nice place in Colorado, a pretty girl sent him a picture of herself in a bikini, and he had neighbors that left him alone. Everything was looking pretty good until he woke up to find two people in his house that were planning on killing him; one was an old coworker and the other was an old boss.

From a shootout in Tijuana to a strange base in Dulce, New Mexico, Steven has his hands full just trying to stay ahead of the god that wants him dead, the girl he's finding himself more and more smitten with, and new allies that may or may not be up to any good.

Some days it's hard to be one of the HENCHMEN

Contents

01 | It Doesn't Stay In Vegas

The desert outside of Las Vegas, Nevada is brutal under the best of circumstances. If you never leave the casinos you never really get a feel for how damned hot it gets out here. Heat mirages are rising from the endless asphalt ribbon and even the buzzards have decided to hang out somewhere that doesn't suck as much as this place does.

"We're in." Frank's dour voice over the comm link seems nonplussed to the point of being bored. There's a hint of derision there, too, like he can't believe he just wasted his skills on *this place*.

"These computers blow," Jean pipes in.

Frank and Jean are our infiltration team. Jean's the bouncy one. He thinks he's tough but he's really not. Frank's blasé demeanor isn't an act; he probably really is bored right now.

"Good job, gentlemen. Now drop the security grid and get me into their secure area. Let's get Jacob out of the heat before he melts," Eve says beside me.

Eve takes up most of the free space in the front seat of the van. She's our nominal leader, although we tend to be more democratic than most evil outfits. She's every inch a supervillain, seven feet tall, blonde and dangerous. I've been working with her for about six months and she's still largely a mystery to me.

"Roger that," Jean says happily. "These guys are set up with DOD specs, so it'll take me a minute."

I look over at Eve and grin. "I'll bet you five bucks it takes him ten minutes."

"I'll take that bet," she says.

Three minutes later Jean's voice comes over the comm. "I'm through. Want to know the formula for New Coke?"

"God, no," I say and hand Eve her fiver.

"Good," Jean says. "They don't have it here. I'm looping the security cameras and routing all the phone calls to this room. Ready Frank?"

"I'm good to take caller number five," Frank says.

"Holler when you're all set, guys. Jacob, make yourself scarce," Eve says into her mike. She looks at me and adds, "I hope Jacob's mob buddies made good ID badges."

"Does yours list your height?" I ask, peering at my ID badge. My picture looks like me, but I hate looking at pictures of myself so my eyes slide across it. My brownish hair is poking out in the picture and I look like I have rings under my eyes. Photogenic, I ain't.

"Yeah, seven feet," Eve says. "I got a good picture. How's yours?"

"Looks like me, I guess," I say. "I always thought I was taller than five eleven, though."

She peers down at me from behind her aviator specs. "Hmph. Try getting on a plane or finding a dress when you're seven feet tall."

"I'm nowhere near seven feet tall and I've never shopped for a dress," I tell her.

"That's probably for the better," Eve says with a laugh.

"Steven, Eve," Frank's voice says. "I think we're ready for you guys. We've got the codes. We'll meet you at Special Projects, it's up on four. Just follow the signs when you get in."

"Nice work, gentlemen," Eve says. She slaps my shoulder and it immediately goes numb. "Let's roll."

I shift the van into gear and the old Ford shudders and groans at having to move *and* run the air conditioner full blast. It picks up quickly and we can see our destination sparkling in the distance. It's a trick of the light, you know, the sparkling. The buildings are actually dirt brown; it's a combination of the heat mirages and the gypsum in the stucco that makes them glitter.

On the way in, a man on a loud Harley blows past us going the opposite direction. The pipes on the damned thing rattle the windows when he rolls through.

We both tense up slightly when I turn the van in. This is the first of many places where we can get ourselves in trouble.

The sign on the road simply said Anodyne. That's it. No "Anodyne Engineering" or "Anodyne Advanced Projects" or "Anodyne: Spending Your Tax Dollars", just *Anodyne*. If this was on the Vegas strip the name would make you think it's a bar or some damned hipster nightclub.

It's neither of those things, obviously. Well, duh, I guess. Why would someone put a nightclub a fifty miles from Las Vegas? Anodyne is a research and development facility that specializes in various types of advanced armor. Most of their stuff will never get used by the military – the cost is too high and Congress critters don't like to pay to keep soldiers alive – but with any luck we'll find a good use for some of it.

Anodyne is comprised of five buildings on about a two acre lot. The whole place is xeriscaped so there's no grass, no trees, and the only shade is a tin roof propped over some poles. There's a chain link fence with concertina wire covering the entire facility and we have to go through a guard post to get in.

The guard is a fat, bored looking guy dripping sweat and sucking down a Coke like it's a lifeline. He's got about a dozen empty cans all neatly stacked in the window and dark shades on. This is the type of person who believes with all his heart that he's the toughest son of a bitch on the block. The problem is he just can't convince anyone else of it. Even with his dark shades he looks like a kid who found dad's body armor.

"ID," he says when I roll down the window.

Our fake IDs will probably hold up, but it's best to not push our luck too far. If we can get this guy flustered he won't spend much time checking up on us.

"Good afternoon to you!" I say cheerfully. "We've got this load of parts here for Vandelay."

He peers at me over the tops of his knock-off Ray-Bans. "IDs. Now."

I think I'm supposed to be intimidated.

Eve leans over me and asks, "Where do we drop these off, man? They're for Vandelay. *Vandelay.*"

"I still need to see your IDs," the guard says, looking at our van. "And I don't recognize the company you work for. What is 'Rodeo Drives'?"

"Did he not hear Vandelay?" I ask Eve.

"I think he missed it," she replies. She looks straight at the guard and slowly says, "These are for Vandelay."

"I know who Vandelay is. What does your company do?" the guy asks.

"Rodeo Drives makes custom hard drives. We've got a stack of them in the back for Vandelay. Come on man, they're heat sensitive and it's hot as balls out here," I say.

Eve is practically leaning on top of me now, trying to crawl over my seat to look out the window. When she turns to face me we're nearly nose to nose. "What the fuck is going on here?" she asks me.

"No idea, boss."

She looks back out the window. "Do you know what will happen if Vandelay finds out you're fucking around like this?"

"Ma'am," the guard stammers. "I need to see your IDs."

"There is nearly a million dollars' worth or of custom hard drives in a box back there. They are extremely heat sensitive. Do you want to be responsible for toasting a million dollars' worth of drives?" Eve asks, enunciating each syllable of "million dollars."

I didn't think it was possible, but it looks like the guard is sweating more.

"If I show you my ID will you open the gate so we can take this stuff to Vandelay?" I ask.

"Yes, sir. I just need to see your IDs and, if everything looks good, you can go through."

All his attitude is gone now, replaced by a gnawing sense that he's in trouble with Vandelay. A million bucks is probably more than this poor schmuck will make in his entire pathetic life. I show him my ID and Eve passes hers along. The guard looks at them, skimming them quickly until he hits Eve's height.

"Are you really seven feet tall," he asks.

"Not when I'm wearing high heels," she responds with a wink.

He has no response to that so he hands the IDs back and the gate slowly rumbles open.

"Bro," I say, "we won't tell Vandelay if you won't."

He looks both shocked and relieved at the same time. "Deal," he says. "Park around the back."

Some mafia-made ID badges and a little fast talk and we just drove a van into a secure location. Want to know why border security will never work? That's why right there. People are too easy to fool and too easy to befuddle.

Vandelay, by the way, is Peter Vandelay, the Vice President of Advanced Projects at Anodyne. We found his info on the company web site and decided he'd be a good name to drop. He looks like a total cock in his picture, so if he gets busted it's probably just the eternal principle of Karma catching up with him.

* * * *

Around back is a loading dock with a single guy holding a clip board and frantically waving at us. I park the van in front of the loading dock and get out to chat with the guy. As soon as he sees me get out he rushes over and waves the clipboard like it's a magic wand. He's chanting some incantation in corporate speak about matrices and appointments and deliverables.

"Hold up, buddy," I tell him. "I've got the paperwork right here."

Eve gets out and as soon as she walks around the van the guy's eyes lock on her and his jaw nearly hits the ground. She glares at him while she opens the back of the van and pulls out a large box marked fragile.

"*Mikä on hänen ongelmansa?*" she asks me.

"God dammit, I told you we use English on jobs!" I snap at her. "How fucking hard is that?"

She gives me the evil eye and glances at the box in her arms. The guy with the clipboard is getting even more distraught.

"Where do these go?" I ask the guy with the clipboard.

He stammers something that may be an apology or a question.

"The box." I say slowly. "Where does the box go?"

He frantically starts flipping through the papers on his clipboard and muttering to himself.

"I … I can't seem to find a delivery scheduled for today," he stammers.

"Vandelay!" Eve snaps.

"Yeah, they're for Vandelay," I tell him. "Where is the fucker, anyway? He's supposed to sign for this shit."

"Vandelay," Eve says again.

"We get it!" I yell. Pause a beat while she looks appropriately brow-beaten. "I'm sorry. It's the heat."

Eve rattles off something in whatever language she was speaking earlier. Whatever she said it sounds vaguely apologetic.

I turn to the guy with the clipboard. "So, where's Vandelay's office? She can just carry it straight up."

"I'm sorry," he says with his nose buried in the paperwork. He flips the pages back and forth as if somehow, magically, the proper entry will appear. "I just don't see you in here. I'm afraid I've got to call someone about this."

I absolutely cannot let him go any further with this. "Pal, look. We're late, we're hot, she's crazy, and the drives will get totally fucked if we have to wait any longer. Point us at Vandelay's office and we'll put in a good word for you."

He pauses, sweat dripping off his forehead. I can see the gears turning in his head, slowly grinding away at the problem. He's like everyone else that works at places like this: terrified of getting in trouble but desperate for a little positive attention.

"You're not up to anything, are you?" he asks.

"Just delivering some custom drives, bro," I tell him.

"Drives are getting hot, bro," Eve echoes in some non-distinct accent.

"She's carrying nearly a *million dollars'* worth of custom drives that absolutely do not tolerate heat," I say. "And it is fucking hot out here, man. Look, I've got paperwork signed by Vandelay himself."

I hand him the faked paperwork for a fake order from a fake company and he examines it closely looking for reasons to turn it down. We made the order form from scratch by modifying some company's sample purchase order request forms. Vandelay's signature was actually on the Anodyne website, probably to make him look more real, so we copied it and pasted it in place and made it look like a faxed order form.

"Vandelay's office is on three. Go through the loading dock, take the elevator and follow the signs," the guy says. "You'll put in a good word for me?"

"Buddy," I tell him. "You just saved this rat hole a cool mil. I'll shout it from the rooftops, if you think it will help."

Eve is already walking through the loading dock. Those long legs of hers mean she can cover a huge distance in a short period of time and I have to run to catch up to her. The Chairman of Loading Dock Operations watches us, biting his lip and twitching his pen nervously.

Don't worry, pal. We won't mention you.

* * * *

Vandelay's office is on three, but Frank said he and Jean would meet us on four, so I push four and we keep our fingers crossed. Some places require keycards but Anodyne apparently doesn't believe in tiered security and the button lights up.

At least the elevator is cool. God damn it was hot out there.

The elevator hits four and the doors open to relatively quiet hallway. A couple people are bustling around and we get some strange looks, but no one challenges us. I grab a random guy by the shoulder and say, "Which way to Special Projects, pal?"

He barely looks up, just points generally down the hall and says, "That way."

It's always the same in places like this. Office workers treat the delivery people like they're beneath contempt and not even worthy of acknowledgement. That's why you put on coveralls and a name badge if you want to disappear in this type of crowd.

We keep going in the general direction of "that way" and eventually come to door with a plaque that reads "Special Projects" on it. The door opens easily and we find Jean and Frank already rolling up our prize.

Eve sets the box on the table and opens it. Frank and Jean quickly fill it with rolled up pieces of brown and black canvas. Fold the top of the box and we're out the door in less than five minutes. Frank and Jean go right, Eve and I go left.

We need to kill some time before we head back, so we drop down to Vandelay's office. Like I suspected, he's a prick.

"Why would I need a million dollars' worth of hard drives?" he asks when I show him the purchase order.

"I don't know, pal, I just deliver these things," I tell him.

"I'm not your pal and I didn't order these. Take them away," he says.

Who says "Take them away?"

I give him my best hang dog expression and he brushes it off like it's nothing. "What about this purchase order?" I ask.

"Not my circus. Not my monkeys," he says. "Now, get them and yourselves out of here or I'll call security."

I nod to Eve and we take off with Vandelay glaring at us. At the elevator we look back down the hall and see the World's Greatest Jackass stalking off to some meeting or another. We're already out of his sight and out of his mind.

At the loading dock the guy is still there waiting for us. His face drops when he sees Eve still carrying the box. "How did it go?" he asks.

"The first drive he pulled out was busted," I tell him. "Unreadable. Now we've got to take the whole lot back and test 'em. Got a card, man? I'd like our people to communicate directly with you to schedule the return. Avoid any problems, you know."

Everyone in a place like this has business cards, and he hands me his with a conspiratorial smile. "I'll take care of it. Did Vandelay say anything?"

Eve has loaded the box and is already waiting in the van. "He said you did good, buddy. Let's keep the synergy going, bro."

He's still smiling when I put the van in gear. There's a dumpster around the side of the loading dock and I park next to it and make a show of throwing out some trash. When I get back in the van, Frank and Jean are in the back.

Captain America in the guard shack waves at us as we go past.

Down the road a bit is a rest area and a lone biker is waiting for us. I pull up next to him and roll down the window.

"Get the stuff?" Jacob asks.

"We're loaded up," I say.

"Dinner's on me guys," Eve says. "Jacob, it was your plan, where do you want to go?"

I'd expect a scruffy looking biker-type to say he wanted steak or burgers or to just go to a bar so it nearly blows my mind when he says, "I know of a sushi place I'd like to try."

02 | Sushi At The O.K. Corral

Sushi, by any measuring stick available, is the food of the Gods. Gods of all shapes and sizes love sushi, because sushi is made of tasty fish, rice, and true love.

Sushi is an absolute unto itself, and the only thing that can improve it is the display, which is why it's considered bad form to alter the presented sushi in any way other than eating it and enjoying it. Technically speaking, you're not even supposed to add extra wasabi, but that's a convention that Americans tend to ignore. Also, if you're going to dip your sushi in soy sauce, it's best to flip it over and dip the fish side, not the rice side.

Personally, I don't give a shit about the rules of eating sushi. I just want to eat it and I regularly add extra wasabi and dip my rice in the soy sauce because I love sushi so damned much.

This hidden gem of a sushi bar is tucked away up north of the Strip in the downtown area of Las Vegas, away from the hustle and bustle of thousands of people desperately trying to lose their money.

This little place is comfortably quiet, and decorated in the typical understated and elegant way that only the Japanese can pull off. It's a single room, separated into two private areas by rice paper walls with silent sliding doors. We've got tatami mats embedded into the wood floor, arranged in an approximately perfect rectangle, with cushions on them for sitting or kneeling. We're each holding a cup of warm sake and generally basking in the glory of a job well done.

From time to time, a young lady comes in and refills our cups and leaves again without saying a word. I guess in a place like this, it's expected that you will ask for whatever you want, and if something is not up to snuff, you will tell someone. Now and then we hear the guys in the other room - a group of boisterous, tatted-up Japanese guys - laugh or grumble something in their native tongue. That's the thing about rice paper walls: they look fantastic when done correctly, but don't do much to block sounds.

"Man, I have never had so much fun doing donuts in someone's parking lot as I did there," Jacob says, retelling his part in the heist. "I started out by hauling ass, and I mean hauling ass, around the whole complex. Kicked up dust, revved Becky to max, shot a bunny. It was a blast."

This place has rules about dress and Jacob's normal taste in clothing runs perpendicular to their dress code. Motörhead T-shirts and ripped jeans may be haute couture in the real world, but sushi is not the real world. It took some work, but I finally got him into a leather dress jacket and some black pants that weren't too "faggoty."

Becky is his bike, by the way. I think he just likes to be able to say he's going to ride Becky all day long.

"While they were watching this nutter," Jean says, "we had to run through the dust, cut a hole in the fence, and crawl through. I burned my hand on the road."

"If it's any consolation," Eve says, "the air conditioner in the van wasn't very good."

"Yeah, I've got to say I was somewhat less than comfortable," I add. "And that water? Hardly cold enough for my tastes."

"You two suck," Frank says. "I don't think I'll ever get all the dust out of my underwear."

"I'll wash you later," Jean says with a lascivious smirk.

"You guys did nice work on the security systems," Eve tells them. "You deserve some shower time together."

Frank blushes and Jean raises his cup to Eve. "Your wish is my command, boss," he says.

"Right," Jacob says, "like you needed her order to wash him off."

"Care to join us?" Frank asks.

"No offense, bro," Jacob says, "but, and I'm saying this as a friend, your tits aren't big enough for my tastes."

Eve rolls her eyes at that. "Jacob, as big as you are, I doubt there's a pair of breasts out there large enough for your tastes."

"There's a chick with double Fs," Jacob replies. "A man could have a great time with those."

"Is she a porn star?" I ask.

"She's an actress," he says.

"Does she work in porn?" Frank asks.

"She's an actress in adult-oriented entertainment," Jacob says.

"What's her name?" Eve asks.

"Delilah Jugsaplenty," Jacob replies sheepishly.

"She's a porn star," Franks says.

"She's not bad," Jean quips.

"What?" Frank asks him.

"See!" Jacob says with a laugh.

"I saw one of her movies once," Jean says, "she knew her way around a man."

"I cannot believe you watched a movie with a woman name Delilah Jugsaplenty," Frank says.

"It was one of her earlier works. I learned a thing or two from her," Jean tells him.

"Like what?" Frank asks.

"Oh, dear God," Eve adds.

"Like last night," Jean says.

In my best Takei voice I say, "Oh, my."

Frank's anger immediately dissipates and a deep ruby color rises slowly from the collar of his gray shirt. "Oh," he says.

Jean pats Frank's arm. "It was just research."

"It worked," Frank says quietly.

Jacob laughs out loud, a full belly laugh from a man with a sizable belly. Think of Jacob as a hairy version of Santa Claus and you'll get a good idea of the laugh.

Frank is gently leaning against wall and Jean is resting on him. They're both wearing suits, probably picked out by Frank. Of the two of them, Frank's the only one with any fashion sense. Frank *wears* a suit, Jean just puts one on.

Frank is medium height, medium build, medium brown hair, brown eyes. The man blends into every situation like wallpaper. Jean is shorter, with dark hair and a slightly chunkier build. He blends in like hotel wallpaper.

"What was the name of the movie?" Eve asks and immediately takes a sip of her sake.

I stare at her in wide-eyed wonder and then wonder why I should be wondering anyway. Sure, she's a full seven feet tall, can bend rebar with her bare hands, and can probably drink minor gods under the table, but there's someone for everyone, right?

Eve is sitting cross-legged on a cushion, dress draped over her lap, holding her sake and trying to look more like some kind of contemplative blonde Buddha than some warrior who's looking for a little nookie.

"*Balls Out 14*," Jean says.

"Because 13 left so many unanswered questions, right?" I ask.

"I never saw 13," Jean says.

"How did you follow the plot of 14 then?" I ask him.

"I'm sure it was a lot more of 'insert tab A into slot B'," Frank says.

"There were some nice tabs," Jean tells him.

"What about the slots?" I ask.

"Meh," Jean says.

I can't be certain, but I think Eve may be mentally taking notes.

* * * *

This is a different kind of dining than most people are used to. In a normal restaurant, you walk in, get escorted to a table, are handed a menu (or menus), order what you want, eat, dispute the bill over some triviality, pay the bill, and leave feeling you just had a great meal.

Here, we paid ahead of time and are ready to accept whatever the chef decides to send our way. A place like this, you either love sushi or you're boned.

This place specializes in *nyotaimori*, or body sushi, whereby one eats their sushi off the body of a naked woman. It's delightfully decadent.

Because typical *nyotaimori* is just *so last year*, and someone needed to up the ante, this place serves sushi on the body of a naked woman tied to your very own table. It seems gimmicky, and I imagine the restaurant is probably trying to capitalize on the BDSM trend that hit America recently, but the sushi is apparently excellent. And how often do you get a chance to eat sushi off the naked body of a woman strapped to your table? Just be sure to read the fine print that says if you touch or harm her in any way the restaurant gets to mount your head on the wall of shame and toss the rest of you in the dumpster out back.

So far, no one's head is mounted on the wall of shame.

Just so you know, the idea of *nyotaimori*, or body sushi, isn't a terribly traditional Japanese thing. It apparently has happened, but not all that often. Truthfully, even the Yakuza reportedly view *nyotaimori* as being too over-the-top, and vaguely excessive. When the Yakuza, those kind fellows who tattoo their entire bodies with images of Japanese demons, consider a pastime to be over-the-top, you know you've got something that will fit in nicely in America. How a country that introduced tentacle porn to the world can gaze down its collective nose at *nyotaimori* is beyond me.

It's because this restaurant specializes in body sushi that the room currently has no table.

The door quietly slides open and our waitress enters, pushing a low table on wheels. She places it precisely in the middle of us, and we all lean back and enjoy the spectacle.

Most people have never the opportunity to eat sushi off a naked woman, let alone one tied to a table. If you ever have the opportunity, take it. I assure you it's worth the effort.

The young woman's raven hair is shining and draped elegantly across the table. Her wrists and ankles are held with black leather cuffs hooked to the table. Her lips are bright red and her eyes are covered with a black blindfold. She's absolutely still, save the gentle rise and fall of her breasts as she breathes. I imagine she's trained to not squirm, lest she disturb the sushi feast adorning her body. It's obvious by the relaxed way she lies on the table that this is not the first time she's done this.

I like to think she's excited by this treatment, but the truth is she's probably thinking about her history test tomorrow, or how she's going to spend the sizable chunk of change she's being paid for being a BDSM centerpiece for the evening.

In Las Vegas you can get anything with enough money.

"She's buff." Frank says.

"Yeah," quips Jean. "Can we keep her?"

The barest of smiles crosses the girl's lips.

Jacob snorts. "Like either of you would know what to do with her."

"Oh," Frank says with a grin, "I think either one of us could bounce up and down on her for thirty seconds and then go catch the rest of the game."

The girl on the table giggles quietly, trying hard to not move.

We all dig in, taking care to not poke her with our chopsticks as we snatch up delicious fishy treats. The sushi is, of course, excellent. The salmon nigiri melts in my mouth like butter made of fish. It's like the foie gras of the undersea world.

A gentle knock at the door ruins the moment.

After a beat, the door quietly slides open and an older, well-dressed Japanese gentleman stands there. Actually, he doesn't just stand there - he consumes the space. Have you ever met a person, not necessarily a large person, but a person who simply owns every moment, and every space? That's what this guy did: he owned the moment. I really wish I could do that sometimes, but I usually just rent the moment and eventually get kicked out for having too many parties.

"Please accept my apologies for this intrusion," he says, "but there has been an unfortunate mistake."

"What mistake?" Jacob asks, still chewing.

"This girl," the man says, "is supposed to be in our room."

I glance down at the girl on the table. Suddenly, she's tense and looking panicky. I lean in close to examine a piece of sushi on her chest, just a normal guy ogling the scenery.

"Do you know this guy," I whisper to her.

"Help me," she whispers back. Good enough for me. I sit back up, a delightful piece *tako nigiri* in my chopsticks.

"Well," I say, "that's a problem, because our dinner is on her, and she's kind of stuck to the table. So I think we'll be keeping her for the duration."

"Besides," quips Frank, ever the diplomat, "we don't like to share, so piss off."

"This is most unfortunate," our mystery man says, "but we will replace your dinner at our cost. We specifically requested this girl be in our room tonight."

"You can't have her," says Eve. She's got that look she gets just before things start exploding, like storm clouds brewing in her gray eyes.

The well-dressed man frowns slightly and makes a quintessentially Japanese grunt that can mean anything from approval to general disdain, depending on the circumstances. Considering these circumstances, I'm leaning more toward disdain. I'd like to learn to convey displeasure with a grunt.

"You can give her to us and get another dinner, or we can take her."

Jacob jumps up, sniffing a fight on the air. "You can take my dick, fuck nuts," he growls.

I'm not sure what that means, but I sense this will probably not go down well. Since there aren't a whole lot of viable defensive positions from the floor, I start to get up, too. If I can hold back Jacob and the well-dressed man, this situation might not go completely bonkers on us, and we can finish eating.

Before I'm all the way up, a knife is in our guest's hand and heading toward the girl on the table. He's dropping into a kneeling position because the table is so low. I don't have time to stop the knife, so I choose to move the target. I manage to kick the table a bit; just enough that the blade misses her face by an inch or so and embeds itself in the wood of the table.

Again, not a whole lot of good workable positions here. He's on one knee, trying to pull the knife out. She's stuck to the table and there may be more trouble headed our way. With his usual panache Frank defuses the situation.

"Her hair is amazing, it would be a pity to get your blood all over it," he whispers, his straight razor held right up to our guest's throat.

"You don't know what you're doing. You will all live to regret this," the man says, straightening. He bows slightly and backs out the door.

"Get her off there," Eve says to me, "This could get ugly."

Part of me wants to say something witty like "But I'm not done eating yet", but I know it would go over about as well as that time my mom put rattlesnakes in her teacher's desk at school.

Five extremely well-dressed, irate-looking gentlemen show up at our door. The one in the middle is holding a very blinged-out gun, pointed straight at Eve.

"Apologies again," says the guy with the gun, "but we did warn you."

"Last chance," says Eve, calmly pouring more sake, "walk away, and I'll forget all about this trespass." She hasn't even bothered to get up yet.

The guy with the gun hisses. "I will happily shoot you, *baishun.*"

If I had any doubts about what we were dealing with, they left when I looked at this dude. His tie was off and his shirt was unbuttoned to his navel. Normally, this implies a love of the disco era, but when I saw his chest was covered with tattoos, my heart sank. I just wanted dinner. Now I've got a fight with the local Yakuza. The leader glances at the unbuttoned one. His face isn't easy to read, but I would say he doesn't seem happy.

Eve has a similar unreadable face, which usually means she's dropping all pretenses, and things are about to go nuclear.

Jacob is grinning from ear to ear, spoiling for a fight.

Eve calmly rises to her feet and says "Fire away, if you think it will help."

The guy's eyes get big as she stands up and he mutters something about *kaiju.* She stares him down, but he refuses to budge. His ego is on the line. If his companions went back to their mutual friends and told them a woman stopped him, he'd never hear the end of it. You can see in his eyes that he's made the decision.

He fires four rounds from his gun, and every single one of them hits her in the chest. Eve staggers back, the girl on the table screams, and our gunman's buddies laugh out loud. I reach down and grab another piece of sushi, since it's obvious I won't get to finish my dinner.

Eve's dress has four holes in it, which has got to be a wicked pisser since she paid so damn much for it. The laughter slowly subsides when they realize she's still standing. You always hear guys talking about how tough they are, and how they took a bullet and still managed to slaughter the other guy, but it's all bull: you get shot, especially with a large enough round, and your ass is going down. Deep down, everyone knows this, even if they don't like to admit it to themselves. And yet, here's this blonde woman still standing.

Eve puts a finger through one of the holes in her dress and curses under her breath. When she looks up her face is hard. The guy with the gun shoots her twice more – like he's thinking the first four rounds were somehow defective, and the next two will magically stop this tall blonde woman when the others wouldn't. Eve staggers back a bit, but looks up and meets his eyes. He unloads the rest of the magazine into her.

When she hears the click of the empty gun Eve smiles, steps out of her shoes, and launches herself at the guys in the doorway.

The guy with the gun and the older guy are smart enough to move out the way, but the rest go down like bowling pins. Eve stands up, holding one of the guys by the throat. She squeezes, looks at him briefly, and then chucks him down the hall like he's weightless. Bending down slightly Eve grabs the edge of the table, tells Jacob to catch, and casually flips it up. To his credit, Jacob manages to catch the table.

The guy with the unbuttoned shirt has dropped his gun, but he still smells dangerous. There's a dancer's quality to his movements, and his face is completely unconcerned. He's got the look of a guy that's been in lots of fights before and walked away unscathed. His eyes say he's looking forward to doing it again. He's the type that's learned to not rely on a weapon, so when the gun goes away it's an inconvenience to him, but not the end of the world.

Frank takes a lightning-quick swipe of his razor at the button-less wonder. A flicker of movement and blur of motion, and I expect to see the normal spray of red, but Disco Inferno is faster than anyone expected. He twitches back, casually watches the blade swing by, and flashes out a kick that sends Frank falling back.

Someone's been keeping up with his Karate lessons.

The old guy is between me and Karate man. I know I shouldn't kick an old guy, but he's in the way and I'm hangry. Plus, he's a dick. I kick the leader in the side of the knee. As he stumbles toward me I catch him with my right hand, pull his head back and slam a half-fist into his throat. He's an older man, but he's already proven he carries at least one knife and is willing to stab a helpless woman in the face, so I'm not going to play around with him. As he staggers, I push him into Shirtless, and they both tumble through the paper wall. To his credit, the tatted-up Yak doesn't waste time feeling hurt, just springs to his feet like it's the most natural thing in the world.

"Jean, get her off of there!" I yell pointing at the girl attached to the table. I need Jacob in the fight, and he's holding the table up with one hand and trying to unhook her with the other. Jean fights with the clasps. The girl is struggling, which isn't helping things.

"Calm the fuck down! He's trying to get you out and you are not helping!" I yell as I notice Jacob pull his gun out. Eve is somewhere in the hall crushing skulls. Jacob starts firing and things ramp up quickly.

"Jesus, Jean," I yell, "the cuffs are just held in place with carabiners. Just unhook them." I swear some people just have no experience with strapping women to tables. What is this country coming to?

Disco Inferno notices me and throws a punch. Damn, he's fast. I barely manage to block it and the second punch is coming my way. Dodge it, and there's a thrust kick coming in. Slip past and barely catch that before he tries to chop me in the philtrum. I turn my head just in time to avoid the major damage, and catch the chop in the side of the head. Not pleasant, but better than the alternative. I manage to throw and land a punch to his head, and he staggers slightly.

Jean has finally gotten the girl free, and she's working on getting the leather cuffs off while Jean checks Frank's ribs.

Here's the thing about real fighting: Someone takes a solid blow in a sensitive area, and they're going down for a bit. In movies, someone takes a knife to the lungs and keeps on fighting like it's nothing. In MMA someone can take a serious blow and keep on fighting, but they're professional athletes, and you can see solid blows take their toll even on professional fighters. A solid kick right into the middle of the ribs by a trained fighter can push your ribs into your lungs, which usually causes a severe case of not being able to breathe. Frank will be okay, but he's out of it for a bit.

A knife stabs through the wall next to Jean and slides down, razor sharp and shining. The fifth guy has reappeared. Apparently, he was smart enough to think outside the box a bit. As Americans, we're used to the idea of solid walls, and thus never really think of going through them. Not all Japanese walls are paper, but paper walls are definitely more prevalent in Japan than they are in America, and the guy holding the knife and grinning like a maniac exploited a loophole in our thinking.

He tries to stab Jean in the neck, but the girl pulls Jean out of the way. Frank swings his straight razor up and into the guy's balls. I cringe a little.

The look on the fifth guy's face is priceless. It's a mixture of surprise and extreme pain at the sudden and unexpected field castration.

By now the girl has unhooked herself and has pushed the table aside, her face a mask of murderous rage. Everything stops. There's nothing like an angry naked woman to bring things to a standstill. Disco Man looks her up and down, a leer growing on his face.

"It would have been easier if you had just stayed down," he says, pulling a tanto out of a hidden sheath in his suit jacket. The blade is a perfect example of Japanese steel artistry, stunning and austere at the same time. "Just come quietly and we won't have to turn this rape into a murder." Like a sadistic bastard, he holds his knife out toward her, hoping to terrify her. It's not working.

Her right leg, cuff and all, flashes in arc and drops on his wrist. You can almost hear the bones break and the knife clatters to the floor. Before he can react, she's slammed the same foot into his stomach, bending him over. She plants her foot forward, closing the distance between them, then punches him in the back of the head with the left and uppercuts him in the side of the head with right. He falls into the table face first, right into a nice piece of *amaebi*.

"Groovy," Jean says. He's impressed.

Jacob hands her his jacket. It's like a tent on her, but she takes it anyway and smiles a quick "thank you" at him.

The leader is trying to get up now, pulling himself up on the wooden doorframe. He looks terrified and crazy, cursing in Japanese. Eve is behind him, taking the time to smooth out her dress. She has all the time in the world, and she knows it. She taps him on the shoulder and he turns and looks up at her. Eve casually grabs the top of his head and his chin and twists his head completely around. His vertebrae shatter and his muscles and tendons stretch and rip. He has enough time to look shocked before the signals from his brain stop making it to the rest of his body and he collapses in a heap on the floor.

"Well," says Jean. "That just happened."

03 | Sake, Anyone?

"What?" I ask, "What just happened?"

I look at the girl, wrapped up in Jacob's coat, calmly unhooking the cuffs on her wrists and ankles. She's about 5'7" or 5'8" and completely unashamed at her lack of clothes. She's got the body you would expect of a woman who makes a living being naked: a toned hourglass figure, with a light tan and no tan lines. Muscles ripple as she moves. She's strong – mentally and physically - and her eyes are focused on the task at hand. "Who are you?" I ask.

"Jessica," she says, not looking up.

"You're welcome." I snarl. I'm always keyed up after a fight, and grumpy because I don't know what just happened. And I'm hungry. And hangry. And fuck everyone. "What the fuck did those guys want with you?"

"She has a nice rack," suggests Frank.

"It's not that great," says Jean.

Jessica looks up, an eyebrow cocked up.

"They're nice," says Eve, "but no one starts a gunfight over breasts."

"They do in Texas," I say.

"You know, guys, I'm right here." Jessica looks around, dropping her wrist cuffs. She bends over to take the cuffs off her ankles.

"Jacob," Eve says, "please put your tongue back in your mouth."

Jessica tosses the cuffs on the floor. "They grabbed me a few months ago, roughed me up and took pictures of me lying in the gutter all busted up. They said they were sending the pictures to my dad. Apparently he knows something they want to know."

She walks over the guy she lumped and kicks him in the ribs.

"This piece of shit said he'd rape me next time if my dad didn't get back to them. I guess tonight was the night they chose."

"What do they think your dad knows?" Eve asks.

"I have no idea." Jessica responds. "They never said, only that if 'daddy didn't come through, his little girl was going to get hurt again'."

She puts her foot on his throat and Eve steps over to gently guide

Jessica away before she kills the guy.

"What does your dad do?" Jean asks.

"Not sure. Something classified. He'd always say he couldn't talk about it. I used to fantasize that he was in the Mob, but he just worked for the Department of Defense. I found his ID once while he was asleep. It just had his picture and his clearance level on it."

"What clearance did he have?" I ask.

She rolls her eyes up like she's trying to remember something. "Uh, TS, Q, SCI. There were others. I don't really remember."

"That's pretty high clearance, if you're remembering correctly." Jean says.

TS is Top Secret, Q is the DOE version of TS, SCI is Sensitive Compartmented Information. SCI has been likened to a sort of "above Top Secret," but that's really not the case. It's really more like a specialized layer of security on top of TS or Q.

"Why do they think he would help them, even with you on the line?" I ask.

"I don't have a clue. They never told me anything other than they'd cut me up bit by bit if I talked." She shudders a little and gets ready to kick Disco Inferno again.

"Wait." Eve pulls her back. "I really want to know what's going on, and we need him alive to find out what they wanted."

"What do you mean, you need him alive?" Jessica asks.

Jean's looking around for unspilled sake. "It's hard to torture – sorry, 'perform an enhanced interrogation' - on someone who's dead," he says.

Jean finds a bottle that still has some sake in it, and pours it into a cup. He drains the cup and smiles that sad smile that he gets when serious thoughts hit his big brain. "Fuck it," he says. "Torture requires a living, feeling participant to work. The more he can feel the better. For us, anyway."

"Yep," Frank quips, looking a bit brighter. Frank's interest is piqued, as is mine. "It's not often you get to find out something that could be really interesting."

Frank's a bit of a sociopath, but he's our sociopath, so it's fine.

"Where does your dad live?" I ask.

"Albuquerque. It's in New Mexico," she answers.

"Yeah," Jacob rolls his eyes. "We know where Albuquerque is."

"We're going there tomorrow," quips Jean.

"At any rate," Eve looks around, "we had best get out of here, before someone finds all the spilled food, broken walls and dead bodies.

Let's grab this guy and find out what he knows."

She's right. There's sushi and rice everywhere. The wall has a missing panel where someone cut through it. The room and hallway are dotted with three unconscious gangsters and a couple of dead guys. Fortunately, what happens in Vegas stays in Vegas. Also, we've already paid the bill, so we can sneak out the back and blame it on someone else.

Jessica takes a look around at us, Jean drinking sake, me pacing, Frank wiping his straight razor on someone's jacket, Eve still standing with a bunch of holes in her dress. "Who are you people?" she asks.

Jean raises his cup to Jessica and says, "We're the bad guys. Pleased to meet you, ma'am."

"I'm still hungry," Jacob says, rubbing his stomach.

Jessica informs us there's an In 'N' Out Burger a bit north of here that's probably less busy than the one on Tropicana.

04 | Crunchy Rolls

The upstairs is trashed, but the building is surprisingly quiet considering the fight that just went down. We weren't exactly loud, but fights tend to make some noise, and a fight in a restaurant freaks out the staff almost as much as yelling about the finger in your soup - especially a place as clockwork as this one. Speaking of which, our waitress had been by every 15 minutes without fail since we got here, but it's been over 20 minutes and she hasn't refilled our sake. Pity, really. I could go for some sake right now. Might take the edge off looking at the dead guys on the floor.

Eve looks around, grimaces then sighs. "I can't take you boys anywhere."

Frank's getting onto his feet. Jacob is rifling through pockets and stealing watches. Jessica looks a little lost, but that's not too surprising considering what just happened. She's not shaking or crying, though. Jean offers her a drink of what little sake we have left and she drains it straight out of the carafe.

I want a cigarette. One of these fuckers must have one. I quit, but this is looking like a good time to start back up again.

"Jacob, any of these bastards got a smoke on 'em?"

He pauses for a second, thinks, and then strolls over to the old guy. "Yeah, this guy had some. Never heard of the brand, though. Sakura, huh. What the fuck? Want his lighter, too?"

"Sure, why not," I say, although I'd probably get a longer jail term for smoking in public than for assaulting an old man. What the hell. We've already done a number on this place and I doubt I'm going to make it much worse.

The cigarette isn't bad. The lighter is nice.

"Grab that dude with the open shirt." Eve says, glancing around. "Make sure the rest are dead. We need to make this look like a gang tussle gone bad."

"What about her?" Frank is pointing at Jessica. "Can we keep her?"

"Yeah, she's coming with us."

"Do I get a say in this?" Jessica asks.

"Sure," replies Eve. "You can come with us or we can leave you here. These guys still have friends."

Jessica nods. I imagine this this not a good headspace to be in. Either you go with a bunch of strangers who, admittedly, saved your ass, and hope for the best. Or you stay and hope the dead guys' friends don't wonder how you survived.

We pack up and start out. I glance back at Jessica. She's standing there wrapped in Jacob's jacket and staring at a wall. "Smoke?"

"No, thank you." She responds distantly. "I need to get my stuff and some clothes. There's a changing room downstairs. Can we stop?"

"Yeah, sure," I respond.

We move out and hope no one notices.

On the way down the stairs, we find out why things are so quiet: our waitress is sprawled on the stairs with her blood sprayed on the walls. It looks like her throat was slit and she was shoved down the stairs, probably before that old guy first showed up. He almost certainly meant to kill us all anyway.

Downstairs, behind the kitchen, is the staff changing room. The kitchen staff is dead, the head sushi chef is dead, the hostess is dead, the rest of the staff is dead. There's a woman face down on the floor, blood dripping out of the hole in the back of her head. If we turned her over there wouldn't be a hole in the front of her face. A silenced .22, the choice of weapon for thugs who kill waitresses and sushi chefs, uses a subsonic round that rarely goes out the other side of the head; it just bounces around in the skull until it runs out of energy.

"She was supposed to be in your room." Jessica looks distraught. "She wanted to switch because those other guys tip so well, and I didn't want to be in their room. Now she's dead."

I decide now is not the best time to explain about how subsonic .22 rounds work.

Their break room is a typical shabby employee break room, with the requisite laminated posters about minimum wage, OSHA regulations, worker's compensation, etc. I wonder how OSHA would handle complaints about a night like tonight.

Jessica unlocks her locker, grabs her stuff and disappears into the bathroom and comes back a few minutes later dressed in yoga pants, a t-shirt, and a pair of Vans. She doesn't seem distraught anymore. Just empty and broken, with an expression that says "I don't care anymore." She'll fit right in with us.

Frank wanders in, looking quite pleased.

"The schedule for tonight only has two entries, us, and those other guys. That's why there was a minimal staff on tonight. There's no walk-in traffic here. No one's coming in until morning at the earliest."

Jean pipes up, "We're all good."

Jacob looks around. "Since we've got the place all to ourselves, is there any food around here? I mean, it's a fucking restaurant, right? There's gotta be something to eat around here." He's not pleasant when he's hungry. I think it may be a blood-sugar thing, but he won't get it checked out because going to the doctor would be damaging to his masculinity.

"If no one's coming in, we can work here tonight." Eve is smiling, which is never a good thing when she's talking about work. "Find me a sturdy chair and a lamp. And there's got to be a pair or two of handcuffs or rope or something similar in this place."

"Jessica, you said there was an In-N-Out around here?" I ask.

"Well, yeah. It's a few miles or so from here," she replies.

"Good, let's get some food. It's going to be a long night. Have you got a car?"

"Uh, yeah. It's out back," she says, looking a bit lost.

I know what's going to happen next with Disco Inferno. I've partaken in it in previous misadventures, and it's never pretty. It's also hard work. People always get all gooey about the tortured, but no one stops to think about the emotional toll it takes on the torturer. At any rate, I doubt Jessica's ready to see this, and I know we're all hungry.

"Right, then," I say. "Let's go get some big-ass burgers and big-ass fries and big-ass shakes for everyone."

Jean somehow found a sturdy wooden chair hiding out in a corner, and is dragging it into the center of the room as I escort Jessica out.

05 | Tasty Burgers

Jessica's car is a typical college car, nothing exciting, but it has a stereo and the windows roll down, and that's more than I can say of some of the cars I've owned.

Her AC works, which is a good thing in summertime Vegas. Did you know that human testicles have a regular temperature of about 94 to 96 degrees Fahrenheit? True story. As such, when the temperature gets that hot you can quite truthfully say it is hot as balls outside. Vegas in the summertime is much hotter than balls.

All In-N-Out Burger joints are the same: they're bright white and red, and the interiors are sterile to a fault. The food is always good, and there's almost no one ever holding up the line trying to figure out the menu because there are only, like, three things on it.

We order seven Double Doubles, seven large orders of fries, and seven large chocolate shakes. This is America in one greasy wrapper, a tasty amalgam of awesomeness.

"Who's the seventh order for?" Jessica asks. They're the first words she's spoken since we left.

"Jacob likes to eat," I tell her. "I once saw him put down a large pizza on his own and start eyeing everyone else's food. Trust me: it's best to keep him fed."

It's only a few minutes' drive back to the sushi house, and Jessica's quiet the rest of the way in, like she's driving on autopilot. I don't know if this is normal – for her, or for anyone. I'm not sure what it would be like to have to integrate into our little group as a complete stranger. Frank and Jean were already working with Eve when I showed up, and I didn't have any problem fitting right in. Jacob would be happy doing anything that allowed him to stick it to the man, and bust skulls. None of the rest of us are exactly normal, so a regular person may be a little at sea right now.

We get out of the car and I tell her to wait a minute. "You OK?" I ask her.

She wraps her arms around herself and shrugs, head held low. "I don't know. I don't even know how to answer that."

"So, you're saying your average night doesn't entail being assaulted, watching a bunch of strangers casually kill another bunch of strangers, finding out your coworkers have been executed, and eating In-N-Out in a parking lot with strange man you don't know?" I ask.

"Yeah, basically," she mumbles, her expression lightening a bit.

"You need to get out more often," I say, digging into the burger bag. Hunger may be the best gravy, but when you put that gravy on a tasty burger? Perfection. "Here, have some dinner. Everything looks worse when you're hungry."

She toys with the burger, fumbling with the wrapper. It's probably best to wait to go back in. And, frankly, I am hungry. I hope they finish up soon, though, or their shakes are going to be melted.

"These guys are going to keep after me, aren't they?" she asks.

"More than likely. There aren't a whole lot of Yakuza in the States - they tend to work mostly in Asia - but they're expanding. Even if these guys are the only ones here in Vegas, I'm sure they've told someone else what was going on. Even if the rest of their clan doesn't know, it's a sure bet another clan does know. So, yeah, I'd bet someone else is coming along." It's hard to say this, but it is the truth. There is honor at stake. These guys will keep coming back forever to go after a girl whose dad may or may not know anything of any value.

Her shoulders slump a bit. Yesterday she was getting paid a bunch of money to hang out naked and think about what to do later in the day. Today - well, not so much. This is one of those moments that will stretch to eternity and be miserable the whole time. I never know what to say in times like these. How do you tell someone it'll be OK, when it's patently obvious that it probably won't be? It's a simple fact that if she stays here, she's dead, and not in a good way, especially considering what's happening to that Yakuza gangster right now.

The back door bangs open and Jacob comes swaggering out. He's grinning ear to ear and his knuckles are raw and bloody. He sees the bag and makes a beeline to us. He grabs a shake and downs it in one gulp.

"Hey, Jessica," he says casually, like they're old friends. I swear, nothing fazes this guy. He's the type of guy who could grin his way through a car crash, crawl out and calmly pop open a beer and wait for the cops. He's shoves a burger in his face and tries to talk at the same time.

"So mumble grumble fumble jap wumble chomp chomp chomp tough mumble mumble teeth and mumble fuck."

"Jacob, chew your food then talk," Eve says as she walks out, Frank and Jean in tow. Frank's wiping his hands and face on wet-nap he found in the kitchen. Eve grabs a burger and a shake and leans against the car. She takes a bite and a drink to wash it down. "Jessica, your father worked in some dark areas, right?"

Jessica nods. "I don't know exactly what he did. He never talked about it. I haven't heard from him in years."

"Those Yakuza fellows don't know exactly what your dad was up to, but it involved something that scared the hell out of the people working on it. Apparently the government buried the whole thing and tried their best to forget about it," Eve says.

Jean gulps down a bite. "You know, when the people who brought us such wonders of modern life as VX gas, nuclear bombs and enhanced interrogation techniques are scared of something, it must be delightfully terrifying." He's grinning like a kid who just found out he's getting a new bike.

"Do you know how to get hold of your dad, Jessica?" Eve asks her, a serious bent to her eyes.

Jessica finally takes a bite of her burger, swallows it. "I'm not sure. Like I said, he disappeared years ago. He got offered a job in New Mexico and took it. He was going first, and then we'd follow about six months later. We got regular messages for the first month. Then they started getting more and more erratic. About six months in, he just sent a message telling us not to come. Mom assumed he was having an affair. We didn't know how to get hold of him, and we never could get anyone to answer us."

"He's in Albuquerque. Or was. Our friend in there had his last known address," Frank says.

"Well, why the fuck would they go through me to get to him? I haven't seen him in years! I don't know what he's doing! I don't know a damn thing! Why not show up at his doorstep and beat the shit out of him and threaten him?" Jessica's angry now. Most of the time when you hear someone talking about their pathetic daddy issues, they're just being pricks. She actually does have daddy issues, and justifiably so, from the look of things.

"They couldn't go after him directly. If they tried to go directly after him, DSS would've taken them out without thinking about it. All he'd have to do is tell anyone in the government, and all those crazy Yakuza fuckers would've woken up in Cuba. Or worse. DSS takes secrets very seriously, and guards them jealously, especially the dangerous ones. Look at that guy, Snowden. He's done his damage, but they've got to grab him just to send a message to anyone else who's thinking about doing the same thing. If they'd gotten to him before he spilled the beans, they'd have crushed him like an ant for even thinking about it. The gangsters had to get your dad to come to them willingly," Jean says excitedly. It's nice to see him get excited about things.

DSS, in case you're wondering is Defense Security Service. They're the branch of the government that's responsible for maintaining secrets.

"Shit," Jessica grumbles. "I always assumed my dad just got tired of his old family and decided to get a new one." She sticks a fry in her mouth and chews it.

Eve sighs. "Here's the hard part, kiddo. They'll keep coming for you. We couldn't give you to a bunch of degenerate gang-bangers, and we probably saved your life, so we're responsible for you to some extent. You can stay here if you want. Tell everyone we killed those guys and let you go because we weren't interested in you. Give them names if you want - it doesn't matter. We'll help you out however we can. The problem with this idea is they will still come after you for other reasons. Or, you can come with us. Whatever you choose, it has to be your choice."

"What's up with the guy inside there?" Jessica asks her.

"He's messed up. He might live, he might die." Eve says, "He's alive right now. Live or die, he'll never be the same. Personally, I'd prefer that he dies. He was a pretty bad guy - hired muscle - he enjoyed his work. Besides, if he lives he can stir up attention we'd rather not have right now."

"You want to see him?" I ask Jessica.

She ponders a moment, thinking whether or not to answer the question truthfully and finally nods. "I want him to know I won. I want *me* to know that I won."

Eve stands up and straightens herself up a bit. "Let's go in."

Jacob finishes his second burger and heads over to the door, flings it open, and stands there like a royal attendant. It doesn't exactly suit him, but it does help break the mood.

Jean stands next to Jessica. "His name is Hiroshi, and he's been with the organization for ten years. He busts people up for a living. Raped some, killed some. He was planning on doing his worst with you tonight while his buds took pictures."

I walk in first. Eve follows, protecting Jessica like some kind of mother bird. Frank and Jean come bouncing in last, and Jacob shuts the door. We all stand and stare at this busted-up guy duct-taped to a wooden chair. His right wrist is swollen, probably broken by Jessica's kick. His face is bruised from Jacob's fists, and his eyelids are missing thanks to Frank's razor. One shoulder is misshapen and looks like it was crushed in a vise - probably Eve lightly squeezing his shoulder. His head is lolled to one side, and his red eyes are locked on Jessica. To his credit, he's not begging for mercy. He's looking like he can't quite make out what we're up to.

Jessica walks up to him and looks him up and down dispassionately, like he's just a bug pinned to a piece of Styrofoam.

"How does it feel to be on the other side of the beating?" she asks him. "How does it feel to know it's all over?"

"*Kuso kurae, baka buso,*" he chokes out.

Jacob smacks him in the back of the head. "English, motherfucker."

Hiroshi grins at Jacob and I shudder at his missing teeth. "Fuck off, stupid bitch."

Jessica holds up her hand. "It doesn't matter. He doesn't matter." She looks over at me. "Do you still have that knife?"

I actually do, and was planning on keeping it. Hey, it's not every day a nice piece of Japanese steel drops into your lap. I pull the knife out and hand it to her handle first.

She takes the tanto and smiles. He smile doesn't quite make it to her eyes, and she looks scary as hell for a moment. She admires the blade, turning it and watching the light reflecting off it. Like I said, it's a nice knife. Without warning she smoothly turns and buries it to the hilt in Hiroshi's throat with enough force that the tip pokes out the back of his neck. He looks as surprised as the rest of us.

She watches him die, pulls out the knife and wipes the blade on his pants, hands it back to me handle first. "Thank you. I've wanted to do that ever since I met that guy."

06 | Government Security At Its Finest

"Right through there," the guard tells me, pointing to the left. She's 300 pounds of surly TSA agent sacked in a chair and couldn't give a rat's ass if I live or die just so long as I leave her alone.

"Thank you kindly, ma'am," I say and head toward McCarran's tram system. I'm running late, as usual, and the plane to Albuquerque leaves from the furthest possible gate from here.

"No running," she calls after me, but doesn't actually get her ass out of the chair to enforce it.

Frank, Jean and Jacob drove back to Albuquerque since there's no easy way to smuggle stolen body armor onto a plane. It's not a terrible drive, ten hours or so, but it is ten hours in a car with those three and I'd rather stick my hand in a blender than listen to Jacob and Frank bicker about music for ten hours.

Even without the constant threat of terrorism, flying is still an enormous headache, especially when you're trying to smuggle someone out of Las Vegas without anyone knowing who she is. Normally, Jean and Frank could whip up some fake documents, or Jacob could get one of his gun-dealing buds to hook us up, but time is not on our side. Fortunately, we're in Vegas - where, as I said earlier, you can get anything with enough cash.

This is no longer really a Mafia town, but La Cosa Nostra still maintains offices here. Jacob has dealt with them before. A righteous hack by Jean to find an informant gets us new travel papers for Jessica, made while we wait. They won't hold up to any really intense scrutiny, but they work to fool the bored government drones who know all they have to do is not seriously fuck up and they can keep their jobs forever. We'll work up a new identity for her when we get back.

Eve went through the line first, about fifteen or twenty people ahead of Jessica. The tall blonde breezed through security easily.

I have a brief moment of panic when the guy checking IDs looks a little too hard and little too long at Jessica's new license. Maybe she just doesn't look like a Frieda, but honestly, who does? When he called his supervisor over I started planning ways to get the heck out of Dodge. Captain America, protector of life, liberty and cute little puppies, shows his supervisor her ID and points at something. His supervisor, a tired-looking man whose tie tip only makes it to his navel, sighs and adjusts his glasses and peers at her license. He shakes his head and motions to let it go and keep the line moving.

I breathe a sigh of relief, and get my less-than-real ID ready for checking. My fake identity is a little better established than Jessica's. It's a necessity for me. My real self is less than popular with the authorities.

"How was your stay in fabulous Las Vegas?" the agent scanning boarding passes asks.

"I lost about a grand and picked up something that eats penicillin for breakfast," I tell him with a huge smile. "How's your day?"

"Same as ever, man. Endless lines of people. This is my personal Hell, Mr. Sigmon."

The name on my ID is Zachariah Sigmon. I'm a day trader with a tiny group in Santa Fe, New Mexico.

"Hell is other people, bud," I tell him. Treat these guys like humans and you'd be amazed at how easy it is to get through security.

"Indeed it is," he tells me. He circles something on my boarding pass, jots a note, and waves me through.

Eve is going through the scanners when I get in line behind about four thousand people. Shoes off, belt off, watch off, phone out, blah, blah, blah. Eve has to duck to go through the security scanners.

In short order we all make it through the initial checks, the scanners, the metal detectors and all the layered security that will do absolutely nothing to stop a determined attacker and wander to the departure lounge. We don't sit together, and we don't interact.

Wait, what? Why would we act like we don't know each other? Why all the secrecy? We've got an ace computer hacker, an epic building hacker, a guy who can lay hands on almost any weapon, a minor goddess and a relatively young woman with a propensity for violence. We're a tough bunch of mean motherfuckers who are deadly serious about what we do. What are we worried about?

Back during the Revolutionary War George Washington said *"Even minutiae should have a place in our collection, for things of a seemingly trifling nature, when enjoined with others of a more serious cast, may lead to valuable conclusion."* It's a fancy way of saying "watch what you talk about, because even a minor detail can give away the whole game." Nathan Hale of the "I only regret that I have but one life to give for my country" fame - a spy during the Revolutionary War - could probably give you a first-hand account of what happens when the game gets given away. Hale thought he was a good spy, but wound up telling a British agent about his mission and was hanged for his treason. I still find it amusing that people hold up Hale's quote as if he's an example of a great American patriot. Fuck that. If he was a great American patriot, he would have known to keep his mouth shut.

No matter what you see in the movies, no matter how powerful the bad guys are, if it comes down to a fight, there are a hell of lot of people trying to stop you. The whole "you against the world" thing sounds romantic, but the world will stomp you into oblivion in fairly short order. If you want to win this game, you hide your pieces - you hide the fact that you're even in the game. I remember watching The Avengers, with all those good-looking people dressed up in fancy tight outfits. Good movie, but in the end? When the aliens attack and there are only six people who can stop the invaders? The US military would've smashed that invasion. Just like they'll crush my little group if they figure out what we're up to. Hence, the secrecy. We're in this game to finish it, and would prefer to do it completely under the radar.

The flight back is uneventful. An hour and some change. Some ginger ale and some peanuts. I'm toward the middle of the plane, Jessica's somewhere in the back, and Eve is toward the front. When we're taking off a baby starts crying. Eve makes funny faces at her until the baby calms down. The baby's young parents are too grateful to be scared that a seven-foot-tall woman is attempting to play with their baby.

Mostly I keep my headphones on, and listen to 16 Horsepower, and zone out.

We land, trudge through the Sunport (the happiest little International Airport in New Mexico), hoping to hell no one's lost our luggage (they hadn't), grab the bus back to the Airport Parking, get the car (Honda Accord) and hop I-25 to I-40 and head for our little gang's house on the hill.

I can tell Jessica's disappointed when she sees the house. The place has two floors, 4,000 square feet, a full two acres of land, a guest house, a garage, and a workshop. It's not palatial, but it's got what we need.

"So, this is the evil lair," Jessica says, probably wondering what the hell she's gotten herself into.

"Well, I keep my eyes on *Villain Supply*, but I keep getting outbid on the really good lairs, and it's always by some asshole that waits until two seconds before the auction closes who bids and wins," Eve says, completely straight-faced.

"Let's be realistic," I say. "You want to draw attention to yourself? Hire a bang-up architect to design a top of the line base and get an army of contractors to build it. Here, no one will notice what's going on, let alone care."

She's not entirely convinced, I can tell. I wasn't the first time I came out here, either.

"I think Jacob's grilling tonight, if anyone's hungry. Let's get Jessica settled and shown around and get some break time. We'll eat around 7," Eve tell us as she's getting out of the car.

* * * *

An evening of grilled green chile cheeseburgers and Alien Imperial Stout can make everything better. If you've just been party to a mass murder, and executed a Japanese gang member, it may take more than one Alien Imperial Stout. But when you're looking up at the stars, and down on the lights of the city, a couple of good beers can make anything better.

"So, Jessica," Frank asks, popping a fry into his mouth, "what did you study at UNLV?"

She's kind of staring off into the distance, swirling her beer. "I was at the Institute for Security Studies. Homeland security, stuff like that."

"You went to Las Vegas to study national security?" I ask. "I thought everyone went to the University of Missouri for that."

"How the hell do people know this stuff? Why do you know that?" Jacob asks.

"I used to work for the Department of Homeland Security, first as a Computer Security Specialist, then working in Intelligence. We used to look for resumes from University of Missouri," I tell him.

Jessica looks up, stunned that anyone would know anything about her studies. "No," she says, "the DSS program at U of M is more focused on international policy, more large-scale. Homeland security focuses more on the local side of things: terrorism, medical response, things like that."

"Does that explain where you learned to fight?" asks Jacob. "Because I've never seen anyone breaks a guy's wrist with a kick before - outside of the movies, anyway."

"It was Savate," she says. "I studied it in California, in High School. It's French kickboxing."

"French? Kickboxing? What do they teach, surrender?"

Jessica grimaces and sighs. "Ever heard of Gilles Le Duigou? The Savateur that fought Ishima in Japan?"

"Never heard of either of them," Jacob snorts derisively.

"Gilles Le Duigou and Ishima had a full contact kickboxing bout back in the '80s in Japan. Both of them were damn good fighters, but Gilles was tough as nails," I say.

"Yeah," Jessica says, "late in the fight Ishima breaks one of Gilles' forearms. They stop the fight and Gilles tells his corner to tape up his arm, because he's going back in. He goes back in and BAM, Ishima fractures the other forearm. Le Duigou keeps fighting, with two broken arms taped to his sides, and wins with nothing but kicks. KO's Ishima."

Jacob's not a martial arts geek. He just likes smashing heads together. He knows what a rear naked chokehold is, but would probably never do it, because he didn't want anyone to think he was into guys. Old school to the bone. (Not that bone.)

"Is that why you study Savate?" I ask her.

"Nah, the school was close to my house. Convenience was a huge thing since my mom wouldn't drive me. I had to find a place I could walk to. Plus, I thought France was just amazingly romantic, so it kind of carried over."

"Where'd you grow up?" asks Eve.

"Southern Cali. It wasn't the nicest neighborhood, but it was fine," Jessica says.

"France," Jacob says with a huff. "You shoulda just found a tough guy like me."

"Girl's got to learn to take care of herself," Jessica replies. "I saw a friend of mine get her ass handed to her when we were freshmen. Her boyfriend was one of the football players. That whole team was on steroids and would fight at the drop of a hat. He beat her ass one day because she asked him a sarcastic question about football. She finished the year in the hospital, and he had to sit out a couple of games. I saw that, and decided it was not going to happen to me. So I started working out and learning to fight."

"Ever use it?" I ask. I'm always curious. I studied Kenpo and never really had to use it. I'm not a small guy, though, and most people just decide it's not worth the effort.

"When my Japanese friends jumped me six months, ago I put a couple of them in the hospital. Got an extra beating for that. After that, the only time I needed it was when I finally got a chance to beat that fucker down. By the way, thanks for letting me stick a knife in him."

They say vengeance never solves anything, but in my case it made me feel a whole hell of a lot better. Didn't actually bring anyone back, but I did feel like I'd fixed something.

The night winds on until everyone starts slowing down. At around 1am Jacob is passed out in a chaise lounge, Frank and Jean have gone off to bed and it's down to just Eve, myself and Jessica.

Jessica stares out at the sky. "I've never really seen the stars before. Southern California wasn't dark and Las Vegas was nothing but lights. They're amazing."

Eve looks at her, totally confused. "What do you mean you've never seen the stars?"

"I told you, too much light where I lived. You could see, like 10 stars, tops, and I think at least a couple of them were satellites."

"You never went drinking in the boonies?" I ask, incredulous.

"What the hell are boonies? And, no, I never had to go anywhere to go drinking and partying. In high school we just went to each other's houses. In college, well, fuck, it was Vegas, most of the city was a party."

"It was a lot easier to see them before all the pollution, but it's still an impressive sight." Eve says.

We all sit and stare at the sky for a while. There's something about the stars at night, in a place where you can actually see them, that's peaceful. It's almost like the sky is so big that no matter what your problems might be, they're completely trivial. Boss yelled at you? Wife left you for a rodeo clown? Your mayoral campaign is in the shitter because you can't stop texting pictures of your dick to women half your age? Look at the stars for a while and it's, like, so fucking what?

Eve takes a pull of her beer. "Jessica, we should go see if we can find your dad tomorrow."

"I've got his address on an old postcard in my bag." She takes a deep breath, closes her eyes. "Can I ask you guys something?"

I shrug, Eve says, "Of course."

"Why'd you guys save me?"

And there it is. I asked it, Jacob asked it, I suspect Frank and Jean asked it. Eve has her reasons; usually it involves seeing something she needs in each of us. She's very cagey about what she sees or why it's important, though. I've pressed her on it before but she won't give me a straight answer. I guess it's a job and I don't have to get dressed up to do it, so it can't be all bad.

"A little voice told me we needed you. I'm not sure why just yet. I'm just sure we need you," Eve says.

"Like some psychic thing?" Jessica asks.

"Kind of, I guess. I don't know how to describe it."

"This may sound strange, but I had dreams about you. Or hell, maybe it wasn't you." She's nervous now. "I've just had dreams about someone like the two of you and Jacob. Kind of in the shadows, but definitely you guys. There's fire, and screaming, and I was laughing."

"You've got to be careful with dreams and visions," Eve says. "Sometimes you're seeing a future, but sometimes you're just seeing something, and you end up finding a way to make it happen. There was a cop up in Santa Fe a few years ago, decent guy, a bit of psychic prowess that he had no idea he had. He started having dreams about a guy shooting him. He kept seeing this guy's rage-filled eyes and the guy is screaming and pointing a gun at our cop friend.

"Well, one day while he's patrolling, he sees this guy driving around, and he just knows he has to follow him - see what he's up to. I doubt this was a totally conscious choice, but he can't stop, so he follows him around all day. Now, I don't know about you, but you notice it when a cop is following you around all day. The guy just goes home and waits.

"Next day the cop finds him and follows him again. The guy confronts the cop. 'What's going on?' Cop pulls the normal cop stuff: 'You don't need to worry about it.' But the cop backs off and stops following the guy for the rest of the day.

"Next day, cop follows guy again. The guy's getting sick of this now, so he calls the police station to ask what's going on. 'Nothing, as far as we know. We'll ask the officer.' So the cop gets called on the carpet, 'Why are you following this guy around?' No answer. 'Fine, knock it off.'

"So the cop stops, but it keeps eating at him, so he starts stalking around on his own time, using his own car.

"Eventually, of course, the guy notices this cop is still following him and starts to get paranoid. He buys a gun because he's convinced this cop is out to get him. In New Mexico, your glove box is legally a part of your house. Meaning you can keep a gun in it. So this guy's driving around, like most people in this state, packing a gun.

"Finally, after about two weeks of this, the poor guy is completely strung out. He's got a cop following him around, waiting outside his house, driving him nuts. He can't sleep. He can't eat. He's losing it. He walks out one morning, and there's our cop down the street, waiting for the guy to go to work. The cop doesn't know this guy hasn't been to work in a week because he can't focus on anything. Guy walks out to his car, opens the glove box and pulls out the biggest freaking gun our cop has ever seen, and heads toward the cop, gun raised screaming and ranting.

"Cop climbs out of his car. The guy starts shooting. Unfortunately, like most idiots who buy guns to feel safe, he's never learned to shoot, so he misses every shot. Manages to shoot the neighbor's cat, blows out a window, puts a hole through someone's mailbox, and never comes near the cop. The cop, naturally, knows how to shoot and fires two shots, one to the chest, one to the head: both hit.

"Bam, bam. This cop shoots this guy, claims self-defense, gets off scot-free."

"Jesus," Jessica says.

"Yeah. Had he never had that dream in the first place, the dream would've never come true, because the cop wouldn't have put events in motion to make it come true. Sure, he saw the future, but he also made the future happen. If you've been dreaming about us and fires, you may be seeing the future, but you may be seeing a future you make."

"Not that we'd mind laughing while the world burns," I add.

I   yawn.   Beer   and   burgers   always   make   me   sleepy.

07 | Reprioritize, or Mission Creep

I never expected to become a morning person but somehow, against all odds, it snuck up on me. I actually enjoy getting up early in the morning. Drink some coffee, smoke a cigarette, enjoy the quiet. My email volume has dropped off significantly since I fell off the radar, but I still keep getting email about how I can increase both my bust size and my penis size. I'm sure they're totally legit. If I thought any of that crap would actually work, I'd buy a whack of both types of pills, and drop them in random coffees at Starbucks.

It's 6 a.m. and everyone will probably be asleep for a while, so I go outside and enjoy my coffee in peace. In a few minutes I hear rattling around inside the kitchen, and Jessica sticks her head out the door.

"Where are the coffee cups?" she asks.

"Above the sink," I say. "Milk's in the fridge, there's sugar in a canister on the toaster oven."

Jessica comes back out in a few minutes, coffee in hand, wearing one of Eve's shirts, which fits her like a dress. Her eyes are red and bleary and her hair is sticking out in about a dozen different directions. She plops down in a chair next to me and sighs as she smells the fresh coffee.

There goes my quiet morning.

"Sleep okay?" I ask.

"Like the drunken fool I was when I went to bed," she replies.

"Nothing like alcohol-fueled crashing."

We sit in silence for a while, watching the sun coming up over the Sandias. As it comes up, the shadow of the mountains shrinks over the city until the whole of Albuquerque is lit up. It's not a gorgeous town, but this place is home. Plus it's got a great view of the mountains.

"Can I ask you something?" Jessica asks.

"Sure," I say.

"What's up with Eve?"

"What do you mean?"

"Well," Jessica says slowly, like she's not quite sure how to phrase the question. "Who is she?"

"Ah. I'm not entirely sure who or even what she is. I've asked her several times but she never really answers me. I don't know much about her. She's bullet proof, smart, and I get the feeling there's a lot she's not telling anyone."

"Doesn't that worry you?" Jessica asks, shifting to face me. "I mean, here you are doing God only knows what and you don't even really know who you're working for or what she really wants."

"I know what she wants, at least in the short term."

"What's that?"

"She wants to tear the country to ground and let it rebuild itself."

Jessica stares at me in wild-eyed disbelief. She starts to say something, thinks again, sips her coffee and stares into space for a while.

"How is she going to tear down the country?"

"We're planning on killing Congress."

"What?"

"Kill Congress and let the country regenerate itself."

"How is killing Congress going to tear down the country?" Jessica asks.

"They make the laws, set the policies. The laws and policies drive the country. Take all that away and someone or something will have to step in and fill the void. The country will survive. It'll hurt but we'll survive."

"You're insane."

I can't argue that point. "I am, but not in the way you're thinking. All we really want to do is tear out some corruption."

"And take over yourselves."

"No way. Absolutely not. Way too much work. Someone else can step in and try their hand at it."

"So, you're going to kill Congress and walk away. That's your evil plan?"

"Good and evil depend a lot on who wins. Winners are good guys, losers are bad guys."

"What have I gotten myself into?" she mumbles into her cup.

"Eve thought you were important, that's good enough for me," I tell her.

"Does the bus come out here?"

"Sorry, no. I'll give you a ride into town if you want, though."

There's more rattling around, and Jean and Frank come out. Frank only drinks tea; Jean drinks copious amounts of coffee. They're both a bit bedraggled, and neither of them is a morning person even under the best of circumstances.

Looks like everyone's getting up early today.

Jean gives his usual wave and a somewhat cheery, "Good morning."

Jessica nods at him and watches the rest of the gang warily.

"Everything okay?" Frank asks her. "You did show her where the coffee is, right?"

I nod and point to her cup.

"We have tea, too, if you'd prefer."

"I'm fine," Jessica tells him.

"Please tell me you haven't been talking to Steven," Frank says.

Jessica looks at me and back at Frank.

"Oh, dear God. I'm so sorry," he tells her.

"What's wrong with me?" I ask.

"You probably terrified her, that's what." Frank puts on his best safe and innocent expression. "We're not bad people and you don't have to stay here if you don't want to. We're on something of a mission and if you'd like to join us we'd love to have you."

"He told me about the mission," she says with a grimace. "Do you guys honestly think you can kill Congress?"

Eve saunters out wearing her black shirt that says "Super Villain" on the front and "Grovel, Fools!" on the back. She used to wear that around town, and most people thought it was cute or funny. A couple thought she was a dominatrix. The real joke is on them, although I doubt she'd make anyone grovel. Toss them around like dolls; rip their cars apart; hire people to steal their money; sure. But she's not into groveling. Or making people grovel.

"I absolutely think we can kill Congress," Eve says. "Not only do I think we can, I think we need to."

"Why?" Jessica asks her.

"My offer of a ride still stands," I say. "Just say the word."

"Ignore him for now. I'll drive you anywhere you want anytime you want, but let me ask you something first."

Jessica watches Eve warily, nods, and says, "Okay, ask away."

"What do you know about your dad?"

"He worked for some government research facility, lost it somewhere along the line and disappeared."

"What's his name?" I ask.

"Delano. Delano Hayha," Jessica says.

"Okay. Do you have a last address?" Eve asks

Jessica nods. "It's on a postcard, along with a message that said 'Be careful dreaming', why?"

"I'll make you a deal. You don't owe us anything; I just want to make that clear. If you decide to walk away right now, we won't say or do a thing. But, I said we'd help you out however we could and I aim to keep that promise. You could have bolted off into the night and told the first cop you met who we were and what we'd done and you didn't. We're thankful for that. I'm thankful for that. If you want, we can help find out what happened to your dad," Eve tells her.

Jessica ponders the offer. I can see the wheels turning in her head. On the one hand, she thinks we're all nuts. On the other, she's seen us work. She nods and says, "Okay. I'll take your offer."

"Excellent," Eve says. "Find your dad, don't find your dad, we'll help you out. If, after we've found out whatever we can, you still want to leave, I'll understand. I'll even buy you a car and fill it with gas."

"You don't have to do that," Jessica says.

"You didn't have to keep quiet," Eve replies

"Fair enough," Jessica says. "Where do we start?"

"Breakfast is probably the best bet. Steven makes a hell of a breakfast and then he'll take you wherever you want to go," Eve says. Then she points at me and says, "You do what needs to be done, take her around and make sure she gets back safe."

"You got it, boss," I tell Eve.

"What's for breakfast?" Jean asks.

"She's the guest," I say, pointing at Jessica. "Her choice."

"Coffee's fine," Jessica says with a blush.

"French toast it is," I say. "If that's okay with you."

Jessica actually smiles and says, "French toast would be great. How can I help?"

"I'm a lone wolf in the kitchen," I tell her. "You can help by enjoying   your   coffee."

08 | Some Folks Just Need A Beat Down

The address Jessica's dad had written down is for a rental house up in Albuquerque's Nob Hill. It's an ideal location for anyone working at Kirtland Air Force Base or teaching at the University of New Mexico. Living in Nob Hill also gets you close to Central around UNM, which is an ideal place to find hookers and crack.

The rental is a standard-issue raised one-story house designed in the eclectic (read strange) style of the rest of Nob Hill: falling down around itself, yet still costs a small fortune. The house looks like it has tenants, though, which is a good sign. Hopefully one of them will be Delano Hayha.

Out front are a couple cars, a rusty Toyota and a nicely restored Mustang. The Toyota's windows are down, which is the universal sign for "nothing of value in here" around these parts. The stairs leading to the front door shift from side to side when we walk up them.

Yes, stairs on a one-story house. It's Nob Hill, what are you gonna do?

The doorbell doesn't work, so I bang on the door and resist the urge to yell, "Police." There's some shuffling, a crash, some muttering and finally the door opens. The kid who opens the door takes one look at Jessica and says, "We said we wanted you later tonight."

She looks at me. I look at her and shrug. We both look back at the little douchebag who opened the door, standing there in his too-tight TapOut shirt and designer jeans, hair gelled up into a fauxhawk.

"She's not a hooker, dipshit," I say. "We're looking for her dad."

This part of Nob Hill doesn't usually host college students, it's far too pricey. Between the Mustang out front and the kid's designer clothes, though, it dawns on me that daddy is paying for this place and junior is living the dream.

"I could be your daddy, baby." He reaches out to stroke her face, and she slaps his hand away. Stupidly, he gets excited.

"Ooh," he says. "Feisty. I like that in a woman. You know what else I like in a woman? My dick."

Charming lad. Sometimes I weep for the future. Then I remember my folks said the same thing about my generation.

I sigh. I was hoping the two of us together would be sufficient, but I should've brought Jacob along. His mere presence tends to ratchet down situations quickly. Jacob looks mean, but he's actually pretty damned nice. On the other hand, I have seen him head-butt a horse when he was drunk.

"Listen ass-clown," I tell the kid, "we just want to find her dad. Do you know anything about the guy that used to live here?"

He sneers. "No. And even if I did, I wouldn't tell you until she bribed me on her knees." He reaches for her again and she pushes his hand away. Without warning the kid slaps her hard across the cheek. She's so shocked it doesn't occur to her to beat his ass down. The way I see it Eve gave me orders to take care of this girl, so I punch the kid in the head and down he goes. I may not look like much, but I've got a wicked punch.

"Fucking hell!" Jessica yells, rubbing her cheek. "I can take care of myself. We needed him awake! How is going to help us now?" She's pissed, but damned if it didn't feel good to hit that guy.

"Fuck him. Come on, maybe there's a roommate. There are two cars out there, after all," I respond.

The place is furnished in "late-college modern": milk-crate bookcases, beer signs and posters of half-naked women. A couch propped up by a textbook adorns the street wall. The neon colors in the beer signs really bring out the stains in the carpet and the poorly patched holes in the walls.

Someone screams, and a glass breaks. Standing there in front of us is a young woman in shorts and halter top.

Is this the roommate? Maybe, but I've never met a woman who will let you put up beer signs and posters of half-naked women in the living room. She's standing there like a deer caught in headlights. Milk from the glass she dropped is dripping through the floorboards into the basement below. She has a huge shiner on her right eye. Looks like the guy cooling his heels on the floor had a thing for hitting women.

I admit it's probably a bit alarming to walk into a room and find two strangers looking around and your man-boy flattened out on the ground. Still, that milk is going be a bitch to get out of the rug.

Jessica puts her hands up and slowly walks forward.

"Look," she says quietly. "We're not here to hurt you; we don't want anything except information. Then we'll leave and you'll never hear from us again. Please, I need your help."

Maybe it was just the "one woman talking to another woman" thing. Maybe it was the quiet voice and calm demeanor. Or maybe it was the fact that I stayed back and didn't make a threatening move. Whatever the reason was, the roommate relaxes slightly but noticeably. Good thing, too - she didn't seem to be breathing, and the last thing we need right now is two people flat out on the floor.

"Who are you people?" she asks, eyes darting back and forth between us.

"My name is Claire," Jessica says calmly and quietly, "and this is Tyrell."

Tyrell? Oh, fuck it. I can roll with being a Tyrell for a bit.

"What's your name?" Jessica asks.

"Amber," the woman mumbles.

"Amber. My dad's name is Delano Hayha. He used to live here but he's disappeared. Did he leave anything behind?"

Amber shakes her head. We need to leave soon - her eyes are about to bug out of her head. She may actually explode.

"OK. Calm down. It's all good. Do you rent this place?" I ask.

She points at the guy on the floor.

"He rents this place?"

Amber nods her head.

"Okay. Do you know who he rents it from?"

Without taking her eyes off us, she backs over to a desk and quickly grabs an envelope and hands it to Jessica.

"Lobo Fandango Rentals," she reads. "Up on 9000 Spain NE. Know where that is?"

"Yeah," I say, "It's up in the Heights. Not too far."

"Can I keep this?" she asks Amber, who has now started shaking. The boyfriend is starting to groan now, too. It's time to get moving. Amber nods her head to keep the envelope and we start backing out.

I'm glad we parked around the block. Amber's shock should keep her from calling the cops immediately. Although, what's she going to report, anyway? A couple of nondescript white folks thumped her boyfriend and took an envelope? The cops around here won't do a damn thing about it, because it's just college kids doing college things, and who cares? There weren't any drugs involved, so it's not worth their time.

We quietly walk out and drive away.

09 | Data

According to the web browser on my phone, Lobo Fandango is a one-person business. It's wholly owned, operated, and run by a guy named Silvio Goodman, who is apparently a self-styled real-estate magnate. Silvio seems to think he's Trump without the bad toupee. He doesn't realize that Trump handles multi-million-dollar real estate deals while Goodman's deals mostly involve screwing over broke college students.

Silvio's even got a picture of himself on his web site: a short, stocky guy with thinning hair and arms crossed across his chest like he's trying to look tough. Some short guys can look tough - or at least worthy of respect - but this guy isn't one of them. He's trying way too hard to look like he's success personified, leaning on his stock 350z like it's a damn Ferrari.

Lobo Fandango is located in a formerly swanky part of town. Goodman's running the business out of his house and probably using the business to write off part of his house payments on his taxes. The Z is parked in the driveway, so that's a bonus for us. By the way, the vanity license plate on Goodman's Z spells "DOLLERZ."

What a babe magnet this guy must be.

The house is your typical gaudy oversized house, owned by gaudy people who think the décor in Tony Soprano's house was high-class. He's got the requisite neatly trimmed lawn complete with pink flamingo. The door mat spells out *Bienvenido*. I wonder if he's trying to look quaint or just say welcome to the large native Spanish-speaking population in town.

When we get the door, Jessica turns and says, "Can we get some information from this guy before you knock him out?"

I hold my hand up in my best imitation of a Boy Scout salute and say, "I won't smack him unless he really needs it."

She sighs, almost exasperated and says, "Let me handle this one."

Damn. Knock out one stranger who wasn't a threat, and you're marked for life.

She has to ring the doorbell twice before the Lord of the Manor deigns to answer the door. He's shorter in person than I expected, maybe 5'5" or 5'6". He looks at me and frowns. Then he looks at Jessica and smiles, suddenly quite happy to assist us. There must be certain aspects of being a woman that come in handy, most notably the fact that men get really stupid around pretty women. I'm sure it's not all sunshine and roses, but being able to completely warp desperate men with a smile must come in handy.

The inside is as tasteless and bland as the outside; he's decked the joint out in pastel carpets and framed Nagel posters. It's like *Miami Vice* never went off the air. I think I've seen some of the plaster statues Goodman has in those Sky Mall catalogs they give out on airplanes

"What can I do for you today?" he asks her, a twinkle in his eye.

"I'm interested in the property at 420 Hermosa," she asks.

"Let me check this out for you." He sits behind an enormous, ornate desk and moves some papers off his keyboard. He two-finger types a few things into an archaic computer, and waits while it makes a wide variety of clicking and chirping sounds.

I wander over to look at the bookcase. It's stocked with expensive-looking books - a few classics, but mostly real-estate books, self-motivation texts, and other crap. I grab a copy of "The Book of Five Rings for Executives" and start flipping through it. The classic treatise on sword fighting distilled into executive-speak. I briefly studied Kenjutsu, and have read the original version of "The Book of Five Rings." For some reason, I'm always vaguely insulted when I see one of these classic texts converted into a self-help book for lily-assed middle managers. I know I shouldn't get myself worked up about it, but, dammit, ruin your own texts. Go rewrite Zig Ziglar, or something. Leave mine alone.

He looks up and frowns. "That property is already rented."

"Yeah, we know," I say.

Jessica shoots me a look, and sits down all prim and proper in the chair in front of Goodman's desk. "We're ... I'm interested in previous renter. Delano Hayha."

Goodman goes white. "I don't know who you're talking about."

"Please, I need to find out what happened to him." She's giving him the damsel in distress treatment, but it doesn't seem to be working.

"It's time for both of you to go now. I have a very important business meeting."

Jesus, dude. At least try to not look completely guilty.

He stands up, walks around the desk, and holds out his hand to

Jessica. Silvio is a true gentleman to the end. She shakes her head and says, "We're not going anywhere until we find out what happened."

"I don't have anything to tell you." He's getting nervous.

I rip a page out of his book. Damn, it feels good to do that. "Actually, it's probably a good idea if you did tell us. It's not like we're asking for anything important, right?"

He looks from me to Jessica. She no longer looks prim or proper, and there's an angry look creeping into her eyes. The last time I saw that look, my newly acquired knife had to be cleaned.

"I'm not scared of you. You can't do anything to me," Silvio stammers. He's scared, maybe not of us, but he's scared.

"We don't really want to do anything to you," Jessica says.

"Speak for yourself," I say, ripping some more pages out his fake "Book of Five Rings". He's never even opened it. He just keeps it around so he can feel tough.

Goodman's shaking a bit now, eyes darting back toward his desk. "You can't scare me with this good-cop, bad-cop bullshit. Just get the fuck out, now."

I know this guy has a serious Napoleon complex, but no real-estate agent gets like this over a previous tenant. When we got here, I doubted this idiot would know anything, but now I'm guessing he's neck deep in something. I've met plenty of guilty people in my previous life - hell, I've been one of them - and he's got the terrified look that comes from interacting with forces bigger than himself. Usually you see this look on people working with the Mafia, but I've seen it on people in trouble with the government, too. Goodman's got a look people get after they run into people they didn't quite understand, and got in bed with those people over before they fully understood the consequences of their actions. He's hiding something, and he's more worried about being caught by them than he is afraid of us.

But fear is a powerful motivator, and it's time Goodman paid more attention to the immediate threat.

"Oh, you misunderstand us," I say. "This isn't a good-cop, bad-cop thing." I point to Jessica. "This is bad news," then point to myself, "and worse news. Just answer the fucking question, and we'll walk away quietly."

"Fuck you!" he yells, and tries to run around his desk. Jessica hooks his leg, and he stumbles into the edge of the desk. He bounces off and trips himself. She laughs, and he goes bright red. He tries to get up, and she kicks him in the jaw without even getting out of her chair. Goodman goes down again.

I walk over to him and stand on his fingers. He screams like a little girl and slaps at my feet. Jessica squats down in front of him. "Delano Hayha is my father. I'd very much like to know what happened to him."

"He didn't pay his rent, so I kicked his goldbricking ass out! I had every right! It was in the contract! Would you get the fuck off me?"

I think for a second. "No, I can't move right now. When did you kick him out?"

"About nine years ago. He stopped paying his rent! I went over and he was just sitting there, staring off into space. I told him to get his ass out by the next day, or I'd be back with the police. I came back and he was still just sitting there, so the cops escorted him off *my* property."

What kind of slumlord remembers a tenant from nine years ago? Something happened to drill Delano Hayha into Goodman's mind.

Jessica looks pained. "Did it occur to you to call for medical help? I mean, if he was just sitting there staring off into space, something must've been wrong."

"That's not my problem. I need to make money, and he wasn't paying me what he owed."

Wow. I thought I was callous. "You dirty, saprophyte motherfucker."

"You ass," Jessica says to Silvio. "You could've tried doing the right thing."

"I did do the right thing! I made money off my property."

"Aiyah," I say. I picked that up watching some movie and have been using it ever since. It's such a perfect word. In case you're wondering, it's a traditional Cantonese sigh of disgust.

"Fine," Jessica says. "What did you do with his things?"

"I auctioned them."

"Motherfucker," Jessica says. She looks at me "Do you happen to have that knife on you?"

"Of course I do," I say, pulling the knife out its sheath behind my back. I spent some time earlier polishing it to a mirror finish, and honing the edge to a razor. I make a show out of letting the sunlight glint off it before handing it to Jessica. She holds it up and looks at her reflection in it. I have to hide a smile when she adjusts her hair slightly before squatting back down in front of Silvio.

Goodman's eyes go wide as dinner plates. There's a kind of primal terror about being cut that hits right at the cold part of your stomach. I'm honestly more afraid of being cut than being shot; I know it doesn't make sense, but it's true. When you get shot, it does a lot of damage all the way through your body - but it's over quickly. When you get cut, it takes time to die.

I look down at Goodman. "You sold every fucking thing that guy had?"

"I kept a locked box. They were looking for it, so I figured it was important." He promptly shuts the fuck up, like he's said something that he shouldn't have.

"They," she asks him. "Who are *they*?"

He's purses his lips like if he squeezes them tight enough, no more secrets will spill out.

Jessica holds up the knife. "Let me explain something to you, slick," I say. "She will cut you up, and smile while she does it. Since time is of the essence, I'm thinking she should start with your face."

I look over at Jessica and raise an eyebrow in question. She shrugs. "Why not start with an eye?" she asks.

"Good point. No pun intended, Sil. Ever seen what happens to an eye when it gets punctured by a knife? Your eye is mostly water surrounded by a membrane. It's kind of like a water balloon. Puncture it and you can guess what happens," I tell him.

Jessica smiles and says, "Pop."

Goodman has stopped struggling. Faced with the choosing between a possible situation with "*them*," whoever they may be, and a couple of crazies right in front of him, he's kind of freaking out. Fear is a wonderful thing.

At least, it's a wonderful thing to share with other people.

He gulps the biggest gulp I've seen, closes his eyes and says, "In the top right drawer, in the back, under the papers." Apparently the local horror has outweighed the faceless horror.

Jessica opens the door and pulls out a dull gray, seamless metal box. There's a tear in her eye as she cradles it to her chest. "I haven't seen this in years."

"Take it and get out, you sick fucks." Apparently Goodman's not so terrified that he can't speak.

"Shut the fuck up, asshole," I tell him.

"You'll never get it open."

I twist my foot and hear the bones in Goodman's hand pop and grind. I think I just broke a couple of his fingers.

"Is that the only thing left? Do we need to break or cut things to get the whole story?"

"That's it. I told you. I sold the rest," he spits through gritted teeth. Tough little bastard. I've seen people break down and cry over a hangnail. This guy got his hand ground into hamburger, and he's just gritting his teeth.

Jessica hands me back my knife, kicks Goodman in the head, and walks to the door. From a pure security point of view, it would be best to kill this guy and keep the loose ends to a minimum. Murder tends to bring more police attention than assault, though, so I let him live. Goodman's gone limp, so I chuck his name plate in the trash and follow Jessica out the door.

10 | A Day On The Farm

Home may be where the heart is, but it's not always where the quiet is. When we got back, Jessica disappeared into her room. Jacob was busy shooting random things in the yard, Jean was listening to Ministry at top volume, and Frank was testing saws.

Yes, saws.

Frank was testing some new electric saws he'd found, which he intended to use to hack into buildings. They're pretty quiet, normally, but he was trying to find a way to make them quieter. Part of this was muffling the motor; the other part is working with the cutting wheels. The smoother and sharper the wheel, the quieter the cutting. Of course, there are other things involved - like the material you're cutting. Some things just won't be quiet to cut, but the idea is to treat it like a silenced gun: maybe not perfectly silent, but close enough for jazz and government work. If you can cut through a padlock without waking up the sleeping guard, you're probably doing well enough.

He's test-cutting chains and locks, and there are cut pieces all over the garage. We may be all out of locks now.

"New toy, Frank?" I ask him after he's done cutting through a huge padlock.

He flips up his goggles and grins like a kid who just got the biggest damned Lego set in the world. "This thing can cut through a hardened padlock in 30 seconds."

"Sweet. How's the noise level?" I ask him.

"Not silent quiet, but you'd have to be in the same room to hear it."

"Any other new stuff?"

He grabs something that looks like a tube with a bulge at the end. I look at him quizzically as he holds the thing out. Frank pushes a hidden button and three spikes expand on the tip.

"Compressed air grappling gun, had it custom-built by a guy in town. Light, portable, quiet. I can go up a ten-story building with this bad boy."

"Yeah, and quietly cut any locks when you get to the top, right,

Batman?" I like needling him every now and then, but Frank's absolutely amazing at hacking into buildings. It's a lost art form these days. Most people just want to go in the front, guns blazing, and look bold and brazen for the news, no matter how many hats they need to leave laying on the ground. Hacking a building is both art and science.

That place we hit in Nevada? Jacob found it and basically planned it, but getting in? That was Frank's work. He studied blueprints, watched guards, found holes in the security, and exploited them. The holes he couldn't find, he and Jean created. I've seen him spend a week studying a place, and get in and out like a ghost. It's how he made his living before Eve found him - he hit jewelry stores so smoothly the owners didn't even know they'd been hit until they came in and found themselves cleaned out. He can bypass alarms, cut in through a roof, crawl through ducts, climb elevator shafts - you name it.

"You never did appreciate the art," he tells me.

"Of course I do. I'd love to know how to crack a building like you," I tell him.

"Yeah, and I'd love to be able to figure out what people are good at. Like you," he replies.

"What can I say? I'm a real user of people."

"Yeah, but not in a bad way."

"Well, not recently," I mutter. At some point or another, I've used almost everyone I've ever known to get slightly further ahead. "I'm just lucky to work with good people."

"You're lucky, all right."

"Luck is just the intersection of skill and opportunity," I say.

About this time, Eve comes wandering in to look for some quiet.

"Ooh. Nice saw," she tells Frank. "How fast can it go through a lock?"

Frank beams. I don't care who you are, when the boss is impressed with something you're doing, it always feels good. "Thirty seconds for a hardened lock."

"Damn. Nice find."

"He's got Batman's grappling hook, too," I jibe.

"Does he have the Bat Utility Belt, too?" she asks, doing her best schoolgirl impression. Well, a tall, muscular schoolgirl, anyway.

"No, but I do have a Batman costume," he responds.

"Jean's such a lucky boy," she jokes.

Frank grins and blushes at the same time.

"So, how'd it go with Jessica?" she asks me.

"Well, she can handle herself well enough. She seems to have no compunction with beating someone's ass. She seems smart and can manipulate guys by blinking. I say keep her around," I respond.

"I'd figured on keeping her around, thank you. Did you find anything about her dad?"

"His old landlord had him kicked out, escorted out by the cops and left on the street. Sold everything at auction," I tell her.

"Why?"

"He was a couple months behind on rent, didn't respond when the landlord threatened him. Nearly comatose. No one's seen him for years. Jessica found some box of his, but I don't know what's in it."

"The landlord didn't call an ambulance or anything?"

"Nope," I tell her.

"What a prick. Did you kill him?"

"No. He never saw the car, and was out cold when we left," I respond.

"He's a loose end then, but probably not too dangerous. Did anything else interesting happen?"

"Not really. He did seem concerned about '*them*,' though."

"'*Them?*'"

"He didn't elaborate, only that '*they*' were looking for the box he had."

"What's in the box?" Eve asks me.

"I don't know. Jessica didn't open it in the car."

"She in her room?" Eve asks me.

"Yep. Ever since we got back."

"Hmmm. I think I need to pay a visit. You guys enjoy your power tools," she tells us and walks out of the garage.

Guys always enjoy power tools. It's in our wiring.

"I'm gonna grab something to drink," I tell Frank. "You want anything?"

"Nah. I'm good. Thanks, though."

He puts his goggles back on and looks for more things to cut.

* * * *

Jacob was involved in gunrunning before gunrunning was cool. He's managed to keep his contacts over the years, which means we're never hurting for firearms. He's currently testing a monster of a handgun. It sounds like the hammer of God issuing a pride-obliterating bitch slap, and the brass from the rounds is ginormous. When he's finished, he pulls off his ear protection, and admires the gun.

"Is that what I think it is?" I ask him.

"I don't know. What do you think it is?" he replies.

This is a game we play. I grew up around guns, so I'm pretty familiar with them, but he used to sell them, so he's quite a bit more familiar.

".44 Automag," I respond.

"Goddamned right! This is Mac Bolan's gun. You can keep your Desert Eagle! This is class, right here."

"Do you call it 'Big Thunder'?" I ask and smirk. I knew it. He names his guns. "I haven't seen one in 20 years, and never got a chance to fire one. Can I try it?"

If you want to impress a "gun guy" ask to shoot his prized piece, and praise it eight ways to Sunday when you're done. Jacob smiles that huge smile of his and hands over the gun, reverently and delicately like the huge pistol is his child.

The .44 Automag was designed to put the power of a rifle in a handgun. Consider it a precursor to today's .50 Desert Eagle, but it predates the Eagle by quite a bit. If these two guns are muscle cars (and believe me, that's the best way to think of a .44 and .50 handgun), the Automag is an early '70s Hemi 'Cuda, and the Eagle's a Dodge Viper. Just like the cars, the guns are a pair of potent beasts.

Jacob's got a couple concrete cinderblocks set up downrange - the kind you build those industrial gray walls out of. I get a good Weaver stance - one arm rigid, the other loose, one leg back - and sight down the barrel, both eyes open. Breathing slows as I relax and squeeze the trigger on the exhale. One of the blocks explodes into dust. The gun kicks like a mule hopped up on caffeine and crack.

"That, my friend, is a damn fine firearm," I say. It's an impressive gun.

"You've got six rounds left, Hoss," he says with a grin.

Even though I'm prepared for the kick, the next shot still surprises me. I miss the shot because I'm so focused on preparing for the recoil. Every gun is different; even two guns of the same make and model. Even firing the same ammo (not all ammo is the same, it depends on who loaded it) in the same gun will have a different feel from shot to shot. It can take hours to learn how to feel your way through shooting a particular gun.

I relax my muscles, breathe in, squeeze the trigger on the exhale and the second block vanishes.

"Not bad, buddy. You wasted a round, though." Jacob chuckles.

Yeah, yeah, yeah. My dad used to say 'gun control is being able to hit your target'.

"Just wanted an extra dance with your lady," I tell him.

When he turns around to set the gun back down on the table I notice his freshly-painted leather biker jacket. It's got a cow holding a M60 in a roundel, with JAMCAO written underneath it.

"J A M C A O?" I ask him.

"JAMCOW." He responds. "There are enough bikers around here to start up a new MC."

"What's it stand for?" I ask him.

"Janitors of Anarchy Motorcycle Club, Albuquerque Originals," he responds.

"That's a mouthful."

"That's what she said."

Jacob can act like a total hard-ass sometimes, but he's actually a pretty laid-back guy. He likes to bust people's balls, but he can take it as well as he can give it, and that's a rare thing. We've spent hours getting drunk and insulting each other. (It's a guy thing - don't try to understand it.)

We didn't get on terribly well at first and actually came to blows when we met. He's got experience fighting, and has learned some pretty dirty tricks, but I've spent time learning to look for openings and exploit them. I wound up with a black eye and splitting headache. He got two broken ribs, and a dislocated shoulder. That was the first and last time we fought. We've been friends ever since.

We spend some time shooting and swapping gun stories. He told me about the first gun he built: "The Hawgleg" was made out of pipe from the back yard and had a nail for a firing pin. I tell him about the time my dad threatened to shoot a bunch of Jehovah's Witnesses, and we agree that more people should do that. The only thing more universally deplored than door-to-door religious salespeople is Congress. We're trying to take care of the Congressional problem; the door-to-door religious salespeople problem is up to the rest of you.

When we finally head back in, everyone's in the kitchen, snacking on the little tidbits we keep around. Jessica has finally come out of her room, and Jean has finally stopped gaming.

"Gentlemen," says Eve, "welcome back to the revolution. Jessica's dad was apparently involved in some very scary things."

Jessica's holding a small black leather book - a diary of some kind or another. "He didn't detail everything, but there's something truly scary in this town."

"Yeah," says Jean, "it's called Los Betos Mexican Cafe."

Jessica looks confused, but anyone who's been there will agree: that place is pretty scary.

"I don't know what that is, but I doubt it's what my dad was referring to when he referred to the 'destroyer of worlds.'"

Frank can't help himself. "That's the number four on their dinner menu."

"Knock it off, guys." Eve's trying to sound serious, but I can tell she thought it was funny, too.

"My dad worked for some place called Radula, but he doesn't say much about what he did there. His journal goes downhill pretty quickly; it's just rambling about 'dreaming gods' and 'living shadows' by the end."

"Here's what we're going to do: Jean, find out everything you can about this place. You two," Eve points at Frank and me, "find the building and see if we can get in. Jacob, keep blowing holes in things."

"You got it, boss." Jacob's never happier than when he can go blow holes in things.

"What are you two up to?" I ask.

"Us?" asks Eve, "We're going shopping."

11 | Rad

Frank likes to say that hacking a building is no different from hacking a computer: both tasks require you to find alternate ways into a system. All systems have points that aren't necessarily intended to facilitate ingress and egress, but those points exist and can be used for that purpose nonetheless.

Radula is located behind the dollar movie theater on San Mateo Boulevard. It's a single-story, unmarked building in a sizeable lot surrounded by concertina wire. The fences sport signs that let you know that not only is trespassing not allowed, but the *use of deadly force is authorized* in case of trespassers.

"Don't park directly in front of Radula," Frank says as we're driving in. "Let's park in the theatre parking lot and walk back here."

"Yeah, then people will just think we're here to see the latest Jim Carrey flick. Much better," I respond.

As we're walking around the theater to Radula, Frank tells me his theories about hacking buildings.

"Every building has weaknesses. Most security is designed to just make it too much of a pain in the ass for the average person to break in," he tells me.

I laugh. "You're hardly average, right?"

"Right. I've got experience, but nothing I do is exactly rocket science. It's finding the holes in the system. If I need a rocket scientist to get through a tricky part, I call in Jean."

"No wonder you guys get along so well. The family that breaks the law together, stays together," I say.

"Well, that, and the sex is great."

"TMI, bro."

"Get over it, man, love is love. And nude love is nude love. And I love the nude love."

"All right, I get it," I tell him. "How are we going to seduce the skirt off this place?"

"We start by getting the lay of the land. The concertina wire is professionally laid. I've seen places that don't put the concertina wire over the gates - here it's all over. There's no guard shack, and it looks like the main gate is mechanical. I don't see a keypad or anything, so I'm guessing they've got some kind of sensor system, either on the vehicles themselves or carried with the drivers."

"Damn," I say. "I guess I was just focused on the 'we will kill you if you trespass' signs."

"That's what they have them for. Don't get me wrong - they probably will kill us if they find us, but they're hoping they won't have to. First layer of security: scare people into not looking any further. Ignore all that for now and look further. Do you see anyone wandering around? Guards or anything?"

I look. The yard looks empty, almost deserted. "No. All's quiet on the western front."

"There are four cameras, one on each corner of the building. See those little black dots? Cameras. The second layer of security: difficult to fool, but not impossible.

"Everything that happens here happens inside. Notice, you can't see in? The windows are all mirrored, and I'm willing to bet there are blinds on the inside that will make it difficult to snoop. That's their third layer of security.

"It would be nice to see what's going on inside. Whatever's going on in here, they're working hard to keep it quiet without looking like they're keeping it quiet. There's no name on the building - no address, nothing. Either you're supposed to be here, or you're supposed to just keep right on going.

"Let's walk around the perimeter and see if anything pops up."

We walk the perimeter trying to look inconspicuous. I hope people walk around this place all the time, but I kind of doubt it. At the nearest point, the building is a good 50 feet from the fence, and there doesn't seem to be a damn way to look into the place. No one's moving. I'd think the place was deserted, except for the fresh tracks in the dirt parking lot.

"Is it just me, or does this place look almost desperately innocuous?" I ask Frank.

"Yeah, something feels off about this joint," he says.

"The license plates are all New Mexico, though - not a government plate anywhere. Save for the razor wire and the signs, I'd think these guys were selling farm equipment or something and drive by without a second thought."

"Set back in here, away from the main drag, most people have probably never noticed this place. Even the few who did notice probably ignored it," he says.

"It's like a building made of Teflon - kind of a neat trick, if you can pull it off. So, how do we get in?"

"I'm going to assume the place is guarded 24/7, and the cameras may have night vision. My guess is there's a vault on the inside that we'd have to get through, and probably a Mosler safe or two inside that will need to be opened. We'll need a distraction on the outside, go in the back through that door by the AC. Probably need to silence a guard or three.

"Can you crack a safe?" Frank asks.

Moslers are government approved storage safes. Think of a huge hunk of metal with a lock on the front and you've got a good idea of what they are. They're usually guaranteed to take at least an hour to break through and that's if you're not worried about making a lot of noise. Do it quietly and cracking one can take upwards of six hours.

"No. I can barely open those damned Moslers even when I have the combo," I tell him.

"We can probably get Eve to rip the safes apart. I imagine we can have Jean tap in from the outside and crack any computer security. It'll take him time, and we'll need to hook him into the system, since I doubt there's much in the way of external network access." He's still thinking about how to get in. I can see the gears turning in his head.

We're almost around the place and can't afford to take another lap. "Let's head back," I say.

"Yeah. Yeah. I can crack this nut, I just need some time," Frank mutters. I believe him.

12 | You're Going Down

Back at the ranch, Jean is excited, which means he's found a huge problem and a way to either fix it or a way to get around it. Hacker enthusiasm spawned from cracking the uncrackable. I've never hacked a system - I was just a programmer - but I understand the enthusiasm, since there's nothing like solving a problem. That may just be why our country's so fucked up: no one gets excited about solving problems anymore. They just get excited about pointing out problems.

"Radula doesn't even have a fucking website!" Jean tells us while he's pacing around the living room. "That's how far off the grid they are, they don't even have a fucking website! Everyone has a fucking website! Certs mints had a website that told you abso-fucking-lutely nothing about Retsyn. They didn't tell you thing one about what the shit Retsyn is, but they had at a website that at least fucking mentioned Retsyn! Radula? Not a goddamned thing."

"Jean, you know decaf coffee still tastes pretty good, right?" Frank asks him, rolling his eyes.

"I made a cappuccino with caffeinated water, so what? I need energy to work! I am an artist and you don't criticize how an artist works! You may criticize the final piece, but you never criticize the method!" His eyes are manic and his hands are constantly gesturing around the place while he walks.

"Do you have anything useful to say, or should we wait until this passes?" Eve asks.

"I found out what Retsyn is, I found out what Radula does. I am the rat in the wall, stealing the Twinkies from out your pantry!" Jean shouts.

"OK, he's lost it. 'From out your pantry?' Who talks like that?" Jessica asks.

"He likes to get good and wired and the hack the living hell out of things. He does this all the time," Frank tells her. "One time, when he erased our tax bill at the IRS, he was up for a solid week mainlining caffeine. No, I'm not kidding. He'll probably sleep well after the caffeine wears off – which will be sometime tomorrow."

"OK, Jean, tell us what you found out," Eve tells him.

"Radula is so deep black they're like a black hole. They do government contracting, very specialized stuff. I had to dig deep into the bowels of the Internet, but finally scrounged up a posting on Usenet from a guy who said he used to work for Radula. By the way, can you guess how many former employees this place has? Near as I can tell? One! What the fuck kind of place has one employee who was pissed off enough to talk about anything? Even then, this guy made a post 5 years ago and never followed up. He's probably dead."

"Tell us what you know. Please," Jacob asks him.

"Radula was incorporated in 1976 as a government contractor. Their public filings are all heavily censored, which you're not supposed to do as a civilian entity, but they made a shit-ton of money, and if you make a shit-ton of money, you can do whatever you want. Fucking government contracts, man. License to print money. Jessica, your dad worked for Radula for two years back in the early 2000s. According to his tax records, he was an External Integration and Control Specialist, whatever the hell that is."

Why can't anyone have a normal job title these days? I have a friend whose job title was 'Research Evangelist.' I still have no idea what he did.

"So, what did my dad actually do for Radula?" Jessica asks.

"He integrated and controlled external things, *duh*," Jean says like it's the most obvious thing in the world.

"Do you have any idea what Radula does, or what her dad did there?" Eve asks, getting exasperated.

"No goddamned idea. The only thing I can tell for certain is they did some work downtown, and then something scary happened, and the company has been on a downward spiral ever since. There was a serious brouhaha about whatever bad mojo went down. By the way, this was about the time your dad disappeared and the guy that wrote that post said he was excused from the company," Jean says.

"Well, fuck," Jacob says. "We're going to break into that place, aren't we?"

Frank, never one to pass up a challenge, grins. "Damn right we are."

"Guys, I have a sinking feeling in my gut that this won't be like breaking into Anodyne or the IRS building," Eve says, concerned. "We need information, but these guys are pros, and they've already gotten a black eye. They'll be on the ball."

"Ok," I say, "I've just gotta ask, why are we so interested in what her father did? How does that help us? No offense, Jessica, but we've done our bit."

"I told you, I've got a feeling that something her dad did is important," Eve says.

"How can her dad help us?" Frank asks.

"Look, what do you want us to do here? What are we trying to accomplish?" She points at Jean. "Why are you here?"

"I want to change things," he mumbles.

"For the better?" Eve asks.

"There is no way to change the situation for the better. It's all got to go away," he responds.

Eve pauses for a moment. "Right. You can build a sparkling city on top of a sewer, but that won't stop the stench of shit from rising up. You've got to burn down everything and restart from scratch. What do we have here to do that?"

"A computer hacker, an arms dealer, an infiltration expert, a security guy and an unknown quantity with a penchant for kicking ass," I say. "And you, of course. Also something of an unknown quantity."

Jessica raises her eyebrows. I think she's trying to figure out whether or not to be insulted.

"This is a good group," Eve says. "No doubt about it. But we can't change the world on our own. Whatever her dad was doing may help us. You want to kill everyone in Congress? You want to watch the world crumble? You want to see riots in the streets? We need something other than the six of us, some bullet-proof vests and ton of guns."

"Like what? A bomb?" Jessica asks.

"Bombs are for terrorist pussies," Jacob grumbles.

"Exactly," Eve says. "A bomb won't fix things. A bomb just looks like amateur hour. Besides, we'd never get even a decent-sized bomb anywhere near Congress. They'd cut us down and claim we had all kinds of Islamic connections."

"Well, why can't we just keep doing what we're doing? We've got resources, we've got a good place, all the money we need," Jean asks. He's always been comfortable here and, like most people, he's reticent to move outside his comfort zone.

Jacob snorts. "My friends were gunned down by a government goon-squad."

"I was beaten senseless because they wanted someone to blame. Keep people scared and convince them those guys over there are the root of the problem," Frank says. "Works well until you get singled out as one of the roots."

I sigh. "I know of a Senator's kid who got away with murder."

"Right. On all counts. The corruption is so deep you have to burn away everything to get rid of it," She points at Jessica. "I'm sure she's important."

"Didn't you tell me to not trust visions? That we have a way of making them come true?" Jessica asks her.

"Yes. And it's the making them come true part that I'm interested in. I've seen people getting dumber and meaner and generally more psychotic. Trust me, things will get worse," Eve says. "Things always get worse, and you can't fix the problem by exposing the corruption, or killing a Senator, or burning down a city. You've got to think bigger."

"Fuck it," I say, "I've got nothing going on that can't wait. Let's hit the place. At least it won't be boring."

"I'm in. Anything to hurt these bastards," Frank says. I know he's got a good reason to be bitter. I've seen the looks he gets. I've seen the police report from his assault, the one where they said he'd fallen down the stairs. He's just like the rest of us, though, carrying our wounds like armor and using our sins like weapons.

We may all be kind of crazy, but we're all the good kind of crazy.

"Can we blow shit up?" asks Jacob, a gleam in his eye.

"Sorry, Jake," Eve says. "It's probably best to keep this one quiet."

"Well, shit." Jacob sighs.

"Jean, you in?" Frank asks.

"How could I leave you alone out in the wild to get killed? If you can get a wireless link, I can steal everything off their computers." Jean smiles.

"I knew there was a reason I loved you," Frank grins.

"Well, Jessica?" Eve asks. "Are you in?"

She thinks for a minute. "Yeah, I'm in. For now at least."

"Jessica, do you have a picture of your dad handy?" I ask her.

"Uh, yeah. Let me get it," she says and disappears into the back of the house quietly. She comes back with a Polaroid and hands the photo to Eve, who looks at it and passes it to Frank. And so it goes and so it goes until the picture gets to Jean.

Jean looks at the photo for a sec and I can tell he's ready to dismiss it and pass it off when he does a double take and his eyes get huge. "Holy shitballs. I've met this guy," he says excitedly.

"What?" Frank asks incredulously.

"Yeah, yeah. When I lived in that shitty apartment down by UNM, I used to see this guy."

"You mean the shitty basement apartment next to the Rasta

Simpsons mural?" Frank asks him.

Yes, there was once a mural of the Simpsons as Rastafarians painted on a wall in an alley behind the old salad bar place on Central. The mural has since been painted over, but anyone who has seen it will always remember it.

"Yeah, the place with that crazy hippie bitch manager who refused to do anything at all on her day off," Jean says, tapping the picture. "This guy used to hang out in the alley. He had a beard and generally looked like shit - smelled like shit, too - but it was definitely him. I used to give him cigarettes. I always thought he was just some random crazy, because he was always looking over his shoulder and talking about 'them' and how he was worried 'it' might get free."

"*What* might get free?" Eve asks him.

"He never said, but every time I saw him he'd say it was always a good day because 'it' hadn't gotten free."

"When was the last time you saw him?" Jessica asks him.

"Uh, let me think. I moved out of that apartment a few years ago. I saw him the day I was moving. He waved and told me to stay away from shadows."

"He may still be around," I say. "There's a contingent of homeless people down in that area, because the college students give them money and food, and the cops are too busy busting the college students to bother with the homeless. I think a bunch of them sleep in the park down on Coal Avenue, or in the cemetery down on University."

Eve points at Jean, Jessica and me. "You three - go check Jean's old place out. If her dad's down there, it might save us some time. Jacob, we need to get ourselves some quiet weapons. Frank, find me a way into Radula."

13 | Douchebag Central

Like most decent sized cities, Albuquerque has a homeless population. For the most part, they're pretty innocuous, and everyone's usually more interested in the antics of our resident "naked guy" than what any random shuffling derelict is up to. The climate is usually conducive to living outside, too. For a couple weeks in July it's hot as balls, and for a month or so in the winter it gets really damned cold, but mostly the city's pretty temperate. Climate matters when your main domicile is a public park.

Drive down Central Avenue sometime, and you'll usually see some fun sights. Right now there's a homeless woman covered in grime, wearing a thong leotard, with a giant blue Mohawk and roller skates, trying to hitchhike.

Good luck, sweetheart.

We pull into a side street off Central next to the salad bar and park. Jean's old apartment looks like standard-issue shithole student apartments always do - like the slumlords gave up caring a while back, and it's up to the tenants to keep things in shape. In the alley outside his old place there's a hooker on her knees blowing some guy in a suit down the alley.

We let her finish the job because everyone deserves to make a living. As we walk through the alley, the guy in the suit spots us and gets red in the face. How can anyone be pissed off after getting blown? Granted, it was in an alley, but a hummer's still a hummer.

He makes a beeline toward us, fists clenched, and gets right in Jean's face.

"If you tell anyone you what you saw I will kick your ass up one side and down the other," he tells us.

By going straight to Jean, he's revealed an awful lot about himself. He heads to the smallest guy in the group because he wants a confrontation, but he wants it without any real threat. He avoids making eye contact with Jessica, probably because he's actually terrified of women. It's one thing to pay someone to blow you in an alley. It's another thing altogether to interact with a woman who might not do exactly what you want.

He shoots me the occasional glance, but mostly he's just trying to be the alpha dog with the least-threatening person. This way he can feel like a tough guy, and tell himself he pushed around three people.

He's wearing a standard issue suit, probably a middle manager somewhere, and thinks he's the shit. He's a big guy, but you can tell by the way he moves that he's used to using his size to intimidate underlings, and never has to go beyond the threat stage. I love fucking with people like that. Bullies of all stripes deserve to get thumped every now and then - it keeps them grounded.

"Take a hike, asshole. No one cares that you have to pay for blow jobs," Jessica tells him.

He turns on her and puts his finger in her face. "You shut your whore mouth when men are talking!"

I grab his hand, bend it down, turn around and pull his elbow tight into my body. With both hands holding his one hand, I force him into a Chin Na lock. He goes up on his toes and grimaces but doesn't give up.

"Are you going to fuck off or do we need to gut you and leave you in the dumpster over there?" I ask him.

"Fuck you, asshole." He says and reaches into his pocket with his other hand. Probably going for a knife.

This is what you get for trying to be nice.

The position I've got him pulls him off balance, but it doesn't hurt, so I change my hand position and twist his arm forward and around as hard and fast as I can, pulling his hand down and using it as leverage. This makes for a full-on joint lock and it pulls him forward at the waist. By pulling his arm up I can stretch the muscles and tendons - and that hurts. He drops the pocket knife he was pulling out of his pocket, and tries to pull away.

"Do you drive a standard, or an automatic?" I ask him.

"Fuck you." He says.

I pull the arm up higher.

"Standard or automatic?"

"Fuck. Automatic."

"Good," I say. I was planning on letting this guy go, but as soon as the knife came out, it changed the dynamics. I drive my forearm into his elbow. It's not hard enough to cause any permanent damage, but a hyper-extended elbow still hurts, and losing an arm in a fight is debilitating, unless you're a famous French kickboxer.

He plants face-first in the dirt and rolls over, clutching his arm to his side. His expensive suit is covered in dirt. I know his type. He won't tell anyone what really happened, because he's afraid to let people know he was paying for sex from a crack whore, and got his ass kicked. He'll make up some story about getting jumped by at least three guys, and he's not even certain if one guy was breathing when they ran off. Yeah, he got hurt, but he gave better than he got and it sucks having to the do the cops' job for them.

"Get lost, shit heel," I tell him.

He scrambles to his feet and looks at me, utterly pissed off and terrified at the same time. He backs away and stumbles out of the alley. Before he turns the corner he turns and flips me off.

The hooker has been watching this from behind a wall down the alley. I would've expected she'd be gone by now, but she hung out to watch. Everyone enjoys a fight, especially when a douchebag gets a beat down.

Jessica waves her over with the promise of a fifty. Everyone's a sucker for Ulysses.

"Sorry about your client," Jean says.

"Ain't no thing," our lady of the evening says with a toothless grin. No wonder he liked getting blown by her - no teeth makes it hard to bite. "That bastard shortchanged me. He gave me a twenty folded in half, and said it was two twenties. Now I ain't got twenty."

Jessica shows her the fifty. "Help us out and you've got fifty."

The pro smiles and cocks her hips. "And what can I do for you, sweet thing? You got something you want from me?"

"A full-body condom would be a good start," Jessica tells her.

"They sell those at Walgreens?"

"We just want to find someone," Jean says. "A guy used to hang out in this alley. Crazy looking guy. Always talked about shadows and dreams and shit. I gave him smokes. I was wondering what happened to him. You seen him?"

"Maybe. What he look like?"

Jessica hands her the old picture. "This is my dad. I need to find him."

"Last I saw him he had a beard and old tatty coat. I heard someone call him Crazy Eyes," Jean says.

"Shit. That was probably Gonzo. He call everyone Crazy Eyes."

"Damn," Jean says.

Jessica steps closer. "Can you look at the picture? Have you seen this guy?"

The hooker looks closer at the picture and tries to clear the drug blur out of her eyes. She focuses in and you can almost see the gerbil running faster in her braincase. "Yeah. I seen him. He hangs out at the graveyard like everyone else. People leave him alone 'cause one guy tried to mug him and wound up screaming and trying to claw his own eyes out. Dude never even moved. He got the ghosts around him, and they don't like no one talking to him."

"He clawed the mugger's eyes out?" I ask.

"No. Why you so stupid, stupid? Pay attention. This guy never even moved, the guy mugging him just started screaming and trying to claw his own eyes out. People say it bath salts or some shit, but I know better. Ghosts, motherfucker. Ghosts all around that guy," she says.

"The graveyard?"

"Down the street. By the seven elebin."

Jessica hands her the fifty and gets a promise of "anything she ever want."

14 | Zombies and Other Things

Fairview Memorial Park Cemetery is a common hangout for the local homeless population. It's big, dark, and quiet. I doubt the police patrol the place all that much, and the established residents aren't given to talking much, save through Ouija boards and assorted mediums. During the day the place is pretty quiet since the living population moves along so the mourning population won't call the police. After closing time - at 5pm or so - the regular group of homeless people and youthful miscreants move back in to spend the night with the rest of the ghosts in the cemetery.

In here, they're safe from the outside world since the normals don't care for wandering around graveyards in the wee hours. This is the safe place for the mental wrecks and general derelicts of Albuquerque.

Truthfully most of these people are harmless. They've fallen through the cracks in their sanity and wandered off the boardwalk of normal society. Sure, there's the occasional violent loon. The mini-society in the cemetery tends to take care of its own, though, since violence brings down heat. Heat from the police means beatings and Tasers and tear gas.

We watch the back gates after closing time and find a couple of people who might fit the bill. After a certain amount of grime and shredded clothing most people start to look alike - stooped over, no eye contact.

The first guy is a wash, but the second hits the mark.

Hayha is standing under a tree in his grubby coat and full beard doing the homeless shuffle: step to the left, feet together, step to the right, feet together. Lather, rinse, repeat. Jessica takes one glimpse at his sparkling, fever-mad eyes and covers her mouth as her eyes tear up. He doesn't recognize her. In fact, he doesn't seem like he recognizes much of anything around him, but he's definitely watching something and shaking his head no, no, no. His overcoat has vomit stains down the front, and grime dug in so deep, nothing short of the cleansing power of fire will get the gunk out. That same grime has dug into the creases in face, bringing out his age like stage makeup.

"Daddy," Jessica cries, tears rolling down her face. She learned to hate this man by trusting the lies she made up in her own head about him - the imaginary infidelities that drove her mother to poverty and suicide and left her herself working through college strapped to tables as a centerpiece. All it takes is one gander at this guy and you can see his mind was forcibly evicted, probably a long time ago.

"Shit," Jean says. "He looks worse than ever."

Hayha looks up when Jean speaks, some part of his mind clicking into place long enough to realize this guy was nice to him once upon a time, before the gears fail to mesh and he devolves back into mindless torpor.

"You want a smoke, man?" Jean asks him.

The barest of nods says yes. Jean fishes a pack out of his pocket and hands Hayha a cigarette. Grubby fingers covered in caked blood reach out take the cigarette and put it to his mouth. Jean tries to light the smoke for him, but Hayha pulls away from the flame with the kind of jerk only people who have an intimate understanding of fire do.

"It's OK, man. It's just a lighter. It won't hurt you," Jean tells him and slowly tries a second time to light the cigarette. Hayha pulls away again.

"Give me one of those," says Jessica.

Jean hands her one and she lights it up, takes a drag, exhales, and hands the lit cigarette to her dad filter first. "Here, I lit one for you."

Hayha takes the cigarette and puts it in his mouth. The smell or the taste triggers something mechanical in him and he takes a drag and exhales coughing. The second time works better.

The hairs on the back of my neck are sticking up, so I scan around the cemetery to make sure no one's creeping up on us. So far the place is quiet, save for the odd homeless guy and a man with a mechanic's jacket and a ball cap standing in front of a grave.

I keep panning around. The sensation is probably nothing, but my paranoia has served me well in the past, and I've learned to respect it.

The cemetery is largely open space - no real hills, and only a handful of trees to speak of - so it's an easy place to see would-be problems from a long way off. Nothing exciting is going on. I wonder what the guy in the ball cap is doing. Saying goodbye to a loved one, cursing a fallen foe?

My own family's ashes are long scattered to the breeze. My grandfather once told me, "Grief has a half-life. It gets less and less painful, but it never quite goes away." I've found that to be pretty much the truth and I hope the guy standing over the grave finds some solace or something. We're not into graves in my family, just incinerate and toss to the breeze.

When I glance back to the guy in the ball cap, he seems to flicker like fluorescent lights do before they completely kick on. I must be getting tired. People don't flicker. I blink my eyes a couple of times, thinking my vision is going, and when I open them again, he's gone.

"You need to leave here." Hayha's voice is strained, like he's forgotten how to speak. "This place isn't safe."

"Daddy." Jessica steps forward but there's still no recognition of his daughter anywhere on his face. It's like he's taken his past and shoved it down deep. And then parked a car over the entrance.

"You're not safe here. Go." Hayha holds up both hands and I can see the shredded arm of his jacket. It looks like something with a lot of sharp points ripped into him, and he held his arm up to protect himself. Whatever it was that shredded his jacket, it did a number on him, too. There's blood all over the grime on his arm, and his left hand flops around like it's been disconnected from the rest of his body. "It watches me all the time," he says distantly

"Who watches you, Daddy?"

"This whole town is cursed. He's awake and angry."

Jessica tries to step toward him, but he backs away mumbling to himself. Whatever he saw, or did, or had done to him tore something out of his head and it's not coming back.

As he backs away, Delano holds up his hands like he's warding off some vision in his head. We remain absolutely still, quietly watching him back up. Maybe it's a trick of the light, but I could swear I saw a shadow moving in the grass behind him. It's getting dark and shadows are everywhere, but it still struck me as odd. I must be getting tired.

Jessica takes a half step forward and Delano reacts with a loan moan. Some hidden terror is flashing through his head. I really want to know what happened but there's no way this guy is going to tell us. He's just a shell now filled with madness and loss.

"Let him go," I say. "He's gone."

My neck hairs are prickling again, and I can feel this pressure between my eyes. I get that when I'm being watched. It's easy to be paranoid in this place. I've never liked cemeteries. When I turn my head to look around I catch another flicker of movement from the ground, but when I look back it's gone.

"I think we need to get out of here," Jean says. "The natives are getting restless." All around us eyes are turning in our direction, worried that one of their own is in trouble. It's one thing to be in a cemetery. It's another thing entirely to be in a cemetery when it's getting dark, and a couple of dozen homeless, violent, delinquent, and otherwise marginal people suddenly find you very interesting.

Hayha has forgotten we were ever there. He's standing still, staring off into space and talking to himself. I suspect that nothing we say will be louder than the voices in his head. If we try to grab him, we'll have trouble with the rest of the denizens of this place. Jean puts a hand on Jessica's shoulder, and she flashes him a gaze filled with rage and pain. I can't say I blame her. I lost my dad once, and that was bad enough. To find him and lose him again would be devastating.

"We've got to go, kid. If we stay here, we're going wind up being someone's dinner," I tell her as gently as possible. I can tell she's not happy, but she turns away from her dad, her damp eyes hardening, and heads toward the gate.

I resist the temptation to pull out a gun, knowing it will just make things worse. The best advice I ever got from my Kenpo teacher was that it's always easier to avoid a fight than to win a fight. We might be able to win this one, but I doubt it.

We skulk out with our tails between our legs like dogs that just got yelled at for chewing on the couch. No one physically chases us, but eyes track us all the way out. There's an occasional flash of silver as headlights glint off knives. I really really really hope no one starts anything.

At the gate to the cemetery I stop and look back. Delano is gone and the rest of the zombies have done what they do best: faded into the background. From the outside, the place looks peaceful, but I know if we step back in we're going to have to fight our way back out.

Jessica sits stone-faced in the passenger seat, Jean is shaking in the back seat and I've got a sinking feeling in my gut that we've just stepped into something we should have gone around.

"Someone's going to pay," Jessica says quietly. Her whisper isn't helping my mood. Part of me wonders if we wouldn't have been better off leaving her to the Yakuza. We could have walked away and she'd be just another victim in our wake.

Sure. Leave her and never sleep another night again. Fuck.

Fortunately, we've got a package liquor store nearby. I could use a drink right about now.

15 | Figure It Out

●—◉—●

"I'm in," Jessica says while we're all sitting around the living room. "One hundred percent. I don't know what happened to my dad, but someone broke him and someone needs to pay."

"I'm glad to hear that," Eve tells her. "What prompted your decision?"

I immediately start doing the throat cutting sign that everyone knows means "drop it," but Eve ignores me.

"I saw my dad today," Jessica tells her. Her eyes are hard when she says it and they're lit from some fire inside of her. I had figured she was tough when she took out that Yakuza asshole, but she looks dangerous now. Dangerous and unpredictable. Those are two traits I don't like to see in people I work with.

"How was he?" Eve asks.

Jean joins me in the throat slicing gesture and both of us desperately hope Eve will drop it. We know she won't, but hope springs eternal.

"Gone," Jessica says. "Grimy and dirty and gone."

"You don't know what happened to him, you know," Eve says. "It could have been completely innocuous. He might have simply decided he liked heroin."

Jessica glares at her for a moment before deciding it wasn't an insult. "This wasn't just heroin. Someone broke him and I want to know who and why."

Eve nods and points at me. "What happened?"

"Found her dad," I say. "He didn't look good."

"Where was he?" Eve asks.

"Cemetery," Jean says. "That one down by the university that all the homeless hang out in."

"Should we bring him here?" Eve asks. "Would it help?"

Jessica's got her head in her hands. "It won't help. He's gone. Whatever that guy was, he wasn't my dad. Not anymore."

Her eyes are red and puffy from crying and she still looks like she's in shock.

"I'm sorry to hear that," Eve says. "But I promise you a measure of revenge."

Jessica nods and the barest smile crosses her lips. Like the rest of us, she's pissed and Eve found a way to use that.

"Jacob, what's our weapon status?"

"I got hold of a handful of suppressed Walthers," Jacob says with a huge grin. "Complete with subsonic ammo. You won't have much range and the silencers won't last forever so stay out of any firefights, but they'll be great for killing guards."

Most people don't realize this, but there's really no such thing as a silenced weapon. Guns can be quiet, and legally quiet, too, but they're nigh impossible to make silent. The suppressor on the barrel of the gun allows the gas to quietly dissipate. Subsonic ammunition means there's no sonic boom from the bullet.

"Nice work," Eve says. "What's the status on converting the Anodyne material to body armor?"

"Good to go. I got a guy to make some vests for us," he tells her.

"Excellent. Frank, how are we getting in?"

"The roof was spec'd as a helipad, so that's our best bet to get in. The door up there should still work," Frank says.

"Who the hell puts a helipad on top of a one-story building?" I ask.

"Idiots," Frank says. "They didn't grease the right palms, so even though they've got a helipad they're not zoned to have one and that can't land a helicopter on it."

"How'd you find out there was a helipad up there?" Jean asks.

"I waited in line most of the day and asked for the blueprints." Frank tells him.

"Where?" Jean asks him.

"Downtown, city planning," Frank says and yawns. "I spent three hours sandwiched between a guy with a pompadour and an immense woman wearing tights."

"I'll rub your back later," Jean tells him.

"Anything else we should know?" Eve asks.

"The tights were floral," Frank says.

Eve closes her eyes and I can almost see her counting to ten. I'm not sure what she expected when she found us all but I'm sure we're a pain to deal with sometimes. Like that time Jacob decided he was a Cradle of Filth fan.

"About the building," Eve says.

"Not that I can tell. It may or may not have been built according to the blueprints, and it may have changed over the years, but it's the best we've got right now," Frank says.

"Okay. How do we get on the roof?" I ask.

"Grappling gun," Frank says with a grin. "I've always wanted to try it out. Once we're on top, we just need to open the door and we're in."

"Open the door and we're in? I'll believe it when I see it," I say.

"Steven, you have so little faith," Frank says.

"You have no idea," I tell him.

Cracking Radula will take some planning, but nothing overwhelming. Frankly, given what we know - which is jack shit, really - there's not much planning we can do. We need to get in with a minimum amount of fuss and make a wireless setup to get data back to Jean.

"Well, that covers weapons and entrance," Eve says. "How do we get from the fence to building? Didn't you guys say there were cameras?"

"There are, probably night vision at least," Frank tells her. "We need to cover up and make sure whatever guards are in there are focused on something else."

"Could we stage a fight on the sidewalk?" Jacob asks. "People always watch a fight."

"The guards would just call the cops and be done with it," I say.

"Yeah, but when Albuquerque's finest show up and start shooting it would provide a hell of a distraction," Jacob says.

"You do realize they'd be shooting as us, right?" Jean asks.

"Doesn't have to be us fighting, bro. We find a couple of homeless guys and pay 'em to fight."

"That is the most despicable thing I've ever heard you say," Eve says.

"Much obliged, ma'am," Jacob says.

"Bum fights wouldn't keep them occupied long enough," I say and immediately regret it. I glance at Jessica but she's lost in thought and doesn't seem to have noticed. "We need something that will last."

"We could start a fire," Jean says.

"What are we going to set on fire around there?" Frank asks. "The movie theater? A fire would just draw more eyes, anyway."

Everyone stops talking and stares into space.

"Jessica," Eve finally asks, "are you sure you're in?"

"I'm in," she replies.

"I've got an idea, but I doubt you'll like it," Eve tells her.

Jessica eyes her, one eyebrow raised. "What is it?"

"How do you feel about motorcycles and bikers?"

"I like motorcycles, why?" Jessica asks. Recognition slowly spreads over her face and she wrinkles her nose. "Oh, God," she finally says.

"We'll need to get you some leathers," Eve says.

"What's going on?" Jacob asks. Slowly he, too, gets it. "Far fucking out, man."

"There are a lot of bars around there," I say. "It's not hard to believe a couple might feel a bit randy after a night of drinking."

"I am not having sex with someone I barely know," Jessica says.

"I wouldn't ask that," Eve says. "I would never ask that. What about acting like you're about to have sex? We won't need long to get in."

"It's just a show," Frank says.

"And let's face it, girl," Jean pipes in, "you've got it going on. I don't even like girls, but I'd watch that show."

Frank punches Jean in the arm and shoots him a glare. "You're not helping. Jessica, we need a distraction and you and the hairy mountain over there are the best bet. No one would believe Eve and Jacob together; they're too outlandish. I can cut the security, but I need a gunman and Steven's the best bet. We need Jean to hack their computers. Jacob can shoot and blow things up, but this has to be quiet."

"Wait a minute," Jessica says. "Why do I have to be a distraction? Why can't I just go in with you guys?"

"First," Eve says, "the rest of us worked together before so we're comfortable doing this. Second: You're stunning and any man would probably watch you make out with an ape if they thought they might see your tits."

"Yeah," Jessica responds, "but I don't want to make out with an ape."

"Jacob's not an ape, per se," I interject.

"Sure I am. But I'm the ape who gets to make out with the hottie. This must be how King Kong felt," Jacob says.

"Jessica. We need you to do this. You don't have to kiss him or fondle him or anything else, and if he gets too out of control you have my permission to castrate him," Eve says. "If you're not up to castrating him, tell me and I'll rip his nuts off myself."

Jacob leans back, grinning. "I think I've got the best job here."

"Jean. No offense, but you're not much of a fighter. I want you to stay outside, hidden somewhere. We're going to connect a wireless link on the inside. Once the feed is up, you crack that network and steal everything that's not tied down," Eve says.

"I'll have my hands down its pants before you can say 'roofies'," Jean grins.

It's true. He's not much of a fighter. He can crack a computer like no one else I've ever met, but I once saw him get his ass kicked by a 13-year-old girl he was trying to muscle. True story! We were at the Walgreens on Central once, loading up on supplies (aka cigarettes and beer), when the girl in front of us took too much time to check out, asking questions about what kind of Pokémon cards or some shit they carried. Jean tells her to hurry the fuck up. She turns around, looks at him, and punched him square in the balls. While he's lying on the ground holding his nuts, she goes back to what's she was doing. I'm standing there trying hard not to laugh my ass off, and get him up off the floor at the same time. Frank was pissed, but even he thought it was funny when I told him the whole story.

Eve points at Frank and me. "I'm going in with you guys."

I don't care who you work for, or what you do, but it always kind of sucks when you have to work with your boss. It's a well-known fact that productivity goes down when the boss spends too much time with the staff. Everyone tends to get nervous when the head honcho is around.

On the other hand, if the lead starts flying, I can hide behind Eve and not get shot. Try that with your boss sometime.

Time is short so Eve and Jessica disappear to look for Jessica's new costume.

Frank and I each get a fancy new vest courtesy of Anodyne's research and development division. Eve's already bullet-proof, so she'll probably just go with something in basic black. Jacob dresses in his leathers and usual biker accoutrements. Jean tries to look like anyone else wandering around town. Jessica gets a leather vest and pants, courtesy of the local Harley shop.

I must admit, she's stunning. I warn Jacob that no matter how tight her outfit is, I will absolutely guarantee there is something sharp hidden about her person. He's still spending too much time thinking about sticking something inside her to worry about what she'll stick inside him if he's not careful.

Oh, well. His loss if he pushes his luck.

16 | Incursion

Albuquerque at 2 a.m. is relatively quiet, but not dead quiet. The 'Gentlemen's Club' down the street is close to closing time. As we drive to Radula, we see people drunkenly driving home, racing motorcycles down San Mateo or making out in the parking lots of various buildings. The police usually go after the street racers, who never seem to realize they're an obvious target. Damn kids.

We take different cars in case something terrible happens. Jacob and Jessica are on Jacob's hog. Frank, Eve and myself are in Frank's '65 Lincoln Continental, and Jean's in his beater '04 Civic. Jacob's bike is a traditional monster of a Harley, with pipes that shake the pillars of heaven when he revs the engine. He was in - well, Hog heaven - when Jessica hopped on the back, and they tore off. Honestly, I was kind of surprised he didn't just turn right and head off toward a better life in Gallup.

Jean's Civic looks like a bone-stock Honda, but the suspension is stiffer and the engine has been modded eight ways to Sunday. His car doesn't have neon underglow, NOS stickers, or a huge rear wing, but it'll move like it's got a jalapeno up its tail pipe when he punches it. I rode with him one day and he floored the engine getting on Interstate 40. It felt like someone was sitting on my chest. I don't know what was more frightening - his driving, or his constant top-volume Mariachi music.

Frank's ride is a head-turner, but the ride is like marshmallows wrapped in silk, and he only listens to jazz. I used to kid him that a car like his needs Mancini's "Peter Gunn Theme" playing constantly. Yes, it has suicide doors in the back. Yes, it gets about three gallons to the mile. But the '65 Lincoln is an absolutely amazing vehicle. Someday, I need to get one myself. The back seat even has enough leg room for Eve, which is a rare thing these days.

Radula is dead quiet. I mean, no more so than the place was during the day, but the dust has different tracks, so someone has been around. Jean's wireless receiver doesn't have a huge range, so he finds a dark, quiet parking lot, kills the lights, and waits. His car doesn't seem threatening, so hopefully the police will ignore him in favor of the tricked-out rockets on the main drag.

Jacob and Jessica hit next, pull up across the street from Radula. He guns the engine a few times to let everyone know he's there. Jessica gets off, still grinning. I don't know what it is about motorcycles, but I defy anyone to go for a ride and not smile. There's something about bikes that reduce your stress. Ever wonder why bikers are generally so easygoing? Ride a motorcycle, and you'll find out. One of these days I hope to learn to ride one myself.

Jessica is quite the actress - she gets off the bike like a cat. There must be a class or something that women take, because she manages to make getting off that bike a show, like a Mötley Crüe video. I won't say it's a wholesome show, but it certainly is a good show. She sways her hips and strokes her hands up her body to pull off her helmet. She struts back to the bike and drops the helmet in Jacob's hand. Jacob is completely in her spell.

"Keep it in your pants. We've got work to do," Eve says, breaking my reverie.

"Damn," says Frank, "she is good."

"Yeah," Eve says. "Let's get going."

"OK, folks, let's do a comm check," I say.

"Loud and clear," says Frank.

"Online," says Eve.

"I am bored out of my skull," says Jean.

"I'm here," Jessica reports. "Keeping my eyes open."

"I'm sorry, what was that?" asks Jacob.

I seriously hope anyone inside is just as entranced as I was. Okay, okay, this wasn't the most professional moment of my short evildoing career, but Jessica put on a hell of a show.

We sneak around back, silent as clumsy ninjas. Fortunately no one trips over trash, or sneezes. Maybe we're just lucky. We make our way around back, and cross our fingers that no one notices. The fence is electrified, but Frank considers that a minor inconvenience. A few minutes, and he's got a neat hole made in the fence that everyone fits through easily. We creep across the yard, trying to keep in the shadows. There's not much in the way of light here, so that part's not so difficult. The cameras probably have night vision, so our hoods are up and masks are on to prevent any contrast showing.

So far no alarms have gone off, at least not that we can hear.

Frank's custom grappling hook makes a slight sneezing sound and the hook gently arcs to the helipad. I've always been terrible at climbing ropes, and I'm slightly embarrassed when I slowly get to the top. Frank went up the rope like a monkey and Eve made it in two quick pulls. I was the only one that looked like a total klutz.

The door is right where we expected it to be, and is just secured with a single padlock. Every security solution has a weakness. Every damn one of them. This is because security is designed and implemented by people, and people are inherently flawed.

Most of the security is fine. The door is solid metal. The hinges face inward, and the latch holding the padlock is securely welded to both the door frame, and the door itself. This is what kills me: all that work, and they put a basic Wal-Mart special padlock on to hold it shut. At least it's hardened. Eve grabs the padlock and twists, and the whole thing warps and breaks. As she's reaching to open the door, Frank stops her.

"This is too easy, even amateur. We're missing something here," he says.

"Like what?" I ask.

"Why would you go to all the trouble to put this whole thing together, and then secure this door with a shitty padlock?" he asks.

He pulls out some kind of tool that I swear is a leftover prop from *Ghostbusters*. Turns out, I'm not too wrong.

"This will check for electromagnetic emissions, the kind you tend to see when there's an electrical circuit around the door. If you break the circuit, an alarm sounds. I built this out of a *Ghostbusters* toy I found at a thrift store. I call it Mr. Thingy," Frank says.

He moves Mr. Thingy around the door jamb, and the lights stay off. On the bottom right of the door, opposite the door hinge, the arms rise up and the lights go ballistic. Fortunately, he disabled the sound chip, or everyone in town would know we're up here.

"There we go. Hidden at the bottom. It looks like a simple connection alarm. If we break the connection, something bad will happen," he tells us.

"Something bad?" Eve asks.

"Something bad," Frank confirms.

He pulls some metal out his chest pocket and works it through the jamb. "This will keep the circuit closed, even though the door is open," he tells us. He finally gets the metal into place, bends the edge, and tapes it to the door.

"OK, let's hope that was all."

Hope?

He puts his hand on the door, takes a deep breath, and gently pushes the door open.

I hadn't realized my eyes were closed until I opened them. Don't laugh - everyone does it. Granted, closing your eyes in a tense situation makes about as much sense as hiding under your desk when a nuke is going off across town.

Frank steps to the door and sprays something into the air just inside the door looking for lasers. Nothing shines in the smoke, so he motions us all forward.

"Everyone," Eve says into the radio, "we're going in. Let's keep quiet until you get the all-clear."

A smattering of "Rogers" and "okey-dokeys" fill the airspace.

We step into the landing of a small stairway. I cover the stairs in case anyone happens by. As Frank gently closes the door, we notice about four pounds of plastic explosives attached to the inside of the door, presumably connected to the electrical circuit. Hell of an alarm system. Frank tapes the door closed so we don't have to worry about it opening at a bad time.

The landing is small, only about six feet on each side, with a basic set of stairs going down into a dimly lit corridor. I lean over the edge and peer down into a short hallway that extends in either direction. We're probably still outside the main security system.

Eve, being the only one of who's bulletproof, goes down first. She hits the bottom and nothing happens; either there's no one down there or no one's taking the bait. She listens for a moment, shrugs and motions us down. I go first, gun still drawn, and Frank follows.

The corridor is lit with regular fluorescent lights, most of which are turned off. The décor is standard-issue government contractor bland - all posters about "America!" and "You can't untell a secret" and other crazy shit. They're all faded and tattered. Apparently, Radula has fallen on hard times of late. Probably whatever fuckup they had back in the day trashed their reputation enough that they're barely keeping up. Someone's tacked up a sign complaining about the current President. Typical.

You can tell this was once a hot-shit place, but the carpet is worn down, and the paint is scratched up. The whole place looks like it was decorated in the early 1990s.

We quietly creep down the hallway, but so far the place is silent as a tomb.

"Shit. If I'd known this place was wired back in 1993, I wouldn't have spent so much fretting about getting in," Frank says quietly.

"Let's find the network and get Jean plugged in. It shouldn't take him much time to find what we're looking for," Eve says.

We keep walking around, listening for the tell-tale sounds of a server room (computer fans, cold air and random beeps), until we hit on a door labeled "Server Closet." It's convenient when they put a sign on exactly what you're looking for. The door is locked, but Frank seduces it open in less time than it takes most people to open a door with keys.

Inside, we find a setup that was probably state-of-the-art at one point, but has been upgraded piecemeal over the years with hardware found on eBay and Craigslist. They actually still have an old Cathode Ray Terminal (CRT) plugged in, and the network seems stuck at 100Mb/s. I had faster stuff at my old house. I pull the wireless link out of my pocket and connect it to the network using a spare Cat5 cable I find on a shelf. Plug the link into a nearly overloaded power strip, and it's up and running.

"Jean, you should be coming online soon."

There's a slight crackle and he says, "Got it. I can see inside their network. I'll grab what I can."

"Let's find out what else is around here," Frank says.

The place is still quiet. The inside is a single corridor that wraps around the building, with a few doors that go further into the interior. One of them was the server closet; another leads to a break room; and the last is a heavy door with a combination lock and handle with five buttons underneath the handle. This is probably the vault. For the uninitiated, the buttons under the handle are a push-button combination lock. The order and combination you push the buttons in is the combination to the lock. For instance: press the top and bottom buttons at the same time, the second from the bottom button and the first and third buttons at the same time to open the lock. Usually you open the combination lock then the button lock to open the door.

Locks like this are nigh unpickable.

For the time being, though, we need to find out who else is in here. The main lobby is almost on the opposite side of the building from where we came in. There's one guard, asleep, in front of a bank of monitors that showed us from the second we walked down the stairs.

Good thing he's tired, or we'd be pretty fucked right now.

He's your typical rent-a-cop from one of the local rental places. He's wearing a black uniform and boots to make him seem intimidating, with a Glock on his hip. The guard is overweight, balding and, from the smell of the room, badly in need of a bath. He's also snoring like an exhausted pit bull. Frank cracks him in the back of the head with his pistol, and the wannabe lawman is out cold.

No one else is in the place. The video recorder is under the desk, so we pull the drives and head back to the vault.

Like I said, the locks on these doors are basically unpickable, so you either need to know the combination, or have some heavy tools and free time. Eve punches the door and it falls off its hinges, making about as much noise as you'd expect from an eight-foot-tall metal door falling off its hinges. She brushes the dust off her shirt and calmly walks inside.

Frank grins and follows her. I take one last look around and follow through.

The inside of this vault is like the inside of every vault I've ever been in. They all have the same posters, and all of them are a variation on the same theme: Everyone's out to get you. In all honesty, they probably are. The Chinese are busy hacking every damn thing on the planet, and the Israelis will make a copy of your hard drive the second you land in their country. Give any spook worth his weight in salt access to a place like this, and they'll suck out every secret in a heartbeat. Probably leave some tricks behind, too.

There are two safes in the corner, big Mosler jobs, like two slabs of armor-plated dresser with combination locks on the front. Fortunately, these guys follow procedure, and put the "open" or "secured" magnets in place. All but two of the drawers have the "open" magnet displaying. Just for sanity's sake, I pull open the six drawers that are unlocked, and find them empty - as expected.

"Guys," Jean's voice sounds in my right ear. "I found something. I'm sticking the data in the cloud. You know where. This is bad."

"Gotcha, Jean. We're seducing the safe," Frank says as Eve rips the locks off the other two drawers. "Ok, maybe not seducing so much as backhanding. Anyway, we should be done soon."

Inside the drawers are a couple of folders marked Top Secret NF and a few CDs marked the same. Frank puts them in a backpack and we're starting back when the lights go out.

"Did that guy just fly?" Jessica asks.

"What was that, Jessica?" Eve asks.

"Jacob, what the fuck? Look over there!"

"I don't see anything," Jacob's voice rings.

"Over there! The roof!" Jessica sounds frustrated.

"Shit. Someone's on the roof," Jacob says.

I can't see a damn thing in here, so I pull out a glow stick. Break and shake and we've got some light. Eve and Frank take on a freaky visage in the green light. Eve looks nervous.

"Jessica, Jacob. Get out of there. Hit the road. Meet at the fallback point," Eve says. "Don't question it, just go. That goes for you, too,

Jean. Drop what you're doing and get lost."

"Eve, what the fuck is going on?" Frank asks.

"Get ready," she says. "Here they come."

"Here who come?" I ask, pulling out my gun.

"The bad guys," Eve says.

"I thought we were the bad guys," Frank says quietly.

"We're splitting," Jessica says. "Signing off."

We hear the sound of Jacob's bike starting up over the comms, then a click and the silence.

"Here who come?" I ask again.

"Watch yourselves," Eve says, pulling her gun and checking a knife I didn't even realize she had.

I catch a glimpse of a flicker in the doorway. It's hard to tell, but the shape looked vaguely person-shaped. Another flicker, closer this time and Frank doubles over, clutching his stomach. The flicker moves beside him and slams him face first into the table in front of him. I move toward the wall, trying to get some bit of security, scanning all around as I move. There's a flicker directly in front of me, on the other side of a table. Without thinking I kick the table as hard as I can and am rewarded with an "*oof*" as the table bumps back.

Eve flinches a bit, but doesn't move. Her eyes are closed and her face is slack, like she's at the symphony listening to Holst. Another flinch, like something's hitting her. Frank is getting back up, his gun tracking around the room, his head snaps back and he's back down.

I'm glad the glow stick is still going, but I don't know how much the faint glow is helping.

Eve flinches again and her arm shoots out like lightning. She latches onto - something's - throat, and lifts.

Whatever she's grabbed looks like mostly human, but with bulging, jittery eyes and a waxy complexion. It grins at her, its eyes full of madness and fury, and reaches up to grab her wrist. She squeezes, and there's a sickening cracking sound before its head lolls to the side. She drops the thing like a bag of meat.

Frank is still on the floor, blood flowing out of his nose. Eve roughly picks him up, tosses him over her shoulder, and heads for the door. I follow, gun ready, keeping my fingers crossed that there's no more of those things.

There are no emergency lights in this place, and the shades black out most of the outside light, so it's pretty damn dark in here. Someone should file an OSHA complaint.

I toss another glow stick down the hall and keep an eye out for flickers. So far nothing.

We hit the stairs and Eve calmly climbs them, Frank still over her shoulder, looking dazed. I take one last peek around and am starting up the stairs when everything goes black, and I feel myself falling.

17 | Beat Down

The first thing I feel when I wake up is a splitting headache. This is usually a sign that today will not be a good day. Whatever I'm lying on is thin, and lumpy, and cold.

I try to open my eyes and am immediately decide that's not a good idea. Oh, fuck it. I love sleeping anyway, and don't have anything immediately pressing. At least I don't think I do. I'm not entirely certain where I am or what's going on, but I'm also not certain I care. Sleep is a good thing, a sacred thing, and I'm usually loathe to let it go.

"Well, hello, sunshine," a familiar voice says.

I open my eyes, grit my teeth against the headache, and take a peek around. I'm in a cell: bare concrete floor, gray cinderblock walls, and a single bare bulb covered in wire mesh in case I get uppity and decide I want some darkness. This is the downstairs of the building I used to work in. It sucks being on the other side.

"C'mon, man. I don't have all day," The voice says.

"The fuck you don't. You're government, asshole. You've got all the days in world, except for all the holidays you get," I say, rubbing my eyes.

"There is that," he says. "We just got St. Olaf's day off to appease the Norsemen up in Minnesota."

"St. Olaf?" I ask.

"The patron saint of quality leather pants."

"Jesus," I say.

"Yeah, he's got a handful of holidays already."

"How have you been, Captain Willard?" I ask.

"You know my name is not Willard and I'm not a Captain," he says.

"You still have no sense of culture," I say. "How's the stick up your ass? Still there?"

"You know, for someone on the wrong side of the cage, you've got quite a mouth on you," he says. "You never did have any respect for authority."

"Respect is earned, pal. You just thought you deserved it," I tell him.

My head is still throbbing, so I lean back and put my hands behind my head. My hair is sticky, and there's a huge lump.

"Damn it, asshole," I tell him. "Couldn't you have used darts or some shit?"

"As you well know, the darts provide less-than-predictable results, and tend to result in even worse headaches. Besides, I don't really have a lot of time to wait for you to wake up."

The man outside the bars is a former compatriot, of sorts. We worked together at the Department of Homeland Security finding terrorists and preventing them from doing terrible things. I was an analyst; he was a field guy. I pointed him where he needed to go, and he did what he needed to do, usually quietly and efficiently. When DHS needed a problem fixed, they'd call us - or someone like us. Most people think the Department of Homeland Security is responsible for managing the groping mouth-breathers at the TSA, and that's it. In fact, the Department of Homeland Security is responsible for tracking down and preventing domestic terrorist attacks without fanfare and glory. We were also the clearing house for all kinds of dastardly things going on in America. The information lurking in our brains would probably terrify you. The Transportation Security Administration is responsible for separating you from you from your liquids in the name of Security Theater; we were responsible for separating people from their lives.

His name is Wilford Saxton, and he's one of my many frenemies from my past life. I'll always respect him and his abilities, but he and I are about as far apart politically and socially as you can get. He's your standard issue all-American: tall, blonde, blue-eyed, played sports, worships the right God, and always follows orders without question. He'll happily tell you about how he always questions his orders, but his line of questioning is never very thorough, and he always winds up where he's supposed to be. He's the perfect poster boy.

We had a falling-out that came to blows over a mission a few years ago and never worked together again. I had this crazy idea that we were doing something noble and would happily question my orders if they seemed odd. Saxton felt we were doing something noble, too, but always assumed his orders were like words from above and never once questioned them, even when it meant taking out a whole family. I balked at the orders, Saxton followed them to perfection. He pinned the execution of a family on my bad intel. That's when I decked him and left.

"Well, slick. Time's a wastin'," I tell him.

"We need to find out what you're up to," he tells me, coming straight to the point.

"Well," I tell him. "It's like this: I'm going to hunt down your sister and seduce her. It shouldn't be too hard - she's supposed to be pretty easy."

"Don't get cute. I don't have the time."

"She's got a real pretty mouth, that one," I say.

"Here's the deal, buddy. You've been declared a terrorist, and you should remember exactly what that entails."

"I need to hate America for its freedoms?" I ask.

"You do hate America," he says. "And, as you well know, terrorists have no rights under the law."

He's right. Terrorists have no rights under the law. It's not widely spoken about, but if you're a terrorist and you get caught by American forces, you're well and truly fucked. I don't have a problem with this. Terrorists are pussies and not worthy of any kind of remorse.

"Fuck you. I don't hate America. I hate what you and people like you have done to it," I tell him.

"I protect this country from those who would destroy it, and I intend to continue protecting it, by whatever means necessary. Now, I know you killed Bedfellow, and I know you're up to something bad right now. I can't prove it right now, but it's just a matter of time. You've stumbled into something that is way beyond you, and way beyond me, and this is your last chance to get out."

"Bedfellow?" I say.

"Yes. Senator Bedfellow. His son killed your wife and son, and he covered it up. Six months later he's found dead. Doesn't take a genius to figure it out, especially since you disappeared shortly thereafter."

Let me set the record straight: all I did was move a chair.

"I heard Bedfellow hanged himself," I tell him.

"He did. I know you were behind it, though," he tells me.

"Prove it, asshole."

"If I could prove it, you would've been behind bars long ago."

"Then fuck yourself and open these bars."

"Yeah. Neither of those things is going to happen." He grins. "Explain to our friend that he needs to focus."

There's a flicker next to me and then something slams me in the jaw. Damn it. I was hoping there was only one of those things. I should have suspected there'd be more than one. Government philosophy is why have one, when you can have two at twice the cost?

"What the fuck are those things?" I ask.

"Those are the real patriots. They have sacrificed themselves to get a chance to go after monsters and terrorists like you."

"I'm not a fucking terrorist."

Flicker, and another slam.

"You are a threat to this country, and you will tell me what you are doing!" Saxton thunders.

"I told you already, I'm thinking of new and exciting ways to fuck your sister."

Another flicker and I'm hit twice more, once in the gut and again in the jaw. When my head clears slightly, I can tell I've lost a couple of teeth. Shit. I'm going to need to go to the dentist now. I hate dentists.

"He can keep this up all night. He will happily beat you down until the end of his life, and there is absolutely fuck-all you can do about it," Wilford tells me. "This is the new way of warfare, Steven. This is what we use now. We can't use drones on U.S. soil yet, but we can use alternative weapons and alternative tactics. To hunt monsters we made monsters of our own."

"Nice work in Boston, shithead," I tell him.

I probably shouldn't goad him too much about that; there wasn't much anyone could've done to foresee it. Terrorism has gone open-source, and any asshole with a bone to pick can pick up Al Qaeda's free monthly e-magazine, complete with the latest monthly tips on Jihad, what the sexy terrorists are wearing, and how to behead Westerners. When I left government work, they were still trying to find ways to deal with threats like that without raising the fear factor. It looks like they may have found one.

His head droops and he stares at the ground.

"The only way to prevent another Boston, or another Sandy Hook, or another 9/11 is to think outside the box. We must to stop them before they can do anything, and we need to eliminate them quietly and with plausible deniability. You yourself proposed watching news groups and tapping emails," he says.

"So, now you think everyone is a potential terrorist?" I ask him.

"Everyone IS a potential terrorist. Even our own people want to bring down the government," Saxton yells.

"Ever wonder why that may be?" I ask him.

"It doesn't matter. It never mattered. The only thing that matters is they are weak and we are strong, and we will do what we need to do to keep our people safe and fed and happy."

"Keep 'em happy and stupid and you can stay in power forever, right? The only thing you need to worry about is who will fight for you, and you can always find and use those poor bastards that will fight and die for your causes – right?" I say.

"Our causes! Ours! Not mine!" he yells. "I work for the good of the people!"

"What people? All people or just the ones who pay your salary and give you your pittance of power? They'll walk all over you the second you're no longer useful."

"Someone needs to be prepared to sacrifice themselves for the good of the whole."

"And that someone is you?" I ask him.

Wilford Allan Saxton comes from a traditional blue-blood family, with a history of service to "God and country." He's a true believer, a fanatical patriot who has been trained to trust his superiors in all cases. His family has had pastors and soldiers and various functionaries in its lineage. They've orbited the upper echelons, but never made it into the ruling class. Like so many others, his family has sacrificed, believing their sacrifice was for the good of the country, when it was really just to further the goals of the minority that claims to keep the best interests of everyone in mind.

"You should try sacrificing for the good of the whole sometime, Steven," He tells me.

"So should you, Wilford. You've sacrificed plenty of people, but you've never sacrificed anything yourself! How much innocent blood have you spilt to make the country 'safe?' How many times have you tapped phones, intimidated witnesses, killed kids - and called it collateral damage?"

"A new kind of enemy deserves a new kind of tactics," he says.

"You know, I used to think people shouldn't be afraid of their governments - that governments should be afraid of their people - but the government is already afraid of the people, isn't it? You're terrified of the very people you use, aren't you? You're absolutely shit-scared, and you use this patriotic bullshit and bumper-sticker logic to justify walking all over the people you purport to serve."

"I'm not afraid of anything."

"Then why do you have this freak thing smacking me around while you've got me in a cage? Are you still pissed off that I beat you?" I ask him.

"You cheated," he says.

"Fuck you. The only unfair fight is the one you don't win."

"You threw pepper in my face."

"What the fuck do you think those guys you're hunting are going to do?"

I can tell he's fuming. His eye starts to twitch when he gets really mad. We used to verbally spar like this when we worked together. There was a time when we were friends, but he screwed up a mission and pinned the blame on me.

Saxton walks off. There's a flicker, and I get punched again. *Fucking pussy.*

When Saxton comes back, he's got a laptop with stickers all over it: punk bands, mariachi bands, LGBT rainbows. Jean's laptop. There's blood all over it.

"Recognize it?" Saxton asks me. "Look familiar?"

"You son of a bitch."

"Yeah, that's me."

Shit. Shit. Shit.

Saxton looks at me, trying to figure out if I'm breaking. I'm forcing myself to remain calm. One of the first things you learn in the Intelligence world is keeping your head when the situation gets tense. I close my eyes and breathe. Jean's dead, but if I freak out now, nothing good will come of it. That's when I sense a slight puff of air to my left - immediately before the punch slams me in the side of the head.

"Time's wasting, Steven. What are you up to? Who's the Amazon?"

My head feels like it's stuffed with cotton, but now I've at least got some edge. I pull myself to my feet and try to shake the cobwebs from my brain.

"I told you. I want to fuck your sister. I mean hold her down and just go to town," I say.

The puff of air comes from the behind this time and is followed up with a blow to my kidney. Goddamn it hurts.

"We need to know what you're up to, Steven. What were you doing at Radula?"

"You tell me. You're holding that thing like you've got all the answers," I say, pointing at the laptop.

"There's nothing here! It fried itself when we tried to start it up," he says.

Thank you, Jean. Wherever you are I hope there are lots of hot guys and cold beer.

I give him my saddest face. "Gee, that's a crying shame. However will you go on?"

I get punched in the side of the head for my troubles. Some people just can't handle sympathy. It's like they're losing their masculinity or something.

"What the fuck are these things?" I ask again.

"They're patriots. Men who gave everything to protect the freedom you're so casually pissing away. They volunteered for the process."

"What process?"

"These men can walk through worlds," he tells me. "Now tell me, what are you up to?"

I get smacked in the back of the head. "Jeez, I haven't even made a smart-ass comment yet. I catch you, asshole, I'm gonna fuck you up."

I get smacked again, not hard enough to damage, just enough to let me know he's still there.

Saxton is getting red in the face. He must be under some pressure to get this done quickly. "What are you trying to do?"

I stare him dead in the eye, my most serious poker face hiding my smirk. "All right, fine, fine."

Saxton relaxes a bit. I pause and let the tension build.

I sigh and act defeated.

"I'm trying to find your sister so I can fuck her brains out," I say.

I feel a puff of air to my left, and decide to give it the old college try. If he follows his past actions, he'll come in straight, no angularity at all. Invisible or no, he's a rank amateur. If he couldn't "walk through worlds," whatever the fuck that means, I would've beat him down earlier. I thrust two fingers out to where I think his eye will be and pray there's some god or goddess out there that hasn't written me into their enemies list. I must not have pissed off everyone, because my fingers hit something soft and squishy that feels like an eye. From there it's trivial to step to the left, pulling him by the eye along with me. With my left hand, I slam my palm into his kidney and throw a back hand to the side of his head with my right to get him away. Kenpo calls the technique 'Darkness,' and it's always been one of my favorites. Because if you do it right, "darkness" is exactly what the person being hit sees and feels.

Getting poked in the eye hurts. Having it nearly pushed back into your skull is crippling. When you're in that much pain, it gets hard to concentrate, and apparently these guys need to concentrate to flicker in and out, because he's lying on the cell floor clutching his eye and making weird howling noises. I walk over to him and stomp his head until I hear his skull crack.

"Nice work, Steven," Saxton says, clapping lightly. "But you're still in a cage."

"Yeah. But at least this asshole won't be popping me anymore."

"No. It appears he won't," He gestures around him. "These two, however, are just itching to meet you."

There are a couple of flickers next to him, and I realize this could be a very long night.

I plop down on my cot and contemplate my immediate, possibly very painful future. There are two coughing noises, and the flickers flatten out on the floor. Saxton turns and pulls his gun and empties the clip at something down the hall, a look of pure shock and rage on his face. The rage fades and the shock completely takes over when Eve casually walks up and slams him face first into the bars.

Jessica walks up behind her, silenced pistol in hand.

Eve looks around and then peers into my cage. "Such lovely places you bring us to."

"Yeah, well, I like to show a lady a good time," I say.

Jessica shoots someone down the hall and Eve rips the door of the cell out. "You look terrible," Eve tells me.

"You wound me," I tell her through a split lip. "I've never looked as handsome as I look now."

Jessica looks at me. "You look like hammered shit," she tells me, ever the big ball of happy. "What is that thing on the floor?"

"They walk between worlds," I tell her as I lean on the wall and try to act like I'm fine. For some reason I'm extremely dizzy. Oh, right. Lots of lows to the head. Brain rattled in skull. Good thing I wasn't terribly bright to begin with.

What's left of the flickering man is not a pretty sight to behold. His head is smashed in, but that's not the worst of it. His limbs are like ropy muscle - he's as thin as a skeleton - and his skin is blotched with oozing red sores. I get a cumulative case of the willies thinking about that thing touching me, and suddenly feel like I need a shower.

"Nasty," Jessica says.

"Did you find Jean?" I ask.

"Most of him," Eve says. "His head and hands are still missing."

I nod. Take the head and hands, and it makes a damn sight more difficult to identify the body. They were probably planning on just leaving his body out there and telling the Albuquerque Police Department not to worry about it.

"How's Frank?"

"Pretty bad," Jessica says. "He was almost comatose for a while, but now he's just mad as hell."

"Did he go back to the ranch?"

"No, he's outside," Eve says, raising an eyebrow.

"Assume they can find us now. Anyone goes back to the ranch and they'll be greeted by 20 guys with balaclavas and SMGs." That might not affect Eve much, but the rest of us would be in trouble. "Eve, they may not have anything to hurt you right now, but they will eventually, and they've got numbers. We need to avoid that place like the plague," I say.

People like to think of the government as a bunch of inept buffoons, and sometimes that's true. But they've gotten very good at tracking down and stomping on threats. We've probably been branded terrorists by now, and it's a very good bet they're putting on their stomping boots as we speak. It's time to fall off their radar. We need a place to lay low and lick our wounds.

I manage to make it over to Saxton, lying on the floor with blood running down his face. "Can I borrow your gun for a moment, Jess?"

She hands it over to me and I nudge Saxton trying to get him to wake up.

"Wake up, asshole," I say.

He groans, opens his eyes and looks up at us. I aim the gun at his face and pull the trigger. The bullet hits him right in the skull, and the lights go out of his eyes. He's not the first person I've killed, but he is the first person I've killed that I knew personally. Perhaps it was just vengeance for tonight, but it might have been vengeance for all the other shit he's done. I know I'm supposed to feel regret or something for taking another life, but I don't feel a damn thing except "fuck him." Frankly, I'm glad he's gone.

"We need to get out of here," Eve says. "Can you walk?"

"Sure," I say. "Why not?"

There's not far to go to get out of the DHS dungeon. I grab what's left of Jean's laptop, and start limping to the door. Yeah, I know. I never got hit in the leg. I don't need to limp. This is just something men do when women are around. We like to make it seem worse than it is, and then tough-guy our way through it, even though it's really not as bad as it looks. There's a corollary to this: when men refuse to admit that there's any pain at all. Feel free to file this in your 'Stupid Guy Things' folder and move on with your life.

I head for the door at the end of the hall, past the four pounds of C4 stuck to the wall, and head up the stairs, taking care not to step on the wires.

Wait. Man, my head is messed up. I'd swear I just a hunk of C4 stuck to a wall. When I back up I see there really is a huge brick of plastic explosives stuck to a wall. My tired brain catalogs the explosive and promises it will get to the analysis first thing in the morning.

I shrug and keep going.

"I take it you pulled the C4 out of the Radula door," I ask.

"Eve decided it was a better use than what they had planned," Jessica says.

At the top of the stairs, the two on-duty guards are dead, shot in the head. The wires run out of the front door to where Jacob is busy twisting them onto a battery. I've never been a fan of bombs, but I'll be happy to see this place blown to rubble.

We walk across the street and Jacob touches the wires together, completing the circuit. Four pounds of C4 is a pretty significant amount of explosive, but the explosion is muffled from outside. I'm sure if the explosives were placed properly the whole building would dropped down in a nice, neat pile - as it is the center part of the building collapses in on itself while the walls stay up.

I know you're jealous. Everyone dreams of blowing up a building. Just add that to the list of fun things I've gotten to do that you haven't.

"You know," I say, "if this was *Angry Birds*, there'd still be a pig alive down there."

It turns out that as Jacob and Jessica were high-tailing it out of the Radula debacle, they tried to grab Jean. They found him dead, and no one else around - just a dead body with no head and no hands, and no witnesses. They grabbed anything incriminating out of the car, including Jean's other laptop, and tried to keep an eye out.

They had a clean view of the building, so they saw Eve carrying Frank out. They watched her casually jump off the roof with Frank still on her shoulder.

Since Jessica and Jacob noticed only two people walking out, they decided to wait and see who else came out, and got to see me dragged out and dumped in a black Suburban, which tore off into the night. In a panic, they got ahold of Eve, who told them to follow the Suburban. The Suburban headed toward the DHS headquarters down by the airport, where it dropped me off.

I must not have been out for very long, because it took less than an hour for everyone to show up, kill almost everyone, and wire up the place to blow. Figure Wilford only knocked me around for fifteen minutes or so - that leaves me with forty-five minutes unconscious. Damage assessment: a minor concussion, a couple of missing teeth, two black eyes, minor kidney damage, a sore stomach and wicked headache.

Not bad for a stay in the tender mercies of the U.S. Government.

"Where are we going?" I ask.

Jacob leans over the front seat and says "Hotel on Central. Jesus, you look like shit."

Everyone's a comic. "A hotel on Central. That could be good or bad. Hotel Parq Central, good. Crossroads Motel, bad," I say.

"It's the Crossroads," Jacob says, grinning like a loon.

"Great," I say. "I thought only tourists are supposed to be interested in TV show landmarks, and only crack whores are supposed to be interested in the Crossroads."

"It's the last place anyone in their right mind would go looking," Eve says.

"Yeah, unless they're looking for crack or diseases. Or both," I say.

18 | Methed Up

The Crossroads is an old hotel on Central near I25; it's the representative Albuquerque crack hotel you see on TV from time to time. The place is actually a little bit worse in real life than TV makes it look. It's not the worst hotel in town - there are some a bit further down the street that double as meth labs and dens of iniquity. The beds at the Crossroads are usually free of any meaningful infestation, and there's a slightly less-than-average chance of catching something science still hasn't identified.

Oh, well. The Crossroads is cheap and it comes with free Wi-Fi. There's no breakfast buffet, but I don't think I would eat anything here anyway.

We have two adjacent rooms on the second floor with a wonderful view of the scummy pool, and the parking lot. Eve and Jessica got the room with green door. Jacob, Frank and I got the one with the blue door. The blue door is far better. With all the comings and goings around here, we'll probably be invisible, and the fact that we're not actively slinging crack rock and/or hookers should limit our police visibility.

I'm fairly sure the name Crossroads refers to the crossroads between Hell and a slightly worse hell - maybe the Hell of Lost Dreams, and the Hell of Broken Lives. In a certain sense, I'm right at home, but I just wish they had better beds. The authentic Magic Fingers are great, but the beds are six kinds of lumpy, and I wouldn't bring a black light in here for all the whisky in Ireland - the glow would probably blind me. I heard once (and I believe this is a true story), that hotels usually don't wash the comforters, which might explain why the bedspread in our room doesn't actually bend.

In any hotel, you can get a feel for the usual clientele by looking at what's been secured in the room. In a high-class hotel, nothing is locked, which makes it easier to lose the remote. In this place, the ball point pen is held on the desk with a chain, and the paint-by-numbers pictures on the wall are screwed into place. One of the paintings is missing; you can tell by the slightly-less-dirty rectangle on the wall.

The place isn't all bad. It's mostly roach-free, and the owners used the money they got from a TV show filmed here to upgrade not only the exterior paint job, but also the hookers - all the hookers now have most of their teeth. Also, the TVs are new. And bolted to the dressers. And chained to the wall. And the remote is securely affixed to the nightstand. Plus, you can smoke in the rooms, which is probably a violation of some damn New Mexico code or another.

Anyway, it's home, for the time being.

I'm flopped out on one of the beds, an ice pack nearly covering my whole face when Eve walks in, Jessica in tow, with a stack of folders all clearly marked Top Secret.

"Well, these are interesting, but they don't explain much," Jessica tells us. "Is there a school or something these guys go to where they learn how to write without actually saying anything, because this is some cryptic bullshit.

"Listen to this: 'Transferring the Guest's walking capabilities continues to be a source of frustration.'"

"They expect anyone reading the file to be intimately involved in the whole process, and they don't like to share information with anyone who is not currently involved," I say "Part of it is the constant reminders of security, and part of it is a desire to make sure no one can come in take credit for their work.

"Does the file say anything about those flickering bastards?" I ask.

"Flickering bastards?" Eve asks.

"Yeah, those guys that flickered in and out. I don't know what they're supposed to be called, but Saxton said they can 'walk between worlds,' and he had three of them with him. He kind of implied there were more of them," I say.

"Oh, them. They're called 'Phasers', and somehow or another 'the guest' created them, or they created them from him," Jessica says. Reading directly from the folder in her hand she continues. "The Guest was observed to disappear and reappear at various points during his sleep. The techs said it looked like he was sleepwalking. Data gathered before the event indicated The Guest's 'walking' appeared to be, at least partially, a repeatable process. Further analysis led to a breakthrough. The recipient can 'walk' to a limited extent, which may be weaponizable. Unfortunately, the process tends to degrade the subject over time and use. Our best model describes the recipient's total degradation in six months to one year, depending of the recipient. The process is irreversible.'"

"Shit," Jacob says, "Was that even English?"

"Kind of," Eve says.

"Oh, good Lord," Frank groans. "This isn't brain surgery."

"Yeah," I say. "They've got something and they're trying to figure out how to make it a weapon. It's not exactly helping them, but they've had some limited success transferring some capability they wanted to people."

"And the process is killing whoever they transfer it to," Eve says.

"Not surprising. Do you know how many of the original Manhattan Project engineers died of cancer? Or how many of chemical weapons engineers died horribly? Making new and exciting weapons takes sacrifice. No wonder Wilford called them 'patriots,'" I say.

"Wilford?" Jacob asks.

"The nutjob who was running the DHS, uh, interrogation," I say.

"That guy never got laid, did he?" Jessica asks.

"He got mad poontang. He had the looks, the attitude, knew how to play women like a harp," I say. "He acted like Wilford Brimley, and women ate it up."

"Yeah, well. Wilford Brimley is pretty much a badass," Jacob says.

"He's got the greatest moustache in the world, and he's the final boss of the Internet," I agree.

"He's definitely a man," Says Frank.

"Yes, he's dreamy," Eve says, rolling her eyes. She looks over at Jessica. "Tell them the most interesting thing."

"Well, we don't know exactly what's going on, but it's happening not far from here, in one of the older buildings downtown," Jessica says.

"Do we know anything about the building?" Frank asks. He's calmed down a bit, but I can still see he hurts. He spent the first hour in here in the bathroom. This is how men deal with things, so don't get judgmental. Frank's always been a fairly private person, and, like me, he has trouble opening up. He's turned his pain into rage, and his rage into focus. Someone he loved was taken from him and, in his mind the best way to feel better is to strike back at those people that hurt him. He looks like he's all business now, but I can see the cracks in his armor. He'll have a complete breakdown when he feels like he's got the time.

"It's the Simms building downtown," Eve says.

"Figures," I say. "I always liked that place."

Eve digs around in her notes and says, "It was put up by government contractors back in the fifties. Most of the building is rented out to various companies. There's a sandwich shop in the front, and a post office towards the back," Eve says. "Other than that, we don't know a damned thing."

"It's got bluish trim," I say helpfully.

"Did Jean find anything?" Jacob asks.

"We don't know, his laptop is fried," I say.

"Yeah, but remember, he said he was copying something somewhere?" Jacob says.

"Right, the cloud. Frank, what cloud was he talking about?" I ask.

"Of course," Frank says. "Jean had a buddy with a server farm, and he rented out space on it. It's somewhere in Indonesia."

"How did he meet a guy in Indonesia?" Jessica asks.

"He was a hacker. He had friends all over the world," Frank says.

"But he'd never met them?" Jacob asks.

"Sure he did. On the Internet," Jessica says.

"How can you be friends with someone you've never met?" Jacob asks.

"They've met, just not in the real world," Frank tells Jacob. "Look, man, just don't worry about it. He lived in a different world."

Jacob shrugs. He's never been on the Internet, except to ogle naked women. I keep telling him the web has other uses - like communicating with friends, playing games or stealing music and movies - but he's an analog man in a digital world, and he likes to touch the things he steals.

"Did you guys grab the spare laptop from Jean's car?" Frank asks.

"Yeah. We were going to check it out," Jessica says.

"Absolutely do not turn that machine on," Frank says, deadly serious. "If you don't turn it on correctly, we'll have two toasted laptops on our hands."

"What do you mean, turn it on correctly?" Jessica asks him.

Frank sighs. Everyone's getting a peckish and grumpy. It's been a long day.

"Jean was a hacker. He liked to tinker with things, and he liked to keep his secrets. If you boot it up with the battery and the SD card in, it will scramble the drive during boot, zap the RAM and CPU, and use the power it has left start a fire," Frank tells her.

"OK, I'll let you start it up," Jessica says, quickly handing it to him.

It's an older Asus laptop, orange and black with a glowing icon on the front. Frank plugs in the monstrous power adapter into the outlet in the lamp, pulls the battery and the SD card, and presses the power button. It boots up with the usual ROG graphics, and goes into a Linux logon prompt. Frank logs it in with Jean's credentials (user name: BadAss, password 4t3hL0Lzerz!) and we're rewarded with a picture of a guy in a suit with a Guy Fawkes mask on.

The desktop is spotless except for a widget in the upper right corner showing the CPU load, network load and so on.

Jean wrote most of his own tools, like most real hackers tend to do. He also hid them, like most real hackers tend to do. If you don't know what you're looking for, you'll never find it. You can search a hard drive all day, but if you don't know your way around it's all just a jumble of link libraries, shared resources and cryptically named files.

Frank digs around until he finds what he's looking for buried in one of the many /bin directories, and launches a program Jean wrote to get his files in the cloud. He types in another username and password, and we're rewarded with a "Welcome back to Isher, B@d@$$!" screen, and a list of directories. Frank scrolls down until he finds a directory named **nunya** and opens it.

"Nunya?" Jessica asks him.

"Nunya business," Frank replies as the list populates. "Damn. That's a ton of data. Now we just need to find what we need in this crap."

There are a dozen directories, each with between a dozen and a couple hundred files in it. "There," I say, pointing at the screen. "Guesst. Look in that one."

"It's just a guest directory." Frank says, dismissively.

"Stuck in with a bunch of classified documents?" I ask him. "Ever see a guest directory in a classified location, let alone one with a capital G, let alone spelled with two s's?"

"Point well taken," he says, and opens the Guesst directory. "Bingo."

Inside is a single PowerPoint presentation labeled 'Intro to Guestt.' "I would have expected more files," Jessica says.

"Radula probably did a search of the drive trying to delete anything named Guest and missed these two because they couldn't spell correctly. It happens." I say. "Crack it open, let's see what's in there."

PowerPoint presentations always look like PowerPoint presentations, and anything put together by government contractors is guaranteed to look exactly like what you'd expect a government contractor to generate for a government contract: slick and soulless. They're like sets from game shows. Government PowerPoint slide shows give the appearance of excitement and intrigue, but only deliver mediocrity. At least they're succinct.

The downside is, they're cryptic, unless you have the full speech to go along with them. We didn't have the speech that originally accompanied the slides, but we were able to learn some interesting things from the PowerPoint.

Like that "the Guest" was sleeping but shows signs of waking up.

That most of its capabilities cannot be replicated.

That there are dimensions and worlds that touch ours.

And that when the Guest wakes up it will be hungry.

I would imagine burgers won't satiate anything that can travel dimensions, no matter how good the burgers are.

"'It may be hungry when it wakes up,'" Eve comments, "but I'm hungry now. What's good and close?"

"Frontier's down the street. Best tortillas in all of creation," Jacob says.

"Mmm," I say. "Great cinnamon rolls, too."

The Frontier is also a good place to forget about your day.

19 | Information

The next morning is planning. We've come too far down this road to quit now. DHS is probably looking around for us, Congress is still populated by idiots, and Jean is still dead. At this stage in the game we're not sure we can use anything we have, but frankly, we don't have anything else to do. So why the fuck not?

We know what building we're looking for, but have no idea what we'll find when we go in. So some recon is in order.

We follow the usual rules: Frank figures out the building; Jacob and I peek around on-site, Jessica has grown into a coordination role, and Eve reaches out to some shady contacts that we're better off not knowing about.

The building in question is the Simms building - a classic example of mid 1950s architecture stuck in the middle of Downtown. The Simms building is 13 stories (which is kind of odd, if you think about it) of mid-century blue metal sheeting in stainless steel frames.

Honestly: the building looks like a giant elementary school.

Since we're not exactly sure what part of the building we're looking for, Jacob and I hang out in the lobby and keep an eye on people coming and going. Most of the people are run-of-the-mill office drones. Some Pak-N-Mail attendants. The occasional cop. A few tourists looking for the DEA office that only exists on TV.

One door, to an office in the southwest corner, never opens. No one enters and no one leaves, but the mail carrier drops mail in the slot, so someone's in the office sometimes. We'll have to stay late to see if anyone leaves. Since this is probably a government operation, we won't need to be here any later than 5.

In the meantime, we grab coffee.

After a full day of drinking coffee, my nerves are frazzled and Jacob's bladder is full, so he takes off to the head, and I try my best to not vibrate like a meth addict on a bender. Caffeine is a wonderful thing.

At 5 p.m. sharp, the southwest corner door opens, and two guys dressed like security guards walk out. The door closes behind them, and they part ways without saying a word. One heads out a back door. The other heads toward me.

Jacob's just leaving the bathroom as I make a snap decision. By the time I'm bumping this guy and stealing his wallet, I have enough presence of mind to hope I didn't just fuck the whole thing up. Fortunately, our guy is wiped out enough from doing whatever work he does all day that he barely notices when I snatch his wallet. I take a step, open his wallet, pull out the first card I find, close the wallet and drop it behind me. I keep walking and keep my fingers crossed that I grabbed something useful.

As I walk past Jacob, I hear him call out, "Hey, buddy, you dropped your wallet."

The guy spins around - a hunk of meat that thinks he's the toughest S.O.B. on the block, and is ready to beat down anyone who crosses him - until he sees Jacob's crazy-ass biker grin. He takes the wallet, mumbles thanks and high-tails it out.

I keep going out the back and take a look at the palmed card. Damn, I'm lucky sometimes.

I got a voter registration card with a name of Geoff Brance. I calmly exit and speed walk around the building, keeping an eye out of Brance. I catch sight of Jacob, who motions left. Brance is making his way toward the parking garage across the street. He takes the elevator, and I wait by the gate. I reassure myself there's only one way out, and I'm watching it. Jacob grabs his car off the street and waits.

After twenty minutes of waiting, Brance finally rolls out in a beat-to-shit '77 Firebird, blasting some God-awful southern rock. I nod to Jacob, who follows him out over the tracks and back up Central to the Copper Lounge, where he calls me.

Now, at this point all you Junior Birdman Security guys are probably wondering why the hell we're still using cell phones when everyone knows how easy to track someone through their phone. In order to track you, someone would have to know what name you used when you set up your phone. There are more cellular devices in America than there are people, and traces only work when you know what phone you're looking for. So creating a basically-untraceable phone for fun and profit is fairly easy: steal someone's phone, hack the SIM card so your stolen phone looks like another one and set up a fake account.

As long as no one knows to look for you, or what number to check, you're golden.

Right now, we're the only ones who have each other's numbers. Sure, the NSA is probably grabbing all our calls, but they're grabbing everyone's calls. We can get lost in the noise, as long we avoid key words like bomb, terrorist, Allah, etc.

The way Brance made a beeline to the Copper Lounge makes me think he's probably a regular. The Copper Lounge is a used-to-be-nice bar down the street from UNM, far enough away that the college students can't walk down there easily, and because the bar's not directly in Nob Hill or downtown, the hipsters ignore it.

Tonight's not the night to check further into Brance, though. He'd probably recognize Jacob, and I'm too far away to keep an eye on him. I catch a bus back to Hotel Awesome, and meet up with everyone else.

Jessica and Frank are going over building plans when I get in. Jacob is grabbing pizzas, and no one's heard from Eve yet.

"There's something off about this building," Frank says. "The southwest corner office has an elevator, but the plans don't say where it goes. It can't go up, because there's nothing on the second floor that looks like a shaft. That same spot on the second floor is labeled an executive washroom."

"So what?" I say. "It must go to the basement."

"Why would you need a private elevator to go to the basement?" Jessica asks.

"How the hell should I know?" I'm tired and grumpy. Dealing with people downtown is has tried my patience. The caffeine is wearing off, and my head is thumping again.

The building blueprints show an empty space, about 20 feet on a side, with an elevator shaft dead-center against the south wall. There's one entrance - no windows, no closets, no offices. "Is it me, or do these walls look thicker than normal?" I ask.

"Yeah," Frank says. "I noticed that. They're at least twice as thick as they should be."

"Strange layout for an office," Jessica says. "It's just an empty area."

"Maybe they're a phone support place and they need the thick walls to keep people from hearing the screams of the operators going insane," I say.

"Yeah, a phone-support operation," Jessica says. "That explains why they had two guards."

"Maybe they're there to keep people from leaving," I say.

"Did you see anyone else leaving?" Frank asks. "If it was quitting time, why didn't anyone else leave? And what kind of place employs just two guards to stand around in a room all day? I'm telling you, something else is happening in that room."

"Well," says Eve, "we already knew that."

Eve can move like a jungle cat when she wants to. You'd think it would be difficult to miss a seven-foot-tall blonde bombshell, but she can sneak around like no one's business. One second there's nothing, and the next second she's right behind you. I'm convinced it's magic, but she swears up and down she learned how to do her stealthy entrances by reading a book on ninjas.

Must've been better than my ninja books.

"We know they're hiding something. It stands to reason they'd hide whatever it is someplace secure," Eve says. "Did I hear you say you only saw two people, guards, leave the place at 5?"

I nod. "There's someone else in that room. There must be," I say. "You don't hire two guards to just hang out in a room."

Although, I've seen government agencies do things almost as absurd. One place I worked had a bomb shelter with a couple hundred cases of bottled water stocked away. They had to completely restock the water annually, so once a year, everyone got a case or two of bottled water to get rid of the old and make room for the new.

"I asked around," Eve tells us. "No one knows for sure what's going on, but everyone seems to agree that there's another guard we haven't seen yet. No one's seen him, except glimpses, in years. He never leaves."

"Job security," Frank says. "Gotta love it."

"We should prepare for the worst," I say. "We're assuming three guards, one of whom may or may not live there. One of whom seems to have a taste for the Copper Lounge, and another who seems normal, but who we don't know much about."

Frank looks at me. "Isn't it a bit early to say the guy you saw leaving is a regular at a bar when you've only seen him go there once? I mean, it takes more than one point to determine a line."

"Jacob says he went straight to the bar," I say. "While it's possible this was a fluke, guys like this are creatures of habit."

"At any rate," Jessica says, "it's the only possible in we've got, so I say we take it."

"Ok," I say. "What do we do? Grab this guy and beat the shit out of him in the parking lot?"

"I have a better idea," Eve tells us, "If Jessica doesn't mind doing some dirty work."

"You want me to seduce him, don't you?" Jessica asks.

"Yes. Yes, I do." Eve says. "I'd do it myself, but he'll have a better reaction to you. We'll track him for a couple of days, see what we can find out, and then you meet him at the bar and pump him for information. If he's as pathetic as he seems it shouldn't take much. The rest of us will be in place for backup. For added benefit," she points at me, "you're going to start a fight with this guy. And lose."

At this point it's probably a good idea for me to point out what seems obvious in hindsight, but is very difficult to remember in the moment: if a pretty girl starts hitting on you at a bar, and that sort of thing doesn't happen to you much, you're probably being set up for something. Yes, even you. This is an age-old technique for getting information out of men without having to resort to tedious things like torture. There's something in our genes that makes us stupid around women. Spies have been doing this forever, and it's one of the techniques that always works. All a female spy has to do is stroke that ego (with an implied promise of stroking something else), while she's asking you questions about your work. There's even some actual science behind the process, albeit a simple science: start with small questions, things that don't seem important, and gently work your way up. Even if they don't get everything they want, sometimes the small answers give up more information than you might think.

There are other variations on this that work as well. Someone meets you at a bar or a conference and pretends to be your best friend: laughs at your jokes, compliments you, etc. Then that person will slowly pump you for information or, better yet, get you to join his or her friends at a larger table and they'll all work you for information. It's human nature to want to share information, especially when that information seems trivial to us, and we seem to be impressing people with our answers.

Most people involved in the security world are well aware of these tactics, and are trained to be resistant to them. Unfortunately, when you're in the moment it's difficult, because it doesn't seem like you're being pumped for information. Later that night you'll wake up in a cold sweat and realize you just gave the keys to the kingdom to the Latvians, because that woman with nice breasts touched your arm and smiled at you.

Jessica shrugs. "Ok, no problem. We actually had a class about this in college. Maybe I'll get some free drinks out of it. Is he at least not totally hideous?"

"I'm not a great judge of these things," I say, "but he wasn't terrible. He's not exactly dreamy, but all his limbs are in place and he didn't reek of anything other than desperation. Should make it easier for you."

Finally, Jacob gets back with the pizzas and, proving what a prince among men he really is, a case of decent beer.

20 | History Lessons

Over the next couple of days we kept an eye on Brance. He was at work at 8 a.m. sharp every morning, didn't leave for lunch, left promptly at 5 p.m., and drove straight to the Copper Lounge. He always had two drinks at the bar, and then drove to his apartment off Yale, where he stayed inside for the rest of the night. Like a lot of people, he's fallen into a rhythm, and doesn't even realize it.

Frank and Eve watched the Simms Building. Jacob followed Brance around. Jessica and I stayed out of sight. Since she was going to seduce the guy, and I was going to get beat up by the guy, we needed to remain anonymous. We spent time playing poker, watching daytime T.V. and being bored.

On the second day, while I was reading some piece of dreck I'd stolen off the Internet, Jessica came in and plopped down on the bed.

"OK, I get why Jacob joined your little evil cabal: he hates the government, hates the restrictions, and watched ATF guys blow away a bunch of his friends. Frank I get too - he's spent most of his life hearing politicians tell everyone how gays are destroying everything from marriage to the Union itself," she says.

"How's Frank doing, by the way? I haven't seen much of him lately," I ask.

"He's devastated, but won't admit it. Why do guys do that? Why can't he just admit he misses Jean? Eve said he cried on her shoulder for, like an hour last night. This morning, nada. It's like it never happened."

"Men are raised to not cry, not admit anything's wrong," I say. "We're told from a fairly young age to get over it and man up. It's a difficult cycle to break."

"That's fucked up."

"It is what it is," I tell her.

"Why is Eve so intent on hitting the government in the balls? I've asked her, but she dodges the question."

"I'm not completely certain since she's never really opened up about that to anyone, but we got drunk one night, and she alluded to a couple of things," I say.

"Like what?"

"She wants out."

"Out of what?"

"I don't know. She was pretty ripped and just said, 'I want out'," I say. "I never could figure out of what."

"What else?" Jessica asks me.

"Well, I get the feeling she's pretty old - hundred, hundred and fifty or so. She talks about things that happened in the 1800s like they happened yesterday.

"Being a nearly seven-foot-tall woman couldn't have helped, either. She intimidates the hell out of most men."

Jessica lays there thinking for a bit, staring at the ceiling.

"I never had a plan for my life," she says. "Everyone always tells you that you need to plot out what you're going to do and you've got to follow this plan. My mom always told me to get married, have kids - but I wasn't interested in that. I mean, look how her marriage turned out. She drank herself to death my freshman year in college, because she didn't understand what happened to my dad and blamed herself for it. If she'd had a clue what actually happened to him, she probably would've drank herself to death much earlier."

I let that soak in. My mom's still alive. My dad died in a motorcycle accident years ago, but that's better than being driven insane and left to wander Albuquerque in a drug-fueled haze.

"What did you want out of life?" she asks me.

"Same thing as every other guy," I say, "a hot woman who's into bondage and dressing like Velma. Oh, and a fast car."

Everyone deals with problems in their own way. Some people completely break down; others go through a normal grief cycle and move on. I try to use humor to laugh it off and act like it doesn't actually bother me. One of these days I'll get around to grieving.

"Why not Daphne?" she asks me.

"Daphne was the pretty one, no doubt about it, but pretty only takes you so far. At some point you need to actually talk to a woman, and Daphne never struck me as terribly interesting."

"She didn't seem like the brightest bulb on the marquee," she agrees with me. "I've known plenty of girls who felt being beautiful was the most important thing in the world, so it's not just cartoon characters being nitwits."

"I've met a lot of guys who would agree with you. My own dad used to scope out college girls when he was in his late 40s. I was visiting him

110

once in college and pointed out some girl. I tried to explain to him that I lived in New Mexico, and she lived in Phoenix. You know what he told me?"

She shakes her head.

"He told me I was thinking 'buy' when I needed to think 'rent.'"

She laughs. "That sounds like good fatherly advice to me. How did you wind up hooking up with these guys?" she asks me.

"I moved a chair," I say.

"What?"

"I moved a chair."

She stares at me.

"A few years ago my wife and son were killed. Ever heard of Senator Lucius Bedfellow? Sleazy guy, prided himself on always voting in a way that followed Biblical morals."

She shakes her head, no. That's not really surprising. How many people would you guess know who their own senators are, let alone the senators from another state?

"His son was a real piece of shit, like most kids from rich, powerful families tend to turn out to be. Into drugs, gambling, carousing - he had a couple of kids out of wedlock, but his daddy covered it all up. Eventually the younger Bedfellow would've had a public mea culpa, and run for office, and probably won.

Anyway, one day young Chet Bedfellow got his hands on bath salts – the kind you smoke, not the kind you take a bath with - and stole dad's Ferrari to go for a joyride. My wife was driving home, and Chet cut her off and caused a wreck. He was so drugged up he got out of the car and started shooting. Killed my wife and son."

"Jesus, that's terrible," she says.

"It gets better. Like all rich and powerful families, the Bedfellows had a history of covering things up. They planted a gun, and made it look like my wife had started shooting and Chet was just protecting himself. Chet got 90 days of drug rehab for a double homicide, and the Bedfellows poisoned my dogs to remind me not to fuck with them in the future.

"Senator Bedfellow himself used the incident to try to prove people needed guns to defend themselves, and the rest of Congress used it as some kind of political ammunition or another. None of them gave a shit about what had actually happened they just knew they could use it to stay in power. God forbid any of them have to get a real job.

"I waited patiently for six months or so, until Bedfellow scored a major victory, got a huge bribe and his family went on vacation without him. During that time I kept my head low, and acted like the good little beaten-down peon everyone wanted me to be. Like everything else, it all eventually blew over, and all the politicos moved on to the next media tragedy.

"One night when Bedfellow was alone, and I snuck into his house intending to shoot him in the face and disappear to Mexico.

"He lived in one of those huge houses up in High Desert where he could surround himself with other rich people, who would kiss his ass because of his position. Houses are isolated from each other up there, because everyone wants their 'space.' Security is pretty minimal, because they all want their 'privacy.' It was trivial to avoid the security, hop into his backyard, and loop the phone line so the alarms wouldn't go off. The back door was unlocked for some reason, so I waltzed in like I owned the place.

"His house was full of fine, if somewhat uninteresting, art and statues. Nice kitchen - SubZero appliances and copper pots. No one in his family knew a damn thing about cooking, though, because the kitchen was absolutely spotless, and the pots and pans absolutely shone, like they'd never been used. I hate people like that. How do you get through life never cooking? And why the hell would you spend fifty grand on a kitchen that you never use?

"Anyway, the house was quiet and he wasn't in his office - or in the gym, or the home theatre, or the study, or the living room. I finally found him in the master bedroom.

"Did you know public speaking is the number one fear in this country?"

"I'd heard that somewhere," she says.

"It's true, people are more afraid of public speaking than they are of death and this guy had to speak in front of Congress on a regular basis," I say.

"What does this have to do with anything?" Jessica asks me.

"People do strange things to get over their fears. I read an interview with a D.C. madam once, and she said most of her high-dollar politico clients were terrified of speaking in front of their peers. To get over the fear a lot of them would put on women's underwear under their five-thousand-dollar suits whenever they had to give a speech."

"Gross," she tells me.

"Yeah, it probably helped them think they were pulling a fast one on each other, when in fact half of them were decked out in garter belts at any given time.

"So, back to Bedfellow. I found Mr. Biblical Values standing on a chair, dressed in a corset, stockings, and bright-red high heels. He had gagged himself with a big red ball gag, put a noose over his neck and cuffed himself with electronic hand cuffs. He was standing there, masturbating," I say.

"That sounds dangerous. Isn't that how the guy from INXS died?" she asks me.

"Yep," I say. "Well, minus the lingerie and bondage gear."

"What are electronic handcuffs?" She asks me.

"Someone figured out how to make a pair of cuffs with a timer in them for self-bondage. Lock yourself in them, and you're there until the timer runs out or the battery dies."

"I was never into handcuffs," she says. "They're too uncomfortable."

"Yeah," I say. "I prefer rope. It's easier to get off if something goes wrong.

"So, I walked in, planning on saying something pithy, and find this guy all trussed up. I was so shocked, I just stood there and stared. His eyes were huge and he was trying to talk to me but all that came out was 'mumble mumble mumble'."

"I started laughing, and he turned bright red and started to trying get the noose off, but couldn't - because the cuffs wouldn't let him reach around his neck and loosen the tie. I stood there laughing at this guy, totally shocked. He kept getting more and more agitated, and his feet were slipping. He started crying and snuffling, and since he'd gagged himself, he couldn't breathe very well.

"Finally, I walked behind him and nudged the back of the chair with my hip. His feet slipped completely off the chair, and the noose tightened around his neck.

"I watched him turn purple and finally spasm and die. He pissed all over the place when he finally died. I watched him the whole time and waved goodbye when the light finally faded from his eyes.

"The whole thing was kind of anti-climactic. I'd spent months getting ready to pop this guy and disappear, and he had already done most of the work for me. In fact, this was way better than I'd ever planned."

"Damn," Jessica says. "How did Eve find you?"

"Oh, she and Frank were already there. This was back when she was planning on taking Congress out one dipshit senator or representative at a time, so they'd already gone in, about a minute or so before me. That's was why the door was unlocked. Bedfellow was about as corrupt as a politician can be, and he was local, so they decided to hit him first. When I turned around to leave, they were both there in the doorway watching. I pulled out my pistol, guessing they were security. Eve held out her hand and said 'Thank you,' and offered me a job."

"This is a job?" she asks.

"In a way, yes. It's not like I set out to be a henchman, and I can't say it pays the bills, because I don't really have any bills any more. It's still an organization working toward a goal."

"I always though henchmen were supposed to be big and dumb. Expendable," she says.

"I like to think of myself as big and dumb."

Jessica laughs and looks like she wants to say something but decides not to.

"That's the common way of looking at it," I explain, "but Eve says she doesn't want stupid people helping her because they tend to fuck it up too often. She wants smart, capable people who can help her with her goals."

"Why does Eve even need help? She seems pretty capable."

"It turns out that being super-strong and bulletproof is really not as useful as you might think. If you're shaking down drug dealers for money, it's probably sufficient, but Eve's not really interested in that. She's thinking big and wants to hurt the government," I say. "She needed some specialists to help see things through, and stumbled onto all of us. She says she was drawn to us, but I don't know what that means. Anyway, I think you're the final piece."

"It's good to know I'm useful," Jessica says.

"You've proven your skills," I tell her. "Look, Eve is a good boss. She actually cares about us. Sure, this job is going to entail killing an awful lot of people, and probably wreaking havoc on a global scale. Frankly, it's a job I'm interested in doing. The U.S. government was supposed to be of the people, for the people, and by the people, but it's wound up being of the people, for the rich and by the corporations. They don't care about the people anymore, unless the people have enough money or power to be interesting. They keep us sated with bad TV and religion, but it's all smokescreens and mirrors. They're not interested in anything but more power. Not all despots take over with military might; the best ones give you an imaginary enemy, and then distract you with emotional issues."

"I can't say I disagree. I saw what they did to my dad, all in the interest of a new weapon, but how will killing Congress set the change anything?" she asks me.

"All the corrupt bastards will be gone. The corporations won't have their lapdogs anymore. People will be forced to help themselves, and think for themselves. Once the people see what happens to corruption, maybe they'll help to root out more corruption.

"I hate to say it, but at this point change can only come through the barrel of a gun."

"What about the President?" she asks me.

"What about him? People like to say the President is the most powerful man in the world, but he has to go to Congress for anything he wants. Congress is the power in this country - they're the only ones who can make laws, issue currency, and declare war. Granted, the executive branch has been growing in power for decades, but the President still needs Congress to get anything done. Even if it doesn't throw the country into anarchy, Congress needs a cleansing," I tell her.

Jessica thinks about it for a while. She's young and hasn't had as much time to become as disillusioned with government as I have. Her life has been touched, and not in a good way, by government, but not in the same personal way mine was, or Frank's or Jacob's or Eve's was.

I let her walk through it in her head and keep my fingers crossed she agrees. Because if she doesn't, and decides to high-tail it out of here, that will be a problem. I've come to like her over the past couple of days. If she splits, I'm the one who has to kill her.

"You said this Brance guy works with another guy?" she asks me.

"Yeah, at least one that we know of," I tell her.

"Do you think we can get hold of some fast-acting poison, or knockout drops or something?"

"I imagine Jacob has some contacts that could get us something for the right price. Why?"

"If we're going in there, it might be easier if the guys inside are already indisposed. Take them some tainted coffee in the morning, and let it take them out," she says.

Good, she's on board. I wasn't worried. Honestly.

"Good idea. Let's pitch it tonight." I tell her. "In the interim, there's an action movie marathon on the TV. Up for some entertainment?"

We spend the rest of the day cheering on large men breaking the backs of evil doers all over the world. I've had worse times.

21 | It Must Go Boom

We lucked out: Brance is a creature of habit. Leaves at 5 p.m. every day, arrives at the Copper Lounge by 5:30, has two drinks, goes home by 7:30, at work again by 9 in the morning. No apparent friends, no apparent family. He's somewhat congenial with the bartender.

I guess he wasn't paying attention in the OPSEC classes. If he had been, he would have known you should never be predictable. Once someone can predict your movements, they can take advantage of you.

Like we're about to.

Tomorrow night we'll take advantage Brance and he'll love us for it. Jessica will seduce the secrets out him. I'll probably get punched and everyone will get a drink. For a brief, shining moment in time, Brance's tiny life will expand and he'll be the man he's always pretended he is.

"We need some artillery," Eve tells us, pointing at Jacob and me. "See what you guys can dig up tomorrow. It's not much time, but I'm hoping Jacob's contacts will come through."

"What kind of arty do we need?" Jacob asks her.

"A shotgun, with some incendiary rounds. Sawed-off, preferably," Eve says.

"Dragon Breath," Jacob says sagely. "I know a guy."

"You want incendiary rounds in a sawed-off shotgun?" I ask, incredulously.

"Trust me. You need to be able to conceal a double-barrel shotgun, and you need to be able to hit the guy behind the desk hard. He's not human," Eve says. "I'm not completely certain of what he is, but he is most definitely not human."

"What makes you say that?" Frank asks.

"It's a feeling I get sometimes," she replies. "You're just going to have to trust me on this one. We can smell our own."

Smell our own? One of these days I really need to sit down and press Eve on exactly what she is and what she wants. I've tried it before and it didn't work, but hope springs eternal.

"Sawed-off's gonna make a huge racket, boss," Jacob tells her. "Do we want everyone in the building to know we just slaughtered someone?"

"The walls are double thick, the door is pretty hefty, and that's a fairly loud building," Frank says. "If the door is closed, you should be good."

Eve points at Frank and nods. Decision made, I guess, even if I don't think it's a great one.

"You'll have three targets to take out," Eve tells me. "Deal with the guy behind the desk first, then worry about the guards. You'll have armor, but keep your head down."

I guess I'm going in. Probably alone.

"Why not go in force?" Jacob asks.

"The door is a huge choke point. If we try to go en masse, we'll be sitting ducks," I say. "The only option we have is to be sneaky."

"Speaking of which," Jessica says, "If I can get Brance working for me, I can take him coffee in the morning. We spike it with something and that could eliminate a target - more targets, if I bring in coffee for everyone."

"Won't he get curious if you show up in the morning bearing coffee?" Frank asks.

"He meets some girl at a bar and she brings him coffee the next morning?" Jessica says. "He'll let everyone in the office believe he banged me the night before. It doesn't matter that it didn't happen. All that matters is that his buddies think it happened."

"Ok, good plan. Jacob, check with your contact, see if he's got anything that will work. I don't care if it's lethal or nonlethal, so long as it's fast-acting and can be hidden in coffee," Eve tells us. "Frank, there's a keypad out in front of the door, can you seal the door with it?"

"I'll need a closer look at it, but probably," Frank says. "At the very least, I can probably trigger the lock and smash the keypad with a hammer."

"Good enough," Eve says. "We need to do some shopping. Jessica, you need to seduce a guard, so we need to find you something appropriate." She points at me, "We need to find you a cheap suit so you can blend in."

"Ooh, goody. " I say. "Can it be something from the J.C. Penney polyester line?"

"It will be something suitably tacky," she tells me. "Now, how about dinner?"

22 | Walk On The Luxurious Wild Side

Meeting with any of Jacob's friends is always an adventure. If you've never had the opportunity to hang out with a contingent of people popularly referred to as "gun nuts," you certainly need to. They're great fun, and usually have a whole assortment of toys at their disposal. Mr. Smith, as he insists on being called, is one of Jacob's many contacts in the weapons-dealing and general anti-government world. He lives way out in the middle of nowhere with the rest of the survivalist types. It allows him space so he can quietly test all kinds of crazy weapons.

Mr. Smith' house is set far off the main drag, hidden behind a small forest and over a hill. The main drag, by the way, is dirt and gravel, and is completely impassable in the winter. Or after it's rained. Or if you don't own a four-wheel-drive vehicle.

These guys are never what you expect. For some reason, I always expect gun and explosives dealers to be twitchy and hairy, like bears hopped up on crystal meth and armed to the teeth. The truth is these guys are generally smart, well spoken, and often ex-military. Mr. Smith is clean as a whistle, and he looks like the quintessential ex-Marine-gone-mountain-man, right down to his pressed flannel shirt and khakis. His hair has obviously grown out since his days in the armed forces, but the discipline has remained unchanged. Actually, he kind of looks like the Brawny Guy.

The new Brawny Guy one, not the guy from the Eighties with the porn mustache.

Also, he drives a Land Rover which is the vehicle of choice for people who want to go anywhere at any time and not spill their macchiato.

Jacob and Mr. Smith go way back. I'm not certain how or why and I really don't want to know. There are aspects of Jacob's past that are probably better left alone. I'm kind of the outsider here, so I keep my mouth shut and listen.

"Jacob, my old friend. How are you today?" Mr. Smith asks. Damn, even his speech is formal.

"Doing well, buddy. Doing well."

"I trust your friend here is safe."

"I can vouch for him. We've been working together," Jacob says.

"Thank you. I appreciate that. Just know - he's your responsibility."

I have a bad feeling about that. Jacob gives me a knowing smile that says, "I'll make it quick, buddy."

"What can I do for you gentlemen?" Mr. Smith asks.

"We need some specialized tools. Do you have a sawed-off shotgun and some Dragon's Breath rounds?" Jacob asks.

"Kind of pedestrian, but I think I can help you. I trust you have payment."

Jacob holds up the brief case. It's a Fendi. More to the point, it's a Fendi full of cash. Even more to the point, it's a Fendi full of cash we stole from a drug dealer. What's the point of working in villainy if you can't occasionally show the other villains who's the boss? We found a couple of guys last night doing a brisk trade in crack down the street from the motel. I shot one of them, and Eve crushed the other's skull. Most of the time the crack dealers don't keep much cash on them, but we lucked out. They hadn't had a chance to turn their profits back into more crack, and with the High School District Track Meet in town, they'd had a banner evening.

What? You think you need to be a pro athlete to get "performance-enhancing" drugs?

We netted about 50k last night. Should be enough for what we need.

"Cash is always good, and I must say I approve of the case. But I have to ask. Any idiot can procure a sawed-off shotgun and Dragon's Breath rounds with minimal trouble. Why come to me?"

"There's something else," I say. "Do you have any sort of fast-acting anesthetic or poison that can be dissolved in coffee?"

Smith looks mildly offended. "Gentlemen, I usually only deal in physical weapons. I find toxins beneath me. Still, come into my parlor. I may be able to find something you'll find useful."

His parlor is a library bigger than some of the houses I've lived in, filled floor to ceiling with every book imaginable. Leather-bound volumes with labels printed in gold, all immaculately maintained and presented. Arms dealing is a lucrative business, apparently.

"Did you read all these, Mr. Smith?" I ask.

"Of course not. Who would want a library full of books they've already read?" he replies.

Mr. Smith offers us Armagnac, which is like brandy for rich people. It's quite good.

Smith walks over to a bookshelf in the middle of the room and pulls the corner of a book. The whole shelf swings out, revealing a well-lit room stocked with guns, knives and all manner of explosives.

"Gentlemen," he says, "welcome to paradise."

I feel like a kid in a candy store, and Jacob is positively giddy. There are all kinds of tools of destruction in this place. The walls are lined with guns, knives, swords, and other accoutrements of killing. The weapons vary from the mundane, if rare, Franchi SPAS-12 to the more exotic, including a pair of KGB-issued silent pistols.

The silent pistols are just that, silent. They're two-shot derringer-type pistols that are literally and truly silent.

Smith's arsenal is broken into heavy weapons — rocket launchers like the RPG-7 and heavy machine guns, shotguns and assault rifles from every nation, pistols like the silent pistols, and bladed weapons. If I ever win the lottery, I'm coming back here.

"Do you have any explosives?" Jacob asks.

"No, I sold out of all my explosives last week. Someone bought 50 pounds of C4 earlier this week."

"Who buys 50 pounds of C4 at a time?" Jacob asks.

"I never reveal the identities of my other customers. You know that, Jacob."

Jacob looks hang-dog, like the kid who was just chastised by his favorite teacher. "I know. Sorry."

"Anyway. Let's see now. You need some common items, and some less-than-common items." He carefully grabs two vials of clear liquid and holds them up to the light. "Things like this are not normally my game. I find poisons to be less than…sporting, but these came across my desk as extras, and I decided to keep them."

The vials are a few inches long and made from completely clear, colorless glass, topped with what look like brushed aluminum caps. There's nothing about them to indicate that each one is lethal. I've never been a huge fan of poisons, either, but I'm also not a huge fan of being gunned down in some office downtown.

"What are they?" I ask him.

"This is a one-off custom poison out of Japan. It's a mixture of blowfish toxin and few other choice chemicals. A few drops will incapacitate a full-grown man in 15 minutes. Several drops will kill in the same amount of time. It has no taste, no smell," Smith tells us.

"How much?" Jacob asks him.

"Fifty," Smith says.

"How much for the gun and the shells?" Jacob asks him.

"I'll throw them in gratis," Smith says.

Fifty grand is no small amount of money, but we've got the cash, and we need the goods. "You've got a deal," I tell him.

We shake hands and Jacob hands him a briefcase full of cash. He doesn't care where we got it any more than we care where he came across a toxic arsenal. The world is a scary place full of scary people. Often, the less you know about things, the happier you'll be.

"Needless to say, this substance does not come with instructions or any kind of documentation," he says as he wraps one of the vials in silk and places it in a leather satchel. "I don't think I need to warn you that this is dangerous. I can vouch for its efficacy, though. I saw it tested on..." He pauses. "Well, let's just say I saw it tested on an individual of less-than-savory character. The results were impressive. With a dose of ten drops, the subject was incapacitated within twelve minutes. Termination was within fifteen minutes. It was quiet and effective. His nervous system simply shut down and he collapsed in a heap. Please take care with this substance."

Imagine that: an arms dealer with a conscience.

He hands the satchel to me and walks toward the back of the room, where he pauses and selects a filigreed, breach-opening, sawed-off, double-barrel shotgun. The metal is polished silver, and the stock burnished redwood. Someone loved this weapon, and made it into a work of art. Smith presents it to Jacob like a sword, bowing slightly as he hands it over. He then reaches into a drawer, selects three shotgun shells and puts them in a bag. As he hands it to Jacob he says "Do not use these anywhere that can burn. Shells like these burned down half of Arizona a few years ago."

"I'm sorry to be a bother, but you wouldn't happen to have any flechette rounds, would you?" I ask him.

"Of course. How many would you like?" he replies.

"Three would be great."

He goes to another drawer, pulls out three more shells, and hands them to me.

"Gentlemen. It has been a pleasure doing business with you, but I have another appointment soon and it is imperative that my clients do not meet each other."

"Thank you, sir," I respond.

We walk out of the parlor fifty thousand dollars lighter, but with some exciting new toys.

"Let me see that shotgun," I tell Jacob.

We trade packages and I get my first good look at the double. It's about 18 inches long, and the barrels were cut by an expert. The filigree work is a stunning representation of *Ragnarök*, complete with Thor fighting the *Jörmungandr*. I'm keeping this gun. No matter how this plays out, this will become my Mjolnir.

23 | A Hot Chick, a Tough Guy, and a Valkyrie Walk Into a Bar

5 p.m. is still early by Albuquerque bar standards. Hell, 5 p.m. is early by any bar's standards, which is a good thing. I'm sitting at the bar, nursing an old-fashioned and waiting for the action to begin. Eve and Jacob are sharing a table in the back. Frank's downtown, keeping an eye out for Brance. He'll text us when he leaves. As soon as Brance gets here, Eve or Jacob will text Jessica so she can work her magic.

I'm sitting a couple seats down from where Brance usually sits. I like to believe we'll blend in, but there are only six people in the bar, and we're three of them, so we'll just have to see what happens. In the interim, I'll finish my old-fashioned and probably drink another one. The bartender is your regulation-issue bartender, not too trendy, not wearing horn-rimmed glasses, just making good drinks. I'll have to become a regular.

At 5:10 Frank's text comes through: *The fat man walks alone.* Brance isn't that fat, but considering the NSA is watching everything, we're trying to be at least somewhat under the radar. Granted, *the fat man walks alone* is pretty childish, but the phrase is common enough that it should get lost in the noise. We could have said anything: "I like burgers" or "Donkey Kong kicks it old school" would have had the same effect.

That's crypto for you in a nutshell. All cryptography is essentially scrambling a message, and sharing a key to unscramble it. If you all agree on the message from the get-go, you assign whatever meaning you want, and the message will make sense to each party. Since we all know each other and see each other every day, it's easy enough to exchange the key.

Brance makes it to the bar about 20 minutes after Frank's text comes through. He walks in and sits in his favorite seat. At this hour of the day, he can easily have his pick of the bar stools. I find myself idly wondering if that's why he comes in at this time every day.

If Brance works in security, he's used to routine, since routine provides security.

Well, kind of.

The process of maintaining organizational security is routine; the process of maintaining personal security is to break routine. I know - it's a contradiction. Think about it this way: in an organization routine is important because it means there are steps that everyone goes through to make sure no one gets access to something they shouldn't have access to. The routine means you always do the exact same thing in the exact same order: sign in, check the log, open one safe, close that safe, open the other safe, close it, lock the first door, lock the second door. The fixed routine drives a lot of people nuts, but it is the structure of the system that provides the security to the system, because the structure is designed to make it automatic to follow the routine. People who work in that system for a long time tend to develop habits that follow the system.

Ironically, personal security requires the exact opposite. When you become predictable in your personal activities, you become inherently less secure, because now someone can figure out where to get you and probably have a very good idea of when you'll be at a particular location. So, there you go: follow the security routines at work and become as unpredictable as possible when you leave.

Geoff Brance probably follows all the routines at work to a T. He has the appearance of someone who has become so inured to the system that the routine of it has become second nature. He also looks like someone who's not into thinking in general.

Frankly, I love people like this, because they make it so damn easy to exploit them.

As soon as Brance walks in, I catch Eve out of the corner of my eye fiddling with her phone. The last two nights he's been here, he's stayed for exactly 45 minutes, had two drinks and eaten pretzels. He always sits in the same place, always has the same drinks, and always pays exactly fifteen dollars for two drinks and a tip. Forty five minutes sounds like a lot of time, but that really isn't that much time to set up everything we need to do, and pump this guy for information.

Brance looks briefly at me, like I'm invading his space by simply being in the bar, and orders a scotch on the rocks. He calmly sits sipping his scotch, eating pretzels and watching the game on one of the TVs behind the bar.

Jessica arrives about five minutes later and she looks incredible. She's wearing a black dress, cut low enough in the front to attract attention, but not low enough to attract the wrong kind of attention. She's showing some cleavage, but just enough to make you want to see more, not enough to make you believe you've seen the whole package.

The dress is cut to just above her knees and, while it isn't skin-tight, it is definitely fitted down all the way down and shows her curves to amazing effect. There's a sash around the waist that ends in a bow tie that dangles off the front of her right hip. She's got black hose and heels, and looks like someone who's not just important, but someone who knows what she wants. Her lips are a deep, but somehow still subtle, red. She's stunning.

More importantly, she's smart and dedicated.

If she wasn't half my age I'd...

Well. Fuck.

Jessica asks Brance if the seat next to him is taken, and as soon as he recovers a bit of his composure, he shakes his head "no."

She puts her purse down next to Brance and sits on the stool between us. The bartender is in front of her in the beat of a heart, asking for her order. It must be nice to be attractive. Unfortunately, it's nothing I've ever experienced.

She looks at Brance, and tells the bartender she'll have what he's having.

Brance actually looks proud of himself for a moment, like he's just gotten validation from the Goddess of Drinks that he made the correct beverage choice.

"What kind of Scotch?" The bartender asks.

"Whatever he's having," she responds.

I think I just saw Brance smile and blush.

When the bartender asks to see her ID, she makes a show of getting up and bending over to get her license out of her purse. Brance's eyes zero in on her, and he looks her up and down her long legs, his eyes following the seams on her stockings. She knows this is happening. She knows exactly what she's doing, and she gives me a knowing smile when she stands back up to hand the bartender her ID. He glances at it and hands it back. Jessica repeats the whole process to put her ID back before she sits back down, running her hands across her ass to smooth her dress out.

Brance thinks he's smooth. His eyes are back straight and center before she sits down. He's obviously an expert at surreptitiously ogling women. He tries to act calm and debonair, but all he can come up with is "I like your pantyhose."

I can almost feel her eyes rolling from here.

She pats his hand gently and says, "They're stockings, sweetie."

Jessica looks at him and smiles. I think it was *Starship Troopers* that talked about the idea of weaponizing a woman's smile. It's a wonderful idea, but Jessica's would probably be considered a weapon of mass destruction. Jesus, she orders the same drink and smiles at him, and he's already all hers.

It's time for me to make my move.

"Hey," I ask her, "Why Scotch?"

She shoots me a look that would peel paint, and looks away.

"Seriously. Why scotch? I mean, you look more like a Cosmopolitan type of chick," I tell her.

I've been glared at by pros, but Jessica's gaze is withering. Brance is starting to get a little irritated that she's not paying attention to him anymore.

"Excuse me," he says. "Is this guy bothering you?"

This is the standard guy way of trying to get focus back on us. We're all about the chivalry, especially when that chivalry could lead to sex.

"No," she tells him, putting her hand on his hand. "He's just another drunk asshole. Let it go."

"Seriously," I say, ignoring their conversation, "let me at least buy you something more appropriate for a girl as fine as you. Scotch is for hairy old women, not at all like you."

"Fuck off, asshole," she tells me.

Brance is starting to get edgy.

"Come on, babe. Why do you want to hang out with a loser like this guy?" I ask, gesturing to Brance. "I'm a VP. I can take you where you want to go."

Brance starts to get up, but Jessica puts her hand on his arm again, and he calms down a bit. But it's not going to take much to get him riled up again.

"My BMW is a convertible," I tell her. "At night the stars are amazing, if you follow me."

I catch a glimmer of smile from her before she points at me. She starts to say something but I interrupt her before she can get it out. "Come on." I tell her. "I get it. I like to slum too, sometimes, but you could honestly do so much better."

Brance is up, and he's got a knife in his hand. It's a small one, maybe a four inch blade. But I was expecting to get slugged, not take a few inches of steel in my gut.

Most martial arts expose you to dealing with knives at some point or another, and Kenpo is no different. Like most systems, we trend toward avoiding the conflict whenever possible, but responding quickly when we have to. I don't want Brance going to jail tonight, and I can't afford to let him get kicked out right now, since I need Jessica to get some information out of him.

Brance is holding the knife out in front of him, which puts the knife close to the target (me), but leaves him somewhat exposed.

Did you know you've got a nerve that runs along the inside of your arm? It's called the radial nerve, and it hurts like hell when the nerve gets hit. It doesn't hurt when you hit your radial nerve yourself, but it hurts when someone else hits it for you. Like any nerve strike, it feels like an electric shock when you get hit, and whatever is in your hand winds up on the floor.

I chop Brance in the arm and he drops the knife. This isn't some huge chop where I bring my hand way up and yell "judo chop!" before dropping my hand down in a big arc. This is more of a straight-line punch - but instead of using a fist, I hit his arm right above his wrist with the edge of my hand. He drops the knife and backs up a bit. I immediately kick the knife under the stool and out of everyone's line of sight just before Jessica slugs me.

Getting hit in the jaw fucking sucks, but I'll take it over a solid shot to the nose any day of the week. She's got one hell of a roundhouse, and I'm on my ass before I completely grasp what just happened.

"That was a cheap shot, asshole," she says. This gives Brance an out: if he thinks I cheated, he won't lose "man points" for letting a woman step in for him. In fact, good ol' cognitive dissonance is setting in right now, and he's convinced himself that not only did I fight dirty, but he let Jessica hit me because I was beneath his worth.

"You bitch," I tell her from my solid position on my ass. Her face darkens and I worry for a second that I'm about get hit again. Brance steps in and kicks me in the ribs. Nothing breaks (because he doesn't know what he's doing), but the kick doesn't feel good either.

There's an art to taking a dive in a fight.

Yeah, it sucks. Everyone wants to win, and be a rock star, but sometimes you have to lose the battle to win the war. Such is the difference between tactics and strategies. The strategy is to get Jessica to empty this guy's skull of all his secrets. The tactic is to make him feel good about himself by taking a dive and not fighting back. The art of using tactics to accomplish strategies is having the presence of mind to think about the ultimate win, while you're sitting on your ass in a bar holding your jaw.

Jessica puts an arm on Brance's shoulder and says, "Come on. This guy's not worth your time. Let me buy you a drink for saving me, hero."

That's an awful lot of ego stroking in one sentence, and Brance sucks it up like a man in the desert who's just been handed a tall glass of water. If he hadn't just pulled a knife on me, I'd almost feel sorry for him. She's playing him like a violin, and he's just happy someone's plucking his strings. He must've forgotten that age-old adage about pretty women picking him up in a bar.

I've got another saying I like to live my life by: if you're looking around the room and can't figure out who the sucker is, it's probably you.

Jacob walks over and roughly pulls me to my feet. "You'd better get out of here, asshole. This is a classy joint and you're nastying up the place." The bartender nods and reaches for the phone.

I remember hearing a story once about a Karate school owner who had some problems with a guy around town. One day he comes across the guy, and beats the living shit out of him. No provocation, nothing - just walks up and lays into him with a ton of witnesses around. The school owner got a slap on the wrist, because he said it was all in self-defense, and the witnesses agreed with his story. Now, how in the name of Holy Thor do you instigate a fight, beat up someone who wasn't doing anything to you, and get off by claiming self-defense?

Here's how. The whole time the owner was knocking the snot out of this guy, he was busy yelling things like "please don't hurt me!" and "oh, God, why are you doing this?" The witnesses heard this, and their minds connected dots that weren't there. Voilà, a school owner got to thump someone with no repercussions.

Here, everyone saw me drinking before anyone else came in. Saw me generally being an asshole with Jessica, saw her slug me, and connected the dots. This guy pulls a knife in a bar, and suddenly *I'm* the bad guy.

Jacob pulls my arm behind my back and shoves me out the door. The door slams behind me, and I hear faint clapping from inside. All he did was push me out a door I wanted to go out anyway, and he's suddenly a hero to everyone else in the bar, too.

It'll be a while before they're done in there, so I head over to the Route 66 Diner and grab a shake before wandering back to the motel.

24 | Okay, That Was Funny

About 8 or so Jacob and Frank make it back to the motel. Frank is his usual unflustered self. Jacob is grinning ear to ear and flashing a wad of cash.

"How's your jaw?" Frank asks me.

"Not bad. Nothing's broken and all my remaining teeth are still there," I tell him.

Jacob said the place started to pick up around 7ish, and was still going strong when they left. Brance was being treated like a hero, even though he didn't do jack shit, and was apparently eating it up. Jessica was still laying it on thick, and when Jacob and Frank left Brance had his arm around her waist and she was leaning into him. I wonder if he even stopped to think about why this young lady was so busy asking him about his work. I'll bet you he just thought it meant she was interested in him.

I guess some guy decided to openly challenge anyone in the bar to arm wrestling, and took out Jacob and almost everyone else before Eve stepped in. You know you're in a great place when spontaneous arm wrestling matches start up. I would've loved to be there for it. If he could beat Jacob, he would've whooped me, but it still would've been fun. Eve flattened the guy and he immediately decided he was completely, madly, totally in love with her.

Good luck with that, dude.

Frank and Jacob played pool and eventually wound up challenging some guys to a game. I had no idea about this, but Frank is a pool shark, and paid part of his way through college hustling people at various bars around town. I had figured Jacob would play pool - he looks the part - but finding out Frank was a pool shark completely blind-sided me. I imagine it blind-sided a bunch of other people, too. That explains the straight razor: people tend to get pissed when they feel they've been hustled. I imagine more than a few people got a nice scar in the parking lot of the Billiard Palace trying to take him on.

Jacob flashes a wad of about a grand or so. "This guy's amazing!

Seriously!" Jacob slaps Frank on the back and Frank staggers forward a bit. Jacob never did understand his own strength.

Frank smiles and, ever the gentleman, says "I couldn't have done it without Jacob. Anyway, when the ladies get back, dinner's on us."

Like we didn't have a short ton of money squirreled away in a dozen different accounts. It's the thought that counts.

Jessica and Eve make it back about an hour later. Jessica is pretty hammered, and Eve is glowing.

Jessica "walks" straight up to me, puts a finger in my face and says "If you ever call me a bitch again, I'll cut your balls off."

I stare her dead in the eye and tell her "If you ever punch me in the jaw again, I'll give you paper cuts on your nipples."

She backs up and wraps her arms around her breasts.

"How'd it go with Brance?" I ask her.

Jessica makes a face, shivers a bit and says "That guy was all hands. I need a shower and I'll tell you." She shudders again and heads back to her room to shower.

"Eve," Frank says, "why are you glowing?"

Eve blushes a bit. "I had a really good drink, that's all. And I won an arm wrestling match."

"That's not enough to make you glow," Frank says. "Who was he?"

She thinks for a bit and comes to a decision. "That guy that was arm wrestling? He had a very nice truck with a well-appointed camper."

She looks around at us. "What? A girl can't get laid anymore?" she asks.

I grin, Jacob laughs out loud. "You got laid in the parking lot of the Copper Lounge! Outrageous!"

"You go, girl!" Frank tells her.

Everyone else at the bar thought Brance was a hero, and people bought him drinks all night long. Jessica stayed with him, constantly stroking his ego. Somehow or another the story morphed from the truth - he pulled a knife and got chopped, and Jessica knocked me out, to: I pulled a knife on Jessica, and he saved her from the raving lunatic rapist. People were howling for my blood. Someone drew a composite sketch of me and they hung it behind the bar with a note that says "poison this guy's drink."

Pity. I really liked that bar.

About half an hour later (Jesus, how long does it take a take a quick shower?) Jessica comes back in wearing a tight gray shirt, a black skirt with suspenders and a pair of unlaced Vans. I've never seen a skirt with suspenders, and I must say it's a nice look.

"I'm hungry, guys. Where can we eat?" she asks.

25 | Last Supper

—●—◎—●—

Street Food Asia on Central serves pretty much the food you expect it would serve, only a hell of a lot better than you expect it will be. I once spent an entire dinner trying to convince the manager to invest in luminescent noodles so they could serve Glo Mein, but to no avail. She felt things like the carcinogenic chemicals used in luminescent sticks might kill the flavor of the noodles and, possibly, the diners. Like most of my great ideas, this one died on the vine. Someday science will help me realize my dream of eating glow-in-the-dark noodles. It has to happen sometime.

Eve gets a green curry with beef dish, Jessica gets a Bangkok street noodle bowl with chicken, Frank gets a Saigon rice bowl with beef and shrimp. Jacob, never a huge fan of Asian food, gets Pad Thai, and I get a Tokyo street classic: tempura calamari. We also have, of course, many appetizers: summer rolls from various countries, won tons, and various wraps.

While we're waiting for dinner and drinking tea, Eve grills Jessica about Geoff Brance.

"He doesn't know a damn thing about what he's guarding. All he does is show up every morning and make sure the elevator doesn't move. No one comes in, no one talks. He's on guard duty with one other guard, name of Albert Mills, and their lead, who he only knows as Mr. Robinson. Brance and Mills never really hang out. Apparently they had a political dispute of some kind," Jessica says.

"How did he wind up with this job?" Frank asks.

"His assignment is a punishment of some sort or another. Apparently a general accused Brance of groping his fifteen-year-old daughter. They couldn't prove anything, and she denied the incident, but he was reassigned to this dead-end position to get rid of him. He's only got five years left, and he'll be able to retire with full benefits, so he just keeps his eyes on that brass ring," Jessica says.

"Do you think he actually groped that girl?" Eve asks.

"Considering how many places his hands wandered on me, yeah, I bet he did," Jessica says. "He's a pretty sad, pathetic guy. If he wasn't such a freak, I'd almost feel sorry for him."

"Does he know anything about Robinson?" I ask.

Jessica pauses for a moment to take a drink of her Mai Tai. "Not much. Robinson is always there before either Brance or Mills show up, and he's always there after they leave. Hell, he may live in that room," she tells us.

"If what they're guarding is so important, you'd think there'd be more people," Jacob says.

"That's the thing. They don't know what they're guarding. They don't have a damned clue. They just show up at the appointed time and leave at the appointed time," she says.

"If the place is really super-secret, he may just not have wanted to tell you," Frank says.

"When I put my hand on his leg he admitted to liking midget porn. He told me all about his previous posting guarding something up in Dulce. He would've happily told me anything I wanted to know, if he knew it himself," Jessica tells him.

"It's possible that whatever they're keeping an eye on fell through the cracks. These things happen. Look at Radula. That was some dark stuff, but the project wasn't new and sexy and it just kind of got forgotten. It's also possible that place is so classified that the people guarding it don't have the need to know," I say.

"The only thing he knew for sure was that if the elevator came up, they were to immediately call a number and press a button on Robinson's desk," Jessica says.

"What does the button do?" Eve asks. "Where does the number go?"

"He doesn't know where the number goes, just that the number must be called from the phone on Robinson's desk. He has no idea what the button does. I got the impression from talking to him that they're mostly concerned about that elevator coming up. He's been at that posting for five years, and the elevator hasn't moved at all," she says.

"Did you ask him what he thought was down there? Usually there are rumors, or something," I ask her.

"He suspects it's some kind of nuclear or biological weapon, but doesn't know and doesn't want to know. Apparently before Mills came in, Brance worked with another guy who asked Robinson what was down at the bottom of the elevator shaft. The guy never came back, and no one ever saw him again."

"So he's into midget porn?" Jacob asks.

"He thinks of it more as a strange fetish, but yeah, he's into midget porn," Jessica says.

"I didn't even realize there was such a thing as midget porn," he tells her.

"So, where is this button on Robinson's desk?" I ask.

"It's right on top. Should be easy to find, because Robinson's desk is spotless. His desk has a button and a phone on it, and that's it."

"Do we know anything at all about Robinson?" Frank asks.

"He never speaks, except to tell Brance and Mills what they're doing wrong. He always wears a black suit, white shirt and black tie. He's always immaculate, and he can sit absolutely still for hours at a time. He once went three whole months without saying a word to anyone. If Brance or Mills slouches at all, Robinson lets them both have an earful about respecting their positions. He seems to believe whatever they're guarding is the single most important thing on the planet."

"Nice work," Eve says. "It sounds like Brance actually doesn't have a clue."

"Sounds like a lot of government employees I knew," I say. "I once worked here in New Mexico with a woman who used to go all the way back to California for her dentist, because she didn't think her insurance would work in a foreign country."

The waitress brings our food and the conversation stops for a bit.

I eventually ask Eve a question that's been on my mind for a while. "What are we going to do after all this is over?"

She ponders a bit while finishing chewing and says, "I don't know. I hadn't thought that far ahead."

What does Lex Luthor do after he finally takes over? What does the Joker do after everything's rubble? Move on to bigger and better villainy, or assume the mantle of ruler and move on to the day-to-day tasks to administering the new domain?

"What do you want out of life?" Jessica asks her.

Eve sighs. "I want to see people free to make their own decisions, and to be responsible for those decisions."

"Everyone is already free to make their own decisions," I say.

"No, they're not," Eve says. "They're free to make some decisions within a tiny range of acceptable decisions. You can't live outside the system, because the system is completely pervasive. Look at it this way. What if you don't want to buy new clothes all the time, or pay attention to religious fanatics, or make your own decisions about what you hold dear? Everything about our world is tightly controlled and regimented for most people. They do what they're told, and tell themselves they're free to stop doing that whenever they want. But what happens when you decide to stop doing what you're told? What happens when you decide you don't believe in what you're told the majority believes?"

"You wind up tied to a fence in the middle of nowhere and beaten half to death?" Frank says.

"You see your friends killed, because they sold things the system doesn't want them to sell?" Jacob asks.

"Exactly. The system won't tolerate gross differences," Eve says. "And that's a terrible thing, because it forces people to live narrow lives and have narrow minds."

"How is eliminating Congress going to change all that?" I ask her. "Sure, they're a bunch of corrupt bastards, but that won't change basic human nature."

"No, Congress is a symptom of the disease, but it's not the disease itself. Remember, Congress makes the laws of this country, and all laws are designed to tell you what you cannot do. The one primary thing they don't want you to do is think for yourself, and they've become experts at preventing you from looking up and realizing you're slowly being squeezed to death. Any time there's even a hint of an uprising, they find things to make you afraid of. Terrorism, gay marriage, abortion, taxes. None of these are the root of any problem and, no offense to Frank, none of them are actually serious problems. What is a serious problem? People have started to see these miniscule things they hold dear as the most important of problems, and have been trained over decades to never budge on what they hold dear. People need enemies. They need something to rally behind that will let them get over their bigotry, and unite. This country, as it stands now, is not a single entity. We're 300-plus-million special-interest groups, and we'll all fight tooth and nail to make sure our special interests are carried out.

We want a way to force people to work together toward a common good. Eliminate the government and it will have to be rebuilt. People will have to do that."

Serious talk for a serious night.

"Hey, Jess. Did you ever serve food like this?" Jacob asks.

Leave it to the big man to break the mood.

"Spicy noodles would have been a little hot for Nyotaimori. Also a little public. I worked private affairs, not public restaurants," she says.

"What if we paid?" Jacob asks.

"Still no," Jessica says nonchalantly sucking up a noodle.

"Damn." Jacob says.

"How long had you been working there, by the way?" I ask.

She looks at me curiously and takes a sip of water. "A couple of years, why?"

"Sorry if this comes off wrong, it just seems like you're smart and could have done anything you wanted. Why get strapped to a table so people can eat sushi off you?" I ask.

"Not that he's complaining about the view, am I right?" Jacob says and slaps me on the back.

Jessica blushes and I'm pretty sure I did, too, but she says, "It was work. There's not much in Vegas jobwise, so I could have been a cocktail waitress and gotten groped by drunken assholes or worked where I did. It was pretty easy work; it's not every job where you can lie around and get paid for it."

"Lying around getting paid would be great experience for a government job," Frank says.

"Well, that's ultimately what I wanted and that's why I studied what I did, but it takes forever to get into those positions so I was kind of stuck for the time being," Jessica says.

"Literally," Jacob adds.

"The straps came off every night, big guy," she answers with a smile. "What about you? What did you do?"

Jacob puffs up his chest and says with great pride, "I was in an MC."

"An MC?" Jessica asks.

"Motorcycle club," Jacob responds.

"Yeah, I know. I've seen *Sons of Anarchy*," Jessica says. "What do you do in a motorcycle gang?"

"Club," Jacob says. "It a motorcycle club."

"Semantics. What do you do in a motorcycle club, for reals?" Jessica asks.

"Ride bikes, of course."

"That's hardly a career," she says. "How do you make money riding motorcycles?"

"We, uh, sold stuff," Jacob says, kind of sheepishly.

"Stuff?" she asks.

"Guns, among other things," Eve says.

"It wasn't that big of a deal," Jacob says.

"The ATF appeared to disagree with you," Frank says.

"Wait. What?" Jessica asks.

"We were meeting up with his group to get hold of some weapons several months ago," I say with a sigh. "We had heard about him and his group of well-groomed miscreants from a friend of a friend."

"Well groomed?" Jacob growls. "I've never been well-groomed."

"He thinks anything beyond shampoo means he's a metrosexual," Frank quips.

"Damn right," Jacob says.

Jessica stifles a laugh and says, "Go on."

"Anyway," I say. "We heard about these guys and we needed some guns, so Eve and I went to meet up with them. Everything went smoothly until the ATF showed up and started shooting. They picked the biggest target on the field and just opened up on her."

Jessica looks at Eve and whistles. "I imagine that didn't go too well."

"I ruined a shirt," Eve says simply.

"Everything went to shit in a heartbeat. One second we're exchanging some money so we can exercise our Second Amendment rights and the next there's lead everywhere. I hit the dirt, Eve just stood there and took it, the bikers..." I say.

"Club members," Jacob interrupts.

"Right, club members," I say, rolling my eyes. "The club members opened up on the ATF. It was like the Wild West for about thirty seconds. When the dust settled I looked up and it was just me, Eve, and Jacob in an empty field full of dead guys and guns."

"That's so cute," Jessica says, needling Jacob. "You guys took home a stray."

"He thought we were in on it at first," I say.

"He's a hell of a scrapper," Jacob says, slapping me on the back again.

"You guys got in a fight?" Jessica asks. "You seem so close now."

"It's a man thing, baby," Jacob says.

"We got in a fight," I say.

"Okay," Jessica says, "I'll bite. Who won?"

Jacob and I look at each other, wondering how to respond. It wasn't a clear-cut fight.

"I dropped him with a punch," Jacob says holding up a big, meaty fist, "but he got right back up and kicked the ever loving shit out of me."

"I got a minor concussion, he got a few bruised ribs and a hyper-extended elbow," I say.

"It took a while," Eve says, "but we finally convinced the big lug we weren't responsible."

"What happened then?" Jessica asks.

"We loaded up the guns and the money and got the hell out of there before more agents showed up," Eve says.

"Got to meet Frank and Jean later that night. I'm sorry about Jean, man, I gave you guys shit, but I loved him like a brother," Jacob says. "We've all been together ever since."

Frank pats Jacob's shoulder and whispers a quiet "Thanks."

Jessica's face softens and she says, "I'm sorry, too. At least we got the bastard responsible."

"He was a bastard," I say.

"Where'd Eve find you, Frank?" Jessica asks.

"He and Jean took out an ad in *The Alibi*, it's a local college paper, advertising their skills. Everyone thought it was a joke, but it turned out it wasn't," Eve says.

"An ad?" Jessica asks.

"Hack computers and buildings, will travel, legality not a problem," Frank says wistfully. "We thought we were Bonnie and Clyde."

"Which one of you was Clyde?" Jacob asks with a grin.

Frank shoots him a look, but smiles. "Ain't tellin'," he says.

"I sent them an email and we met up. I needed some skilled infiltrators," Eve says. "The rest, as they say, is history."

We spend the rest of the evening chatting and joking. Eat, drink, and be merry, for tomorrow we may die.

26 | Running Late

Downtown Albuquerque is like any other downtown in any other city at rush hour. It's full of important people doing important things. It's also full of randomly placed one-way streets. I always forget if it's the even numbered streets that go north, or the odd numbered ones, so I'm almost always late. Plus, I never carry cash, so parking is a pain in the ass.

At any rate, I'm late finding parking, but still have the hustle of youth, so I manage to get a coffee before I need to get to work.

I've got on a cheap-ass black polyester suit, a gray shirt and a maroon tie. I've also got a shoulder bag full of random shit, a vest made from Anodyne's finest weave under the shirt, a sawed-off shotgun under my jacket, and a really dope pair of shades.

One of my first job interviews when I moved to Albuquerque was a job I found in the back of *The Alibi*. Actually, I found two numbers that I called. One was to be a phone psychic. I figured I could lie to people about the future as well as anyone else, but the job required I take a class for $400 or something like that, so I nixed that.

I called the other number, for a company that said they were looking for managers. Here I am, fresh out of college thinking I can be a manager. Turned out the job was to wander around to various businesses and try to sell them random crap: kids' books, stuffed animals, pencils with motivational messages on them, stuff like that. I would be a manager of myself. I rolled out with a guy who was one of the more-experienced salesmen, meaning he'd been there for 6 months, and we hit every office park down Carlisle and sold absolutely nothing. I left for lunch, and never went back.

I guess I wasn't cut out for management.

Point being, these random door-to-door sales guys are commonplace around here. They all wear cheap suits because they want to look professional, even though they have no money. They all carry shoulder bags filled with an assortment of things no one wants, and they all try to go into places where no one wants them to be. It's perfect cover.

It's 9:15 am when I get into the Simms building. I miss Jessica going in, but catch her coming out. She's wearing the same dress she was last night at the bar, but now it's wrinkled and her legs are bare. Her hair is less-than-perfect. She looks like she's doing the walk of shame.

"You're late," she says when she sees me outside.

"Good morning to you, too," I say.

"I see you had time to get a coffee," She tells me, her hand out. I hand her the coffee. She takes a sip and wrinkles her nose. "Jesus. Next time get some coffee with your cream and sugar."

"I like my coffee to taste like coffee candy," I tell her. It's true. "How'd it go in there?"

"That Robinson guy is a serious nightmare of a boss. He glared at me the whole time, and he looked like I had offered him a dead rat when I tried to give him a cup of coffee. He actually told me to get 'the poison' away from him."

"'The poison'?" I ask. "Think he knew what was in it?"

"It didn't seem like it, he just pushed the cup away, but didn't warn the other guys to not drink it."

"Did Brance buy the story?"

"He was in seventh heaven. He was about to shout it from the rooftops that he fucked me last night," she says. "He actually tried to give me a kiss when I left."

"Is he a good kisser?"

"I gave him the head turn just before he could plant one," she says. "I don't think his buddy Mills will need the coffee. He looked like he was about to have a heart attack."

"He is, or something just as bad."

"Well, yeah. I guess so."

"Did they both drink some?" I ask her.

"Yeah, both of them took a sip before I left. Neither acted like anything was off. Do you have my shoes?"

I pull her Vans out of my bag and hand them to her. She leans on me and switches her heels out for more comfortable shoes.

"Oh, God. That's much better," she says.

"I'd better get in there. Eve's in the café. Jacob's across the street and Frank's been looping around the block," I say.

She takes her necklace off and hands it to me. "I found this in my dad's box. I don't know what it is, but maybe it'll bring you luck."

She hands me a necklace on a silver chain. Dangling off the chain is a longish charm that doesn't quiet look like it belongs on a necklace. The pendant is about six inches long and painted bright red. It's got a rounded top that she's attached the chain to, and the top tapers down a point, almost like a blunt dagger. I put it around my neck and loosen my tie to drop it under my shirt.

"Thanks. I'll get this back to you."

"Good luck," she says. "See you soon."

She looks nervous for a moment, fidgeting with her hands and shuffling her feet. Without a warning she reaches up, gives me a kiss on the cheek and disappears without saying a word. Between the necklace and the kiss, I decide there's no way this operation can go South on me.

And with that, I walk into the Simms Building.

27 | Den Of Things Best Left Alone

The Simms building is its usual beehive of activity. There are a bunch of offices in this building, most of them full of people doing normal things like processing insurance claims and selling packing supplies, and everyone starts at the same time.

Of course, *saying* you're starting at 9am doesn't necessarily mean you're *actually* starting at 9am. New Mexico is the land of *mañana* and promptness just doesn't exist here.

I keep my eyes open for anything out of the ordinary and weave my way through the foot traffic. Most people are in real suits while others are in jeans and T-shirts. Everyone recognizes my uniform, though, and they go out of their way to avoid making eye contact for fear I'll try to sell them something. One guy bumps into me, probably on purpose, and gives me his best "bring it" face when I turn to see what was up. I don't have the time or the inclination to deal with him, so I mutter a "sorry," and keep moving.

I hear him say, "Fag," as I walk away shaking my head.

To make things look right, I go into a few of the open places on the first floor and half-heartedly try to sell the poor people inside a book or a pencil or something. Each of them gets that *look* as soon as I walk in the door. It's the look that everyone gives salesmen, homeless crazies, and political canvassers; the look of horror that something less than human has walked in and must be dealt with.

I actually did manage to sell a copy of "Goodnight Moon" so maybe I have a bright future in sales ahead of me.

It takes about ten minutes, but I finally make it around the door that I've been subconsciously avoiding. The lobby is clearing out as people finally decide to get to work and the door lurks in front of me like a gray monolith. Once I step through it, there's no coming back.

I take a beat to catch my senses and get into the right headspace, and open the door.

Inside it looks like every other government office I've ever been in. There's an American flag in the back of the office on the right, a New

Mexico flag on the left, and pictures of the current President and Vice President on the walls. There must be a million of those pictures printed up every four-to-eight years. You know how Election Day is always the day after the first Monday in November, but the President doesn't take office until January 20? I think that's because they need the time to print all the pictures for all the government offices.

Brance is on the left, decked out in his black BDUs and vest. Mills is on the right, dressed exactly the same way. Robinson is at his desk in the middle of the room, right behind a mural of the US Seal on the floor.

"We're not interested in anything you have," Robinson says by way of introduction. Mills and Brance both glare at me. There must be a school security guards go to that teaches them the "cop face": the expression they get when they talk to anyone in anything even remotely approaching an official capacity.

Robinson has mastered the "you're completely beneath contempt" expression that officials of all stripes seem to perfect over time. He's wearing a dark suit with a dark tie, and he's moved his coffee to the extreme corner of his desk to get it away from him like it was some kind of poison. I know it's Starbucks, but it's not poison. Well, I guess it is poison, but he doesn't know that. Some people are so hard to please.

"Well," I say, getting all into sales mode, "let's not rush to conclusions. You have kids? I have books for kids you wouldn't believe."

Brance peers at me. "Hey, didn't I kick your ass last night?"

The hell you did, dumbass.

"Sorry, man, I'd had one too many drinks, I was way out of line," I say.

"Dumbass."

He's holding an H&K MP5SD, a common submachine gun that various military groups use. It's the suppressed variant of the standard H&K MP5. He has a Taser strapped to his waist, and a bullet-proof vest on, so it's probably not a great idea to antagonize him.

"Whoah," I say. "Is that a machine gun?"

"It's an assault rifle," he says derisively.

Actually, it's a submachine gun, but we don't need to debate technicalities right now.

"That is cool, man. Where can I get one? It'd be great for home defense, am I right?"

"These are not for civilians," he tells me. "And I doubt you could handle it anyway."

Just in case you're wondering, the MP5 is actually a very well-behaved weapon. Almost anyone can pick it up and find it relatively easy to fire.

"It is time for you to leave," Robinson says.

Jesus, when is that drug going to kick in? I hate making small talk.

"No, wait. I have got to show you some of this," I tell him, walking over to his desk. I start pulling things out of the bag and setting them on his desk.

"This book," I say, pulling out a copy of some kids' book. "Kids love this book."

I keep pulling things out: a cheap-ass MP3 player, a teddy bear, a calendar with Studs of the Year, an Asia CD, an extremely low-end tablet computer that may or may not work, a pair of fake Oakley sunglasses that look like the real thing. Each thing I pull out, I drop on his desk and with each new thing Robinson scoots back a bit further.

Clean freaks are so easy to push around.

The phone is on the left and the button is right in the middle. I'm trying to put things between him and the phone and button, and so far it's working. I pull out a 32oz tumbler, and manage to push the button off the desk.

Brance and Mills are starting to look glassy-eyed. Thank God.

"Look at this. Every office needs pencils, right?" I say pulling out some sparkly pencils. "There is no reason a pencil can't be fun, right? Sparkly, man, they're great."

Robinson finally holds up his hand. "Something is not right, here."

"No, it's cool. They're supposed to sparkle," I say, "Look, I've just got a couple more things here. C'mon, man, you've got to find something interesting in here. Please, if I don't make a sale today I'm gonna get canned."

Robinson shakes his head. "First that girl comes in and brings him coffee," he says, pointing at Brance. "Now, you're here. Not one single soul except the three of us has been here in years, and now we have two visitors in one day. What is going on here?"

Remember how I said security is a human issue, and most humans don't understand or care enough to maintain the security protocols as they've been laid out? It's because most people can't think their way through the problem. Unfortunately, every now and then you come across someone who takes it seriously, and can think through the situation. Deceive, inveigle and obfuscate, I guess; there's no backing down now.

"What's going on is you are missing out on some seriously good stuff! Look. Seriously, what do I have to do here to get you to buy something?" I look over at Mills who's swaying slightly. Brance is about to fall. Once they go down, Robinson will know something is up and that will be bad.

"All right, I get it," I say. "You don't want to deal here, I get it. Look. My company just got us some cards, so if you ever, and I mean ever, want anything, you call me and I'll get it." I make like I'm patting my pockets, looking for business cards that I don't have.

Well, I have one, but it says "World's Best Lover" and I don't often give it out.

As I reach down with my right hand to look in my back pocket, I nod toward Brance. "What's going on with that guy?"

Robinson calmly looks over at Brance and says completely nonplussed, "It appears he is dying. Pity, I hate having to find security guards." As he glances over, I pull the sawed-off shotgun out and point it at his head.

The right barrel is loaded with a Dragon Breath shell, and the left is loaded with a flechette shell. Honestly, until I started hanging around Jacob I had no idea there were so many different, fun kinds of ammunition you could get for shotguns. Not long ago we both got crazy and decided to see what we could shoot out of his Mossberg 12 gauge. Silly putty worked remarkably well.

Modern double-barrel shotguns, or "doubles" as the cool kids call them, don't use the old-fashioned dual trigger model anymore. They've switched over to single selective triggers that can be manual or automatic - meaning you pull the trigger once, and one barrel fires; pull it again and the other barrel fires. Mine is set to fire the Dragon Breath round first, followed by the flechette round.

I also have two extra rounds for each in my coat pockets. Dragon Breath in the right pocket, flechette in the left. I can remember this by thinking "Fire sets things right, and flechettes leave nothing left." It's important make things as simple as possible to remember, because when you're in the middle of a stressful situation your mind turns to mush. The less thinking you have to do, the better off you are.

Robinson glances at the shotgun pointed at him, looks at me, and smiles. When someone smiles at you when you've got a double barreled shotgun pointed at their face, it sends a chill down your spine.

This is that moment where I should say something witty, but nothing comes to mind and, frankly, I don't have anything to say to this guy so I just pull the trigger.

And a tiny burst of flame comes out the right barrel, followed by a puff of smoke right out of a cartoon.

No plan ever survives contact with the enemy.

I pull the trigger again and this time it works. The sound of the 12 gauge flechette round going off in this tiny room is deafening. Thankfully the door is shut.

Robinson, still sitting in his chair rolls halfway across the room, spinning the whole way. He's still spinning when the chair stops rolling.

"Goddamned right!" I yell before I notice the chair is still spinning around toward me. As it spins back to face me I see Robinson still looking at me. His tie is shredded and the front of his shirt is torn. He calmly brushes the tiny daggers from his face and shirt and glares at me.

His arms and legs bulge and rip through his shirt and pants then split into tentacles. His face distorts into something not quite human, almost like an alien trying to imitate a human when it's only read about us in books. The face continues to change and winds up monstrous. Its huge eyes are bright orange, the color of traffic cones, and have sideways slits splitting them. Its skin is a deep rubbery green and smooth as latex. When the Robinson-thing smiles it has a mouthful of needle teeth all pointing different directions. In the past few seconds he's grown, and I'm now staring up at a ten-foot-tall monstrosity with eyes like dinner plates and waving tentacles.

The day started out so well, too.

He slams a tentacle into me and the gun slides across the room, and I go sliding after it. I feel like I just got hit with 400 pounds of pissed-off calamari. Before he can completely clobber me, I roll out and get my feet under me, and pull a shiny Japanese blade from inside my coat.

First rule of fighting: never go for the gun. I don't know why this is so difficult, since we see it all the time in movies. How many times have you seen the protagonist go after the gun, only to have the bad guy pummel the hell out of them? It always happens: you go for the gun, you get clobbered. Besides, the gun's empty and I've got the only shells in my pockets. Dragon Breath in the right, more flechettes in the left. Now I've just got to get past Ugly with the tentacles, grab the gun, reload it and hope to hell the next round is not a dud.

Against - well, whatever the hell this thing is - a knife is small comfort, but it's better than nothing. Big ugly swings a tentacle at me and rather than backing away or trying to block it, I duck under the swing, move in and slash at what would be a rib cage on a human. On the way back I follow with a slash at the base of the tentacle. Cutting the skin on his side is like trying cut tires with a butter knife, but the slash at the base of his tentacle (tentacle pit?) cuts deep. His rubbery skin gives way, and some dark green viscous liquid spews out. He shrieks and smacks me with another tentacle that I didn't even see coming. I slide on my butt across the floor, and he wraps tentacle around his wound.

It's always best to press the initiative, so I shake the cobwebs from my head and get up and try to close the gap without getting swatted again. We're both leery of each other now. I know he can hit me at will, and he knows I can hurt him. He's stronger, though, and I'm not looking forward to what will probably become a long fight.

We're squared off again. I'm low, knife out front, ready to cut anything that comes too close. He's upright, four tentacles holding him up, four waving around. It's actually kind of hypnotic. I'm looking for an opening when a voice yells, "Duck."

I immediately think, "Where?"

I look toward the voice just in time to see Eve kick Robinson's desk at whatever Robinson has become. I hit the ground just in time to see the desk fly across the room and smash into Robinson. The desk pushes him into the wall, and I can see parts of his body swell as the blood moves around.

You know, I don't think this guy has bones.

He picks up the desk with his tentacles, and flings it back at Eve, who punches it out of the air.

Eve's in jeans and boots with a black turtleneck completing the ensemble. Easy enough to move it, but not an outfit that screams "I'm up to something bad." Her hair is back in a ponytail and her eyes are angry gray. She holds herself loose and ready for a fight.

"You stink of them," Robinson says.

"I told you to use the Dragons," Eve tells me.

"I did!" I tell her. "It was a dud!"

"What? You didn't bring any more?"

"Of course I did."

"Then use them!" Eve yells.

Yup. Brain went to mush.

Eve charges Robinson and puts a fist between his eyes. He flies back into the wall, and rebounds like nothing happened. He wraps tentacles around her arms and tries to pull them off, so she kicks him in what may or may not be his nuts. Whatever she hits, it works, and he unwraps her.

I'm honestly completely enraptured by this fight.

"Get the gun!" Eve yells.

Shit, yeah. The gun. It's in the corner and it's actually clear for the moment, since the fight is on the other side of the room. Getting between these two would be bad news.

I get the gun, eject the spent shells and reach into my right pocket.

Fire sets thing right, flechettes leave nothing left. Both shells are still there, thankfully. Since the flechettes didn't do a damn thing last time I used one, I load both barrels with Dragon Breath rounds and snap the barrels back into place. When I close the gun, it cocks it and I'm holding two barrels of fiery fun in my hand.

"Hey, Squishy!" I yell.

Robinson loses focus for a moment and Eve shoves him away. When he's clear of her, I pull the trigger, and a huge tongue of flame leaps out of the right barrel straight into Robinson. Since Dragon Breath rounds don't have a great deal of tactical value against regular targets, I pull the trigger again and watch another tongue of flame lick Robinson like a lover.

He goes up like a candle. He's shrieking like a siren and spinning around, a living firework. Well, hopefully a dying firework. I hope there's no fire suppression system, but I know there is. Maybe we'll be lucky and it will be on a different line, but I'm not keeping my hopes up.

Yep, there it is. The sprinklers go off and give us a nice little rainstorm inside the office. Fortunately, the downpour doesn't seem to affect Robinson, who is still pirouetting and spitting flames everywhere. Unfortunately, a fire alarm is probably going off somewhere.

The rain doesn't last long, but it does mean we need to get moving with a quickness.

After Robinson finally dies out to a smolder I tell Eve, "I had no idea squid could catch fire like that."

"He's not a squid."

I look at her, standing there looking extremely pissed off, glaring at the thing still squirming on the floor. I'm soaked and this place smells like bad seafood.

"You knew what he was, didn't you?" I ask.

"Yes," she says. "I'm sorry I couldn't tell you. He would've known if you knew what he was."

"What?"

"They just know. They can always tell," she says.

"OK, I think I just got lost somewhere," I tell her.

Eve sighs. "Don't worry about it. It doesn't matter. Besides, we need to get moving. That fire may have set off alarms somewhere."

I'd like to press the issue, but she's right. Just because we don't hear alarms here, that doesn't mean they're not going off loud and clear somewhere else.

Eve is bent over her phone, tapping something. "See what you can do to get that elevator going."

The elevator door is fairly obvious. They're kind of hard to hide, unless you live in Wayne Manor. What isn't obvious, though, is how the damn thing works. I've never come across an elevator that doesn't have buttons somewhere. Even if you need a key to turn it on, every elevator has at least one button somewhere. This is just a blank wall with a couple of doors in it. I hope the controls weren't on Robinson's desk, because that's in pieces on the floor.

I find when my brain is frozen it's usually best to step back, relax and smoke a cigarette. I light up a smoke and revel in the fact that I'm not only smoking inside, but in a government installation. Oddly enough, I'd probably be in more trouble for smoking in here than I would be for discharging a firearm, setting a man-like thing on fire, conspiring to kill two other guys, or any of the other myriad things I've done this morning.

"Are you smoking in here?" Eve asks.

Is this a trick question? Eve's normally pretty on the ball and I didn't think this was difficult to figure out. I give her my best perplexed expression; take a drag and say, "No."

She shakes her head and tells me, "Just make sure you take the butt with you. We don't want to leave any more evidence than we already have."

I nod and look closer at the doors. With all the soot, and cracks from desks and monsters being thrown around, I completely missed a small hole near the top of the doors.

"Hey," I say to Eve, "Come look at this."

Eve puts her phone away and comes over. She's tall enough to see what it is.

"What do you make of that?" I ask her.

She looks at the hole for a moment, wipes her hand across the hole to brush away the soot and muck. "Shit."

She runs her hands through her hair, leaving a streak of soot on one side. She's stressed and angry, and that's a bad combination for everyone around her. She punches the gray cinderblock wall and shatters a few of the bricks.

"All this work and the damned thing is locked! Fuck!" She yells, "Fuck! Fuck! Fuck!"

The hole is definitely some kind of keyhole, but the key is round and smooth.

"Maybe we can open it up and climb down," I say.

She brightens up a bit. "It's worth a shot."

Eve pushes her fingers between the doors and pulls them apart like they're weightless. The dark down in the bottom of the shaft is intimidating. I grab a flashlight off Brance's corpse and shine it down the hole. The light doesn't reach the bottom of the shaft.

"Jumping down is probably not a good idea," Eve says.

I shine the light around. The sides of the shaft, save for guide rails, is completely smooth. There's not even a cable on the elevator cab. I say a silent prayer to Odin that they didn't just cut the damn cable, and call it good. Usually they put ladders in these things, but apparently the low bidder saved a few bucks by not putting one in.

Or maybe they just didn't want anyone climbing out.

"Do we have any rope?" I ask.

"Nope, unless you're hiding some," she says.

"Nope. Ropeless. Think Frank could hack it?"

"Maybe, but he and the others are heading out. It's just us."

"Damn," I say. "Let me look at that keyhole again. Is Robinson's chair still in one piece?"

Eve grabs Robinson's chair and steadies it while I stand on it. The hole is small, slightly larger than the diameter of a pen, and completely unremarkable when I shine the light in it. I've never seen a key that could fit this kind of lock. This is why standards in industry are so important. If it was just a regular damned key, I'd still be out of luck, because I don't know how to pick even a regular lock.

All this way, and all we needed was just a bit of luck.

Shit! That's it. Luck. I start grabbing furiously at my chest. Eve thinks I'm having a heart attack and tries to grab me. As soon as she lets go of the chair, it decides to move, and I wind up on my ass. Again.

Fortunately Jessica's good-luck charm is still there. The size is about right. I grab the chair and pull it back over. "Sorry," I tell Eve. "Steady me again."

I put Jessica's good luck charm in and it fits perfectly, but does absolutely nothing.

"Is it in all the way?" she asks.

I resist the temptation to be an ass. "Yeah." I try turning it and it turns smoothly, but nothing happens.

"Damn it!" I yell and yank the charm out of the hole.

As soon as I pull it out we hear a motor start and the shaft shudders slightly. I hop down and we look down the shaft together. We still can't see anything, but something's definitely moving down there.

"Good job," Eve says.

I look at her and roll my eyes. "Yeah. Totally meant to do that."

She clasps my shoulder and smiles. I clip Brance's flashlight to my belt, and she grabs the other one. We take both the MP5s from Brance and his partner. They won't need them anymore. I almost idly wonder what kind of man the other guy was. Brance was a filthy savage, but who was this man? What did he do to get stuck in this place acting as a hired gun for some kind of monster?

We grab the extra magazines, too and I forget about Mills.

After a couple of minutes I start to worry that the elevator's broken. Seriously, how long could it take to get an elevator up here? It's not like Albuquerque's well known for its fabulous underground caverns. This damn thing must be coming straight up from hell.

When it finally arrives we find ourselves staring at an industrial green box with failing lighting and tattered cloth walls. Neither of us moves.

"You realize," Eve says, "that this thing hasn't been serviced in probably ten years."

"Yep. And when it was last serviced, it was probably done by contractors or government employees."

"After you," she says.

"No, no. I insist. After you. You're more likely to survive the fall."

"Not from this height, I'm not."

I decide to be a gentleman for once in my life. I close my eyes and step into the elevator. Hell, a quick death from falling is probably better than winding up in a cell in some Saharan shithole, which is what DHS will do with us if they ever catch up to us.

The elevator bounces slightly and my heart stops momentarily, and then it's all over. I open my eyes and Eve is staring at me.

"Wouldn't you rather see what's going to kill you?" she asks.

"Are you coming?" I ask her.

She steps in and the elevator bounces a bit but stabilizes. There's a duplicate keyhole on the inside so I put Jessica's key in, and say goodbye to the world as the elevator starts down.

28 | Hades

It takes about five minutes to get to the bottom of the elevator shaft, and it's perfectly silent the whole way down. Part of me almost wishes there was at least a Muzak version of some horrid pop song playing. Actually, a Muzak version of "We're Not Gonna Take It" would come in handy right about now. Might help take my mind off of the fact that I'm in an elevator shaft going God only knows how far down, into a place that's been shut off for God only knows how long, for God only knows what reason.

You know what the problem with God is? Knows everything, but won't tell you jack shit.

The elevator finally stops in front of two industrial green doors that grudgingly slide open part way before Eve pulls them apart the rest of the way.

"We're in Hell," I say, "I just know it. Look at that couch. No sane human would make a couch out of lime leather."

We step out into poorly-lit lobby, complete with that hideous couch, ten-year-old magazines, and a receptionist's desk behind safety glass. The lobby is only slightly disorganized - a couple of magazines are on the ground, and the coffee table is obviously misaligned, like someone bumped into it. About half of the fluorescent bulbs have failed, and a couple of them are flickering.

Ever since I saw the movie *Aliens*, flickering fluorescent bulbs freak me out. At least whatever backup power supply they're using is still running. They probably tapped into the city's power, and put in some kind of generator or another down here, too.

There are no signs explaining where we are, just the receptionist's desk (complete with a name plate that reads "Bethany Daniels") and a sign-in sheet, with a ballpoint pen chained to the desk.

Eve picks up the sheet and stares at it for a minute. "Look at this. The last entry is date 9/3/05, some general or another. He never signed out."

Behind the glass I can see someone's purse, a chair pushed into the middle of the office, and a computer. The computer's monitor is facing away from me, so I can't see what's on it. There's a door to the right that's closed and latched from the inside with a sliding lock. There's also a bell on the ledge in front of the desk. On a whim I ring the bell. In the tomblike silence of the place, it sounds like I just rang the bells at Christ Church Cathedral in Dublin.

Eve looks like she's going to smack me.

No one comes out to help us, which isn't surprising. I try the door and, of course, it's locked. "Eve," I say, pointing at the door.

She puts down the sign-in sheet that she'd been flipping through, and turns the knob with ease – like it wasn't locked at all. The door opens quietly when she gently pushes on it. We both wait with bated breath, but no alarms go off, and no guys with guns come running.

I check my MP5 - make sure the magazine is full and there's a round in the chamber - and switch it off safety. The weapon is well-maintained, and probably hasn't been used much in its lifetime. I pull the stock to my shoulder, take a deep breath, lean into the open door, and look into the hallway. The hallway is empty and there's no sign of anything or anyone.

The flickering of the fluorescent lights is messing with my head. I keep thinking I'm seeing shadows flickering across the walls. It's got to be all in my mind, because there is not a damn thing moving down here except Eve and myself, and we're not moving too much right now, either.

Time to nut up or we'll be here forever. And I can think of an infinite number of places I'd rather be right now.

We both walk into the hallway and try the door to the receptionist's cage. Locked. Not surprising. In a place like this, all the doors are probably locked. Secret installations still follow the adage of "minimal exposure." It's likely that if there were multiple projects going on down here, people working on one project knew absolutely nothing about any of the other projects.

Down the hall to left, behind the receptionist's room are the bathrooms. Across from those is the break room.

The break room still has someone's desiccated lunch sitting on one of the tables, complete with a knocked over Coke can, a half-eaten sandwich, and a bag of chips. The Coke is dry and sticky, and the mold growing on the sandwich has long since expired. There's a drip in the sink where someone needed to fix the tap. Apparently, no one's been around to fix it, so drip, drip, drip, drip.

At the end of the hall are the secure doors. Think solid steel doors, solid steel frames - the walls are probably steel, too. Eve would probably have trouble with these. The doors are just numbered 1, 2, 3, with the usual government warnings about trespassing and its terrifying consequences.

"Well. Which one?" Eve asks.

Shit. Each one has a keyhole, but if I know these people - and I do - if I put the key in the wrong one, the lock's memory will erase itself. You know how at some hotels if you put you key card in the wrong door the lock will erase what's on the key? This is the exact same kind of technology. Under normal operating times if you accidentally erase your key you get a lecture about security protocols and they eventually reset the key. If we choose the wrong door here and it erases this key, we're are totally out of the game, since there is no one that will reset this key. We get one shot, and it had better work.

"Somewhere around here there has to be a map, or something. Can you open that receptionist's cage?" I ask her.

Eve effortlessly rips the door handle off the receptionist's cage, and pushes the door open. There's a slight ping as the latch on the inside gives up. "Ta dah," she says with grin.

Inside the receptionist's cage we find our first body, presumably of the receptionist herself. She's collapsed under the desk, clutching a dead BlackBerry to her chest. There are no real signs of struggle. Her Diet Coke can is still on the desk. Her glasses are right next to a half-finished crossword and an open diary. Whatever happened in here, it missed her completely, but she was too terrified to ever leave and probably died when something scared her quite literally to death.

There are two video monitors in the room: one showing the ground-level office above us, which was probably just the first layer of security for this place anyway. The other has a locked Windows XP display. Fortunately, the upstairs is still quiet, although heaven only knows how long that will last.

Contrary to popular belief, hacking a computer when you're sitting right at it isn't the easiest thing in the world. If this one is set up correctly, it will lock out the account after five incorrect attempts. That lockout duration may be as little as fifteen minutes, or may last until an administrator unlocks the computer. Since the administrator is either dead, or long gone, that would mean a permanent lockout.

If you're sitting right in front of the screen, and have physical access to hardware, it's possible to use any number of password reset utilities that circumvent Windows security. Or, you could just go straight for the gusto, and boot another live operating system that will pretend Windows doesn't even exist. All that takes effort, and I'm fundamentally lazy and tend to prefer to use social engineering to hack a system. Social engineering is great, because as hackers say, there is no patch for human stupidity. Unfortunately, I don't have any hacking tools or other operating systems with me right now.

So, how do you use social engineering on a dead person? Simple. You put yourself in their shoes and take a look around. DSS would sweep a place like this frequently, so it wouldn't be an obvious hiding place. Under the keyboard is out; a Post-It note is out.

"Eve, can you look through her purse for anything looks like a password? It might be on the back of a business card, or a Post-It Note or something like that."

She rustles through the purse for a while, pulling things out, commenting on the dead woman's lipstick (trashy color), wallet (Hello Kitty? Really?), vibrator (bad design, weak motor), cigarettes (ugh, menthol).

Eve opens the wallet and pokes around. "Her name is Bethany Daniels. She's 32. I don't see any pictures of kids or a husband, probably single and childless. One picture of a dog. Looks like a pit variant sound asleep on her back with her feet in the air."

Eve flips through Bethany's diary. "The last entry is dated 9/20/2005. It's pretty shaky, but it looks like she wrote down her password and something that looks like 'fuck you.'" She shows me the diary.

"Let's try it."

I type in 14 characters and the screen unlocks itself.

In case you're wondering, the password was mypassword0831. Not terrible as these things go, but it could have been better: MyP@ssw0rd0831 would be just as easy to remember, and quite a lot harder to guess.

While I'm entering the password, Eve keeps flipping through the diary. "This is terrible. She was down here all alone for over two weeks." She flips back until she finds September 3, 2005. "Listen to this: Her co-workers bugged out, and told her someone needed to stay to let the rescue team in. They left her here to die."

Apparently Bethany kept her hopes up for a couple of days, until they cut the phone. She had a little moment of joy when they sent the elevator back down - until she realized it was locked, and she didn't have a key. She spent the rest of the time avoiding the shadows and sneaking out to go to the bathroom and get water. They left her down here to rot.

"Oh, no," Eve says.

"What?"

"She had a date the night they locked her down here. She was so excited. It was her first date in a couple of years. She had her dress all picked out and everything."

"Does it say who the lucky guy was?" I ask her.

"No, why?"

"I was just thinking we should find the guy; tell him he wasn't stood up."

Eve puts the diary back where she found it and flips back to the last entry, like the room is a mausoleum, and she doesn't want to disturb the dead any further than we already have. She closes her eyes and says something under her breath.

The screen still has some kind of custom government software running on it. You can always tell government-contracted software: it looks terrible, but it works most of the time. This one looks like some kind of scheduling app designed to be more secure than Outlook. Of course, secure software is only secure if you actually use it like it's designed be used.

The day on the screen is September 3, 2005 and there's only one appointment scheduled - room 3 at 2pm for General H. Hapablap. Room 3 is referred to as "The Sleeper." Room 2 is "Angels Above," Room 1 is "The Hole."

"What do you think "Angels Above" is?" Eve asks. "Think it could be aliens?"

"Possible," I tell her. "They're not that exciting, though. Their weapons aren't all that spectacular and we can't recreate their power supply, so they're basically useless to us."

"Wait a minute. There are actually aliens on Earth, and you know about them? And you never said anything?" she asks.

I look at her for a moment. This is the one of a very few times I've ever seen Eve excited, and she's giddy as a schoolgirl. I never pegged her as the type to get excited over aliens.

"I'm sorry," I say. "It honestly never came up, and I don't think too much about it anymore."

"They're real?" She asks.

"Yeah. Great big eyes and everything. They have a deep and abiding love of black licorice."

"Why are they here?"

"They sent out ships in every direction, one of them stumbled across us. Pure accident," I say.

"Do they know anything?"

"They know they're tired of deep space and they like black licorice. Other than that, they're basically long-haul truckers who've found a truck stop and thought we'd be an easy conquest."

I look her in the eyes and she looks crushed.

"I'm sorry. It's just how it is. They just kind of do what they do. They're not all that different than us - same motivations, similar weaknesses. Their technology is more advanced, but that doesn't mean the average individual is more advanced. Humans can make some pretty amazing things, but that doesn't mean your average sofa slob knows a damn thing about making circuit boards."

After all the build-up most people have about aliens, it's disappointing to find out they're not magical or wise or uplifting. I was just disappointed I wouldn't be able to fly their ship.

"Come on," I tell her. "Let's see what's behind door number 3."

Door number 3, the lair of the Sleeper, is the last door on the right, and it looks exactly like the others. If I'm wrong, the key will probably get wiped and we'll be stuck down here forever.

"You're sure it won't open Room 2?" Eve asks.

"I don't know, it might. It might only open 1. I'm hoping it only opens three, because that's the one I think we need."

29 | Dreamer

I put the key in the hole and pull it out. For a moment, my heart drops through my stomach when the door does absolutely nothing. Before I start to panic, the door quietly slides apart, and we are the first people in eight years to see what the spooks who ran this place called "The Sleeper."

The room is square, about a hundred feet on a side, and packed with various flashing lights in a cacophony of colors. Tiny lights flashing in the near darkness, like stars lighting up the dusk sky. There's a hum from the fans of dozens of computers. Dropping from the ceiling and scattered around the room are strange looking instruments designed to do or measure God only knows what. Some of them are straight out of a mad scientist movie.

The corpse of a dead security guard is curled in a ball right in front of the platform, lying in a brown pool of dried blood. Eve turns him over and his eyeless face is covered in dried blood and scratches, like he clawed his own eyes out and his mouth is still agape in a silent scream of terror.

A few feet from the security guard is a guy, probably a tech from the look of him. The back of his head is blown off and a dead hand is still gripping a Colt .45. Colt .45 the gun, not Colt .45 the beer.

"Damn," she says.

"Yeah," I reply. My normally free-flowing flippant comments have abandoned me for the time being.

All around the room are signs about not throwing things. Someone has taped a child's picture of a sleeping man to one of the computer monitors, complete with his dreams in a thought bubble. There are rolling chairs scattered around the room, like someone got up in a hurry and didn't look where he was going. A woman's shoe lies in the middle of the floor. A couple of coffee cups are tipped over, and there are papers strewn around the place. An open folder, the first page stamped *TOP SECRET* lies open next to someone's wallet.

"Whatever happened here happened fast," I say. "They didn't even have a chance to pick things up."

I'm focused on the computer stations. I used to work with systems very similar to these, usually trying to harden them against outside threats, and a small part of my mind is disgusted at how many machines are unlocked. I move the mouse on one of the machines, and the desktop pops up, showing me a Windows XP desktop with yellow and black striped borders at the top. The script over the borders proudly proclaims this to be a system that was used for processing classified. That's not a typo. In the secure world, when you work with classified material, you are "processing classified." This place would definitely fail a security audit.

Eve grabs my shoulder.

"What?" I ask.

She turns me away from the computers and points toward the center of the room.

The centerpiece of the room is a raised platform surrounded by an intricate, glowing mandala of concentric circles, spirals, and stylized flames carved into the floor. There are words written in a language I don't recognize, and whole thing pulses and glows like it's a living thing. The mandala is made of blue and white light circling endlessly around, crackling slightly.

Around the platform, about ten feet from it, is a fence made of steel tubing painted yellow with black stripes. The striped paint job is the traditional way of screaming "Don't touch, danger!" and it does a pretty good job of it. You could easily climb over it if you wanted to but the signs all around that say "DO NOT PASS THIS FENCE. USE OF DEADLY FORCE IS AUTHORIZED" are an effective deterrent. This is not a fence to keep something in; any idiot could get through it. This was to keep people out and let them know business was meant.

In the center is a man, calmly watching us.

He's an older gentleman in a double-breasted suit and fedora. He's leaning at a jaunty angle on his cane. His suit is dark navy with gray pinstripes, and is absolutely immaculate. If you think about it, this is pretty impressive feat for someone living underground for nearly a decade. Come to think of, the whole look screams 1930s, which was an amazing time for suits.

"Well," I say. "This is kind of anticlimactic."

Here I'd thought we were looking for something terrifying - something worthy of all the secrecy, and an abandoned underground base. Hell, this place was guarded by a monster! This should be a terrifying moment. Instead, all we get is a guy in a nice suit.

Granted, it's a really nice suit.

"Uh," I ask, "Just out of curiosity, where'd you get the suit? And do you suspect they might have one in my size? I'm, uh, asking for a friend, you understand. He's my size."

He looks at me for a moment, exuding cool.

"If I tell you, will you let me out of here?" he asks.

"What's keeping you in?" I ask him.

"Magic. Science. Whatever," he says. "All you need to do is break the circle, walk over and shake my hand. Or you could just toss me that baseball."

I walk toward him and Eve stops me. "Don't cross the lines. You'll collapse the circle."

"What happens if I collapse the circle?" I ask.

"You release me," the man says.

Eve points at him. "Collapse the circle, and he walks free."

"Isn't that the point of coming here?" I ask.

"Yes," The man says. "Listen to your boss."

"Excuse me?" Eve says.

The man eyes me. "I'm terribly sorry, madam. I had assumed it was the other way around. Listen to your henchman."

He's slick, I'll give him that. I've never actually been called a henchman before, but it's far from the worst thing I've ever been called. I guess henching is as good a job as any these days. I don't get dental insurance, but I do get to break into government installations.

"How long have you been in there?" I ask him.

"I woke up eight years ago to find myself stuck in this place."

"Eight years? What have you been eating?" Eve asks.

"Nothing, here. Part of me is outside the circle, and an even smaller part is outside this building. Unfortunately, the parts outside the building are damaged, and no longer entirely reliable."

The shadows seem to come to life and move around us. They circle and form complex two-dimensional shapes, like mandalas and fractals, then seem to explode into tiny squares that reform across the room.

"Those shadows," Eve says, "They're part of you, aren't they?"

"They are me. As much as your skin is you. When they closed the circle, part of me was outside, and the people who built this place didn't realize it. When I woke up, I used those parts to try to free myself, but the circle is too strong. Your people have learned well. For all his fluff and bluster, Bedfellow actually managed to hold me. I can't wait to kill him."

"Wait a minute. Bedfellow?" I ask him.

"He called himself Senator Lucius Bedfellow. He was a tiresome man, but not without his powers. He locked me in here and ordered this place closed when he found I was awake and not fully controlled."

"I've got bad news for you, pal. Bedfellow is already dead. I killed him a couple of years ago," I say.

They say revenge never fixes anything - that it doesn't change what happened, that it doesn't make the pain go away. To a certain extent, they're correct. Pain has a half-life: over time it lessens, but it never completely goes away. My family will never come back to me. I will never have my old life back again. I will never again wake up, and feel like things are safe.

I used to get enraged, thinking about how I was powerless to stop that madman from abusing his power. Now, whenever I get mad or feel powerless, I remember Bedfellow bound, gagged, wearing lingerie and turning purple while he slowly died in front of me. That memory always makes me feel better.

After all, you can't go through life angry all the time.

"You killed him?" he asks me.

I nod.

"Your memories - I must have them. I have waited so long to see him die. Will you share your memories with me?"

I've got a bad feeling about this, but say, "Okay."

"I promise I won't hurt you," he says.

Some of the shadows coalesce into a singular form that looks almost like an amoeba made of darkness. It silently slides across the floor and wraps around my feet. As it slides up my legs I feel a slight chill, but I can tell it's not actively trying to hurt me. I have a moment of panic as it makes its way up my torso and around my neck, but shove the panic down and close my eyes. The shadow wraps around my face and I faintly hear Eve say "Hurt him and you'll never get out of here."

Distantly, like it's coming from down the hall and around the corner through a closed door I hear The Sleeper say, "I promise you, I will not hurt him," and then I'm back in Bedfellow's bedroom. The Sleeper is standing right next to me, watching Bedfellow standing on a chair in lingerie and cuffs and a gag, noose around his neck, desperately trying to masturbate.

The room is just like it was before - overpriced, overdecorated, and desperately detailed. There are large white blocks on the wall that I don't remember from before, and most of the area on the other side of the bed is plain white. It takes me a moment, but then I realize I'm reliving a memory, and must not have looked at those places, so my mind is filling them in with blank white areas.

"My, my, my," The Sleeper tells me. "Lucius was quite the interesting character. What is he doing?"

I look at him quizzically. I had kind of thought it was obvious.

"You'll have to excuse me," he tells me, "I've never really understood human mating habits. Although, I must say, I don't see anyone here for him to mate with. Perhaps you didn't see her? Or him?"

How do you explain masturbation to someone? Hell, for that matter how do you explain bondage, or cross-dressing, or auto-erotic asphyxiation to someone?

"He was into kink," I say.

He looks at me again, confused. "May I dig deeper into your mind?"

Sure, why the fuck not? I'm already standing in the bedroom of dead guy with some kind of supernatural being next to me. It's got to be less painful than trying to explain kink to a god.

I nod and say, "Ok."

He closes his eyes and I feel a slight tingle as he pushes further into my mind.

After a few moments he opens his eyes and laughs out loud. "Oh, this is delicious! Lucius Bedfellow, the man who owned me, the man who controlled me! Did you see him die?"

I nod. "Yeah. It took a while, but I watched the whole thing."

"I must see that. Oh! Look! He's noticed you're here."

Again I get to relive killing Senator Lucius Bedfellow. I get to hear him trying to plead for his life through a gag. I get to watch him drool, and blubber, and plead with me with his eyes to please just let him live - he'll do anything; give me anything.

Just like before, Bedfellow can't give me the one thing I really want. Too bad.

The difference this time is that I have someone else with me. Someone who stares in wide-eyed wonder at the man on the chair. Who laughs out loud when Bedfellow tries to talk, and who claps when I nudge the chair and Bedfellow's high-heeled shoes start to slide off. And when Bedfellow can't stop his feet from sliding because he's chained his own ankles together, the man in the suit applauds and cries "Bravo!"

After we watch Bedfellow die, we stare at him, gently rotating on the rope, until the memory ends and my remembered self gets up to go. Then the memory pauses, and I'm watching myself leaving the room, but frozen in time.

I look at the man in the suit and try to figure him out. On the one hand, he seems to be just a normal guy, on the other hand I am looking at him in a memory. He's wandering around the room, examining things and chuckling to himself. "Who are you?" I finally ask him.

"People in this area of the country used to call me a God of Dreams. The Rememberer. I can be anything I dream up, or anything anyone else dreams up. I've been a destroyer, a builder. I'm chaos and order. I don't have a name, and don't really need one, but you may call me anything you wish if it will help."

"How about Dreamer?" I ask him.

"I do love to dream," he says.

"How did they trap you?"

He sighs. "I love to sleep, and I love to dream. When you're immortal, you can sleep for decades. Dreams become your best friends, because they don't die around you. Try as I might - dream as I can - I cannot stop death in others. She's uninterested in me, but maintains her single-minded intensity with everyone else. While I was sleeping, someone found me. This man you killed coerced some local shamans, what do they call them? Medicine Men. They built the circle around me. I gather I was to be his ultimate weapon."

"You didn't like the idea, I take it."

"It wasn't so much that I didn't want to be a weapon, but I didn't want to be his weapon. I'm sorry about this, but I don't feel much for your kind. You're like shadows to me. You, personally, have given me a great gift, though. I would have preferred to kill him myself, but your memories are so vivid and you showed such great panache when you knocked him off the chair. Thank you for watching him die so I could relive it with you. What became of all this?"

"One of his aides found him the next day and alerted the authorities. They covered it all up, naturally. Made it sound like he died of natural causes - heart attack, I believe. His wife ran for his vacant Senate seat and won in a landslide. She's been mercilessly pressing her agenda to bring Jesus back to the schools, like that will somehow magically fix all the problems in this country. The Senator's aide had snapped a picture of Bedfellow hanging here, and released it on the Internet. Bedfellow's family claimed the pictures were faked. The whole thing eventually blew over and nothing really changed. There have been allegations Mrs. Bedfellow been taking bribes from a half-dozen interest groups, but nothing's stuck. Honestly, she fits right in his old shoes," I say.

"That is how government works now?" he says.

"Pretty much. Government of the people by the rich, for the special interests," I tell him.

"You're a pessimist at heart, aren't you?"

"Not a pessimist, a realist," I say.

"Why do you let them do that?"

"Do what?"

"Take advantage of you? Walk over you and get away with it? This man killed your family and you killed him for it. Why not do it with the rest of them?" He asks me.

"They hold all the cards. They control all the pieces. Shit, pick your own gaming metaphor. They've got all the mushrooms. Our leaders run everything. We can't fight them."

"I can." He looks at me. "You've done me a favor. Only one other person in millennia has ever let me into their mind. Only one has shared a memory with me. Only one tried to help me, and I couldn't help him in return. Back when I was worshipped in these parts, I tried to be helpful, but it got so tedious. 'Please make the crops grow.' 'Please let so and so like me.' The crops wouldn't grow because these people lived in a damn desert. Make so-and-so like you on your own. I'm a god of dreams, not a pimp. And you know what? Not a single damned one of them would ever help me."

"If you've read my mind, you know where to find them."

"I have read your mind. Thank you for letting me do that. Let me out, and I'll happily rip them to pieces," he says.

"What, because I let you out?"

"Partially. Partially because I enjoy it. Partially because they dared to hold me, and tried to turn me into a weapon. They took part of me and spread it around. I want those parts back."

"Okay," I say. "I don't think Eve will take much persuading."

Bedfellow's room dissolves around me, and the last thing I see is him hanging there with his purple face and his bright red lingerie. It still makes me smile.

30 | Of Course It Would

The control room is just as I remember it, and it's a shock to go from the bright colors of Bedfellow's room to the grays and blues of the lab. I know my eyes shouldn't need to adjust to the change in light because my eyes never left this place, but I still have to blink a couple of times to get my brain back on track.

Dreamer is still in the circle, but his suit has changed to a more modern cut. His hat is gone, and he's wearing sunglasses. The changes are not immense - after all, men's suits don't change all that much over the years.

"How did you change clothes so quickly?" I ask him.

"I was never wearing clothes. I just updated my look based on what I saw in your mind," he tells me.

Eve is there, watching me. "Are you OK?" she asks.

"I'm fine," I say. "We were just remembering."

She looks concerned for a moment, like she's wondering if I'm actually me, or if I'm him, but apparently decides everything's all right, and touches my arm. "How'd we do?" she asks.

"Let him out of there and he'll tear the country apart. Partially for me, partially for his own vengeance, partially because he just enjoys doing it." I look at Dreamer. "How do we turn all this off?"

"All you have to do is break the circle," he says.

If you're thinking this would be the perfect time for something to go wrong, you're correct.

Before I can walk across the circle, there's a flicker and fist slams into my gut. While I'm doubled over another hits the back of my head and I find myself facedown. I'm staring at the concrete of the floor and fighting back the cold gray mist trying to take over my vision.

It must have followed us down and stayed hidden. Or maybe it was down here all along. Hell, I don't know, and I don't care. All I know is I hate these damn things.

I start trying to drag myself forward, and see a flicker out of the corner of my eye just before Eve staggers back. Immediately another one hits her from another direction. So we've got at least three of the bastards down here. Eve will be fine – I doubt they could even bruise her. But they can hold her back.

The edge of the circle is only twenty feet away. Standing, I could cover it in seconds. I try to struggle to my feet. Rising makes me feel nauseous and I get slammed in the kidney for my efforts. While I'm lying on the ground, I see Dreamer - and he does not look happy. The shadows are tearing around the room, trying to find a flicker, but they can't do much. At my side, lying on the floor is a baseball.

"Break the circle!" Dreamer yells.

"I'm trying, but I can't get there!" I yell back.

"You don't have to break it yourself! Anything crossing the line will break it," he yells back.

At first, my groggy mind spends precious time trying to figure out what a baseball would be doing down here, before it hits me: techies love toys. I also realize that a ball crossing the circle is as good as anything else crossing the circle. Break the threshold, and the whole thing will collapse. I say a silent "thank you" to whatever techie smuggled this contraband in here, and make a desperate grab for the ball. I manage to get my hand on the ball when I see a flicker in front of me. I grab the ball and pull my arm in as fast as I can and narrowly manage to avoid getting it stomped on.

Behind me, they've managed to get Eve on the ground and are flickering around her, kicking her mercilessly. They seem to have figured out a tactic and are working as a team to keep her occupied. One will flick in, hit and disappear; then the other hits from the opposite side.

I've got one shot at this. I fling the ball as hard as I can and it sails straight and true toward Dreamer. He's got his hand out to catch it. Then there's a flicker and the ball bounces off something and rolls under a table.

I've got to get to my feet if I'm going to have a chance. To do that, I've got to keep my head, and I've got to find a way to slow this guy down a bit. When the next flicker comes I see a boot headed toward my face and barely manage to intercept it before it breaks my nose. Without thinking, I pull the foot toward me with my right hand and let my left hand follow the leg up until it hits something squishy. Lucky, lucky, lucky. If he'd kicked me with his right leg I would have hit nothing but air, but he kicked with the left and I managed to land a solid blow to his nuts.

If you've ever been hit hard in the testicles, you know it hurts. Even if you don't have nuts you know that kicking someone in the crotch will take down pretty much anyone. A glancing blow hurts a lot. A powerful blow will have you lying on the ground crying and wishing you were dead.

I see his face above me, lips pulled back in a snarl, exposing teeth that are much too long. His knees knock together and he starts dropping. I get my arms up and start rolling so he doesn't fall on top of me. Kenpo doesn't teach much in the way of ground fighting, but we do have a few tricks up our sleeves. I send a kick into left knee so he falls away from me, and as soon as he hits the ground I'm on top of him, punching the back of his head for all I'm worth.

One of the guys kicking Eve notices his buddy is down, and next thing I know I'm getting kicked straight backward. While this sucks for me, it's a pretty bad tactic on his part. It took two of those guys to even keep Eve down, and now that she's down to just one, she's managed to knock him back long enough to get her feet partially under her. She's down on her right knee, left foot on the ground, when there's a flicker in front of her. She takes the blow that comes at her like it's nothing and slams her open palm into the attacker's balls and squeezes for all she's worth.

I'm not the one getting hit here, but even I flinch on that one.

The flickering man stops flickering and she uses her other hand to grab his throat. Then she stands up, holding this guy off the ground by his throat and his balls. Eve spins to build up some momentum and tosses him directly at the circle. The remaining flicker man tries to protect the circle just like his buddy did. Unfortunately, the force of a baseball moving at, say, twenty miles per hour, is significantly less than the force of a person moving the same speed. He flickers in just in time to catch his buddy full on in the chest and they go flying, flip over the railing and slide across the floor. As the last guy tries to stop himself, he put his arm up over his head and they both slide to a halt just in front of the circle. I can almost feel their sense of relief.

The last flickering man stretches his arm to get some leverage to get up - and there's a palpable change in the energy in the room. Just like when your refrigerator stops working and you only notice the sound it makes because the sound is gone, the energy level in the room drops off to nothing. It was so pervasive, yet so subtle, I didn't even notice it until it was gone.

The flickering man's hand had broken the circle.

Shadows race to Dreamer and disappear into him, and his expression is almost orgasmic. The last fully functioning flicker man stares up at the God of Dreams above him in abject terror. He tries to flicker out – he's willing to leave his comrades, ignore us - anything to get away from the thing above him.

"I don't think so," Dreamer says. "You all have something of mine, and I want it back."

You know how in movies you can always see energy moving around, or souls being sucked out of things? In real life, you can't see anything like that. Dreamer doesn't spread his arms out to gather his power. He doesn't close his eyes, or anything like that. He just stands there, and the three flicker men clench their fists, grit their teeth and arch their backs in agony for a moment, then collapse into heaps on the floor.

And then it's over.

Dreamer smiles, twirls his cane and says, "I think I'd like to leave this place now. Shall we?"

Eve helps me to my feet and gives me something to lean on as I stagger toward the door. It's shut, which is not surprising, but still opens when I put Jessica's key in the lock.

As we walk out, Dreamer stops at the doorway and turns around. A final piece of shadow darts across the floor and flows into him. He smiles. "I don't think I'll miss this place. I really must learn to not underestimate your kind in the future." And with that he steps into the hallway and the door closes behind him.

"Hold, up a sec," I say. "I want to grab that receptionist's diary."

Eve shrugs and helps me into the receptionist's room where Bethany's corpse still lies. Dreamer notices the corpse and sighs. "If I'd known she was still down here, we might have been able to help each other."

"She didn't have a key to the room, and she was terrified of you," Eve says.

"Pity. I would've loved to have someone to talk to," Dreamer says.

"She died of fear or a heart attack or something a couple of weeks after everyone left," I say. "She probably wouldn't have been a great conversationalist."

While I'm grabbing Bethany's diary I glance at the monitor showing the cameras upstairs and mutter "Shit. We've got problems."

"What?" Eve asks and looks at the monitor. "Damn."

On the screen are Jessica and Jacob, both kneeling hands behind their heads, each with a guy in a black balaclava behind them, holding an MP5 at their heads. The resolution's really bad, but I'm pretty sure Wilford Saxton is standing between and slightly behind them, calmly watching the elevators. How the hell did he survive being shot in the head and blown up?

Sometimes your former jobs haunt you forever.

"Friends of yours?" asks Dreamer.

"Well," I say, "the two on the floor are. The guy in the middle is old associate. I don't know the other two. Saxton's bosses must still think they have a chance at containment if they sent such a small force. They might not know you're out yet."

"Well, let's go take care of the problem," Dreamer says.

"Yeah. I've got a plan. Here's how we're going to do this," I say.

31 | First Floor: Hostages, Dead Things, DHS Agents

Since Eve destroyed the doors on the elevator earlier, it kind of limits our tactics. On the other hand, people tend to believe what they see in front of them, and respond to the immediate threat rather than worrying about the unseen threat.

Years ago, Donald Rumsfeld waxed philosophical about "known knowns, known unknowns and unknown unknowns." If you don't stop to think about it, that phrase sounds like total gibberish, like most of what comes out of government, and he took a beating in the press over it. But there's a certain wisdom to what he said. There are things we know about, and we take steps to control and manipulate those things. In the minds of the soldiers on the first floor, they know the elevator is coming up, and they know that's probably a bad thing.

There are things we may not know about, but have a pretty good idea that they're bad, so we set up ways to mitigate those problems from getting the best of us. The soldiers have an idea that something dangerous is coming up - they're armored, armed and have hostages.

Finally, there are things that are complete unknowns - things we didn't plan for, because we didn't think they could ever happen. Like the fact that I'm riding an elevator up with a god and whatever Eve is.

I'm actually feeling a little outgunned here. Usually I feel like I can handle pretty much anything. But if these two were to turn on me, I'd be well and truly fucked. Hell, if they were to turn on each other, the resultant fight would probably destroy the elevator, and I'd still be well and truly fucked.

Here's to putting yourself in harm's way.

Eve is in the center of the elevator, looking depressed and haggard. We cut up her clothes and messed up her hair a bit, and the general grime from fighting the flicker men makes it look even more realistic. Dreamer is off to the left, and I'm off to the right - both of us hidden next to the side panels of the elevator.

When we hit the top floor I can hear Saxton yell, "Drop your weapons!"

Eve holds up her empty hands and turns slowly around. "I'm unarmed," she says.

The room still reeks of damp squid and there are puddles everywhere.

"Where is Steven?" Saxton yells. He likes yelling - always has. It's his default form of communication when he's nervous or stressed out. I once saw him yell at a bowl of Rice Krispies to shut up.

"Dead," she says. "Those things you sent killed him. I barely made it out myself."

Saxton looks at her for a moment. He's still thinking, hoping actually, that containment is viable. He doesn't know what's down there, but he knows it's his ass if it gets out. I can almost hear the relief in his voice when he says, "Light her up."

Known knowns. I fully expected Saxton would eliminate anyone coming up the elevator, because it would be his job to sanitize the scene. "Sanitize the scene" is a fancy way of saying "kill anyone who knows anything." It's a way we have of using language to make ourselves feel better. You didn't order the slaughter of women and children, "you sanitized the scene." They're not "freedom fighters," they're "enemy insurgents." I didn't "kill a Senator," I "moved a chair."

The Mafia "silences witnesses." The government "sanitizes scenes."

The two guys with guns open up full auto on Eve and lead starts flying. A full auto MP5 fires around 700 rounds per minute. It can empty a full 30-round clip in slightly less than three seconds. Three seconds doesn't seem like a long time, but when you spend that three seconds hoping none of the 60 small, fast pieces of lead being fired from the gun find you, three seconds can feel like an eternity.

When it's all over Eve is slumped on the ground at the back of the elevator. Her shirt is torn to shreds, and what's left of her bra is pretty torn up, too. I say a silent prayer that no one notices there's no blood, lean around the corner, and fire three shots at the guy behind Jessica. She must have seen Eve's signal, because she immediately launches herself at Jacob and body-checks him into the ground before his gunman can react. Jacob's guy gets a shot off that grazes Jessica's leg and I put three rounds into his face. I ditch the MP5 and pull out Mjolnir. Before Saxton can react, I'm upright and headed toward him with the sawed-off pointed directly at his head.

Eve gets up and brushes herself off. I hear her say "I really must get some bullet-proof clothes at some point" just before I squeeze the trigger and twenty hardened steel darts fly at Saxton's face at 2,000 feet per second.

Saxton staggers back about five feet and hits the ground hard and motionless.

Dreamer is looking around the room and standing over the remains of Robinson when Eve joins him, and stares at the still smoldering corpse.

"I do not choose you," she says to the wet charcoal.

Dreamer stares at her and a look of understanding dawns on his face.

"Is that who I think it is?" he asks.

"Probably. You knew him?" she asks.

"I did. He was a loathsome creature. It doesn't surprise me that he would sell his services to anyone. He might've been useful, you know."

Eve shakes her head, "No, he was too unstable and too mercenary. He'd be more of a detriment than an aide."

"Who got him?"

Eve points at me. "He did."

Dreamer looks genuinely impressed. "I must say, you're full of surprises, my friend. You just did the world quite the favor," he tells me.

"Who was he?" I ask.

"No one. Never mind," he replies.

Dammit. What is wrong with these people? You'd think I was asking for their bank account numbers or something. I realize everyone has their secrets, but a little information would be nice.

Jessica is climbing off of Jacob, who looks like he might be in seventh heaven. He grins up at her as she puts her hand out to help him to his feet. "Can we do that again?" he asks her.

She mutters something about men and drops him on his ass.

Dreamer stops looking around and stares at Jessica like he's met her before. She meets his eye and says, "Who the hell are you?"

"I'm sorry. I'm being a bad host," I say, a little grumpy myself. "Jessica, Dreamer. Dreamer..."

He cuts me off. "I know who you are, my dear. I've seen you in the memories of your father."

"What the hell did you do to him?" she asks, stalking forward, a scary looking black knife materializing in her hand.

Dreamer holds up his hands, palms out. "Patience, child. I didn't do anything to your father but try to help him. He was the one who was there when I first woke up. He actually smiled at me, and let me into his mind so I could learn about where I was, and what was happening. He pleaded my case to his superiors – he tried to convince them that I should be released, that they had no right to hold me, that I would never be a slave for them. He even threatened to let the secret out if they wouldn't help me.

"I put two of my shadows on him for protection, but couldn't stop it when they took him next door and broke his mind, something about that room blocked me from entering. They were livid with your father. He'd apparently been writing a letter to you, but it got lost and they could never find it. They got him hooked on heroin, and left him on the streets knowing no one would believe his tale.

"There was much commotion over the next weeks. They'd not only lost the letter to you, but a box with dangerous information in it.

"I tried desperately to keep his mind intact, but there was only so much I could do, trapped down there. I'm afraid the good man that was your father is gone. He loved you more than you could ever know."

"I think the letter wound up in the hands of a group of Yakuza gangsters in Las Vegas. It probably got delivered to them by mistake, and they sought you out," I say. "The box was stolen by the sleazy landlord her dad was renting from."

Jessica's eyes are watery and her face is completely shocked. All her life she'd figured her dad left her and her mom for some damned selfish reason or another: affair, better life without them, whatever. Turns out he tried to do the right thing and got smacked down for it. This is, unfortunately, the way of the world today: no good deed goes unpunished.

When Eve's phone rings, everyone jumps. Well, except for Dreamer, who doesn't seem to be the type to get flustered over much of anything. Eve's ring tone is "Sabotage" by the Beastie Boys, and it kind of seems to fit the situation.

Eve answers it, listens for moment and says, "Ok. We'll meet you at B."

She hangs up and tells us all, "There are 15 guys out in the lobby, the streets are blocked off at either end, and if we walk out there, they'll cut you all down like cattle."

I look around the room. The place is filled with corpses, and the still-smoking body of some damned thing. I should have guessed the response would be larger than just Saxton and two guys.

"So, we have a sawed-off shotgun with one flechette round left; a few MP5s with a couple magazines each; four flash-bang grenades; and body armor. I say we toss the flash-bangs, wait for them to go off and start shooting," I say.

"Yeah, great idea," Jessica says. "I've always wanted to get gunned down in some old building in New Mexico."

Jacob says, "She's right, you know. I want to go out in a blaze of glory, but this ain't the place, bro. They'll tear us apart and piss on the pieces."

"Well, ladies and gentlemen, it has been a real pleasure," Dreamer says, "but I'm afraid it's time I take my leave of you. Thank you very much and again, Jessica, I am truly sorry I could not save your father. He was a wonderful man, and he helped restore some of my faith in humanity. He loved you very much. Never forget that. Don't worry about the men in the lobby. I've been confined for too long and it's time I stretched my legs, so to speak."

I'd really like to say I had a great response to that but all I could muster was, "Thanks, man."

As he turns to leave, he pauses over Saxton's body. "Ah, Mr. Saxton. I see they've done their dirty work."

Then he casually opens the door, waves, steps through, and closes the door behind him. The walls are soundproofed, so the screams are distant and the gunfire sounds faded, like listening to a World War II movie from another room. It doesn't last long and a deafening silence soon descends again.

Out of curiosity, I walk over to Saxton's body. His face is shredded and he's not moving, but the blood that should be all over the place is missing, like it crawled back into his body or never left in the first place. Eve walks over and stands next to me, staring at him. She wrinkles her nose and grunts.

She simply says, "Odd" and then moves off to check on everyone else.

Unknown unknowns.

32 | New Beginnings

I cautiously open the door and look out on the scene of a slaughter. I can't tell how many people Dreamer caught, because there are pieces of them everywhere, indiscriminately torn limb from limb and tossed around the floor. The lobby is riddled with bullet holes and the whole place reeks of gun powder and the coppery smell of blood. They were all firing wildly in every direction, and managed to hit nothing.

A small part of me thinks, "My God, what have we done?" but I choke it down. Dreamer will tear across this country with a vengeance, destroying everything in his path. He never said it, but I have a feeling he won't limit his rage to the government that kept him locked up for long. If you're in his way, he'll rip you to pieces, and smile while he does it.

So why do I choke it down? Why do I have no desire to even attempt to stop him?

It's always easy to say it's the other guy's fault that things are not like you want them to be. It's easy to shut down the government and claim it's in everyone's best interest. It's always easy to place blame on the banal, and claim that's why your life is messed up. Just like all your failed relationships, the only common denominator in all your mistakes and your fucked-up life is you. You elected these people. You held your nose and voted for the lesser of two evils every damned time rather than rising up with a single voice and saying "We deserve better."

Well, now you're going to have the opportunity to make something better. Because I guarantee you the old system will be gone shortly and there will be a vacuum to fill. We'd better learn to put aside our petty differences and work together. We'd better learn to get over our childish fears. The coming weeks will be pivotal for this country, and we'd better learn to step up to the plate and swing with all our might, because if we don't, everything we've come to hold dear will never come back.

"Whoa," Jacob says as he looks around at the carnage. "I've been around weapons all my life, man, and I've never seen anything like this."

"Yeah," I add. "I can see how someone would want to weaponize this. Steal that guy's power and no one will fuck with you ever."

Jessica is looking a little green and leaning on me. I put an arm around her and she doesn't move it, so I guess we're all good.

"What the hell was that guy?" she asks.

"That, my dear," Eve says with a grin, "was the God of Dreams."

Jessica looks at her like Eve's gone mad. "Seriously, who was that?"

"I told you, the God of Dreams," Eve says. "I've always wondered what happened to him."

"Wait a minute," I say. "You knew that guy?"

"No, never met him, but I've heard about him."

I shake my head and wonder exactly what Eve's real plan in all this was. "You and I need to have a deep conversation someday," I tell her.

"You're a good guy, Steven, and I like you. Trust me on this, though, you're way out of your league here. Let it go, and this goes for everyone, pretend you never saw this because you all just met something you were never ever meant to meet."

"But…" I start.

"No buts. Let it go and hope this went unnoticed," Eve says, holding a finger in the air.

"How the hell is this supposed to go unnoticed?" Jacob asks.

"Unnoticed by the ones we want to avoid. They might not realize what happened and I'd like to keep it that way," Eve says.

Jessica stares at Eve, hypnotized like the huge woman is a cobra slowly dancing in front of her eyes. "You are one freaky chick," she finally tells Eve.

"You don't know the half of it, kiddo," Eve says.

We're all standing around in the lobby like a bunch of college freshmen, when a familiar voice sounds over the intercom. "You now have 10 minutes to evacuate the building before the explosives detonate." Eve's voice warning anyone left in the building to get the hell out. Hopefully people will listen.

"We need to leave. Now," Eve tells us. "I had Frank wire this place up over the past couple of nights."

We find the door out the back of the building that Mills used to go through. Jacob kicks it open and we hot foot to it meeting place B, which is our secondary meet-up place in the alley behind the PNM building. Frank's monstrous car is waiting for us, and he's casually leaning on the hood.

"You're just in time," he says, glancing at his watch.

He counts down quietly, three, two, and on one points two fingers toward the Simms building. There's a roar of thunder and a dense cloud of smoke and dust rises into the air. The whole building shudders and starts falling in on itself. Watching a building fall is a hypnotic thing. It's like the whole structure goes from solid to liquid in a moment, but it takes gravity time to figure out how to grab hold of it so it shudders like a bowl full of Jell-O before it splatters.

"I did some planning of my own," Eve says. "I don't know what else was at the bottom of that elevator, but now it's down there forever. If they had some way of stopping Dreamer hidden away down there in that basement, they're going to need some shovels to find it now."

The dust cloud from the collapse is sizable, and some gas line or another has ignited letting loose a hundred foot long tongue of flame into the air.

There are flames in the distance and smoke and dust all around us. The explosion triggered every car alarm in a four block radius and people are running around screaming about the apocalypse and terrorists and the END OF THE WORLD. Jessica starts giggling. The giggling gets more forceful and next thing I know she's into full-blown laughter. She must be letting off steam from this morning, because it's really not *that* funny.

Okay, it's kind of funny, but I'm the kind of person who likes to see the joke in everything. You want in on the joke? Here it is. No one, absolutely no one, will believe what happened here today. The rubble will clog the streets and make getting around in downtown Albuquerque even harder than normal. Someone will be cleaning it up for months to come. All kinds of people will use what happened today to further their own career and fuel their ambitions. A small group of people will make a gagillion dollars and a lot of people will get jobs cleaning up this mess.

Pretty soon I find myself chuckling along with Jessica.

Maybe someone will eventually put two and two together and build a memorial here. Doubtless it will be something maudlin and lifeless, a piece of art for art's sake that is representative of man's temporary nature. Or something.

Personally, I'd prefer a simple plaque that reads "Here's where it all ended, and here's where it all began."

33 | Last Breakfast

Frank's '65 Lincoln Continental is actually roomy enough to hold all five of us, with room for a soccer team in the trunk. They seriously don't make them like this anymore, which is unfortunate. This thing is like a reclining chair on wheels - no vibration from the road, no engine noise, just the smooth sensation of easy movement.

Jacob climbs in front, and immediately starts fiddling with the stereo looking for the one station that plays all Jacob music, all the time. I don't know if it exists, but if it's out there Jacob will eventually find it. In the interim we're treated to ten seconds of every popular song on the radio, and the occasional idiot blathering about Jesus. Frank just rolls his eyes and asks "Where to?"

Eve doesn't even stop to think about. "Waffle House, please."

"Yes, ma'am," he says cheerfully.

I'm starving and thirsty, and ready for some comfort food. While Waffle House will never be considered *haute cuisine*, there are times when you need a huge plate of greasy food and a gigantic stack of pancakes, and this is one of those times. "Balls to wall, man," I tell Frank.

"What is it with men and balls?" Jessica asks.

Frank drops the massive engine into gear and we motor toward Avenida Cesar Chavez.

"'Balls to the Wall' is a phrase from World War II," Jacob says. "Doesn't have anything to do with testicles."

"Yup," I say. "Fighters in World War II had throttles with spheres on them, probably to make them easier to grab. Anyway, when you pushed to the throttle all the way forward, the balls were at the wall."

As we're passing over the tracks we can hear the fire trucks and police converging downtown. There's a plume of smoke rising in the sky. "Hey," I ask, "can you find some news on the radio?"

So far there's only a smattering of panicked theories coming in. Terrorists hit Albuquerque. It was gangs. One guy even said it was God's punishment for our sins. Oddly, he's the closest to the truth. He's partially correct, just wrong on which god and why. I'm not sure

178

Dreamer cares about sins or even recognizes that they exist.

The Waffle House is its usual unironic self: heaps of food; gallons of coffee. The food is always edible, and the people are usually friendly. We get a table off to the side where it's relatively quiet, and order copious amounts of breakfast. While we're waiting, we sit drinking our coffee, quiet and contemplative. People all around us have that shocked look people get when they find out something bad has happened - but it didn't happen to them, and they're desperately trying to find a way to squeeze some sympathy out of someone because, damn, it was such a tragedy. The Waffle House isn't far from downtown, so news probably hit here pretty quickly. There's a little T.V. on the counter and everyone is watching it, even the cook.

The talking heads on the T.V. are proclaiming this to be a terrorist attack, probably by Muslim fundamentalists bent on hurting us because of our freedoms. Scattered reports are coming in about a swarthy man in a suit seen leaving the scene, but no one can seem to locate him. It's like he just disappeared.

I don't recall Dreamer being particularly swarthy, but maybe I just never saw him in good light.

When our food arrives, the waitress asks us if we had seen what happened. We confessed to being downtown and boogying out as quickly as we could. Because I'm a jerk sometimes, I tell her I heard it was Mormon separatists behind the bombing.

We could have also gone with the Muslim angle, but Muslims have a hard enough time in America as it is.

Before we dig in, Eve taps her spoon on her coffee cup in a universal sign that everyone needs to hush and listen. Everyone else in the restaurant is glued to the TV, so we've got a decent amount of privacy. She hands us each an envelope and tells us, thank you very much for the hard work.

Eve raises her coffee cup in a toast. "Gentlemen. And lady. To evil."

We all raise our cups and echo "To evil."

"Do you think he'll do what he said?" I ask.

"Probably," Eve replies, "but not necessarily out of any loyalty or desire to help us. I think his goals temporarily aligned with our goals and that's good enough. If it's any consolation, I think he was genuinely grateful, but I still wouldn't cross him if I were you."

"Did you know him?" I ask her.

"No. Never met him before this morning," she says, sipping her coffee. "I've heard of him, though. He vanished sometime in the 30s and no one knew what happened. Now we know."

"What did he mean when he asked if you chose that thing?" Jessica asks.

"Don't worry about it," Eve replies. "It's neither your concern nor your business. Well, friends. That's it. We've set the events in motion that will change the world. In each of those envelopes is a new identity and a bank account with ten million dollars in it. It's been a pleasure working with you all."

"Where are you going?" Frank asks her.

"I'm just going to take a walk," she says. "I'd like to see what happens now first-hand. What about you all?"

"I've got a place up in Hesperus that I'm going to retire to for a spell," I say. "It's quiet; the neighbors are far enough away to be out of my hair. I miss the mountains."

Jacob finishes his coffee and pours something brown in his glass from a flask. "I think it's time to get serious about JAMCAO. I'm gonna head down south and see what I can find."

"I'm going to drive across the country," Frank says. "I've got a comfortable car and a full supply of truck-driver songs."

"And plenty of money to put gas in that beast now." I quip.

"I don't know what I'm going to do," Jessica says. She looks at me. "Maybe I'll go back to California, or a nice beach somewhere quiet."

"Send me a postcard," I tell her.

"Jessica," Jacob says. "Can you ride a motorcycle?"

"Of course," She says. "What kind of loser do you take me for?"

I'd just like to point out; I don't know how to ride a motorcycle. Oh, well. I've got plenty of time to learn now.

"Just making sure," Jacob says. "You saved my life back there. That guy would've plugged me without thinking about it. I want you to have this." He takes off his JAMCAO jacket and hands it to her. It's about four sizes too big, but it's the thought that counts.

I cover the tab. Frank covers the tip. We all go our separate ways.

For now.

34 | Hesperus, Epilogue

Dreamer was as good as his word. It took a while, but he finally made it to Washington, D.C. and laid waste to everything. He wasn't exactly quiet moving across the country, either. He hit a church in Kansas, literally flattened the place, and filled the heads of the adults with utterly terrifying dreams. He refuses to hurt kids, though.

He's become something of a messiah figure, travelling across the land. Sometimes destroying random things, sometimes building other things. I can't see the rhyme or reason, but I'm not a god, so what do I know?

Congress went on paid vacation after they shut down the government this time, but he made enough noise that they decided to get back together again in a special joint session to decide just what was to be done about this dangerous new terrorist. Even up until the end, they called him a terrorist. It was like their tiny little minds couldn't comprehend a danger that wasn't a terrorist. Whatever they wanted to call him, he was waiting for them when they met again.

He shredded both the House and the Senate. They meet on opposite sides of the Capitol Building and he somehow managed to take out both of them at the same time. He'd told me he'd been a weapon before, but I never suspected how effective he'd be. His shadows swarmed over them, buried them in the dark dreams of their own karma. Some fell to their knees and proclaimed him god. Some clawed their own eyes out, trying in vain to get the visions out of their heads. He flared into shapes out of nightmares and tore people limb from limb.

One senator's aide, a pretty young brunette, tried to run away, but he'd just flicker and be right in front of her whenever she thought she was safe, like a predator playing with his food. She'd turn and run one way and he'd flicker and be waiting for her when turned around. She'd turn to run the other way and he'd flicker and be there, too.

To say he moved like the flicker men is like saying a first-year dance student moves like a professional ballerina: sure, they're both doing basically the same thing. But one is graceful and effortless, while the other has to think about it. He chased her through the madness, and finally casually tore her throat out when he got tired of the game. CSPAN covered the whole thing, since they were on-site for the special Congressional meeting. When it was over the only members of Congress still alive were the ones who swore fealty to him. Then he slaughtered them, too. It was pretty brutal. I couldn't even finish my popcorn while I was watching it.

Considering Congress's approval ratings in the polls, it was unsurprising that the majority of the people didn't have much of a problem with this.

This left the country in something of a lurch. Our system has always been based on the checks and balances provided by the legislative, executive and judicial branches, and now the entire legislative branch of the government was gone. To make things even more interesting, no one in the government had a contingency plan about what should happen if all of Congress was suddenly wiped out. I think they all assumed if the entire legislative branch were to fall, the entire government would collapse. It didn't exactly turn out that way, and there are already greedy assholes all over the country lining up to run in the upcoming special elections.

Thing is, though, there doesn't seem to be a whole lot of interest among the people for actually going to the polls and, you know, voting for any of these guys. It's like a couple of months without hearing about how Congress had screwed up this, that, or the other thing, was like a breath of fresh air. It'll get reformed eventually, but it's been a pleasant time without them.

We didn't quite get anarchy in the streets, which is what I was personally hoping for. Instead, we found regular people could come together for a brief time and take over the running of the country. It was like everyone woke up, and realized they needed to do something other than watch T.V. and complain about things. With any luck, the running of the country will remain in the hands of regular people. Of course, regular people are just as greedy and vulnerable as some of the old families, so we'll have to see how it turns out.

Dreamer's still in D.C. somewhere, though, and everyone knows it. To some he's a hero. To others, he's a villain. So it goes. Every place he went dreams become slightly more real and reality becomes slightly more dreamy. It's difficult to describe. In places where he really went wild, reality became softer, and the dream world took root.

The section of Albuquerque where he tore through Saxton's men is completely sealed off. Actually, the whole damn downtown is sealed off.

For all the sealing-off, things still sneak out from time to time - which isn't terribly surprising. How do you hold in dreams, anyway? Fortunately, the things that sneak out don't last too long. Personally, I think his dreams can't hold themselves together in reality for very long.

D.C. was another matter entirely. He's physically there and the dream world is much closer to the real world. The military has what's left of the city surrounded, and is actively shooting anyone who tries to enter, and anyone or anything that tries to leave. The "important" people were evacuated shortly after the incident, leaving behind only the regular citizens, and no one in government seems to care about them. They've been completely written off, kind of like they were before this whole unpleasantness.

There are rumors of things, half-hidden in the shadows of D.C.

At first the military was more than happy to try to help people escaping, but that all came crashing to a halt when things that looked like people started trying to get out, too. What looked like a woman carrying a baby turned into something horrifying, all teeth and no eyes and it tore three soldiers in half before they took it down with a flame-thrower

Twisted and horrible things, reeking of ill-gotten power and madness stalk the city. At first I had assumed these were just itinerant politicians, but it turns out that may not be the case. Every now and then someone will make a break for the border, and if the military doesn't cut them down, something will wrap around them and drag them screaming back into the ruins of the city.

A couple of teams have been sent in to find out what's happening, but they never make it back out. The last team made it a full half-hour before the surrounding military force reported things coming out of the mist. Gunfire, screams, silence. I understand they're working on sending in some of the newer land-based drones now. We'll see how long those last.

The scary thing about D.C. is the area of... infection? seems to be spreading. Every day, the military has to pull back a little bit. I suspect Dreamer has established his new home there. It was never what you would call a happy city. A lot of bad things have happened there, so I imagine the dreams there are delicious.

I've spent some time researching exactly what Dreamer is. This is not as easy as you would think it would be. In this era we're used to having all information right at our fingertips, but there's very little legitimate information on him out there. Oh, sure, there are plenty of fanboi-type websites dedicated to Dreamer, and a whole slew of charlatans who just made some stuff up and are trying to cash in on it.

There's very little in the way of hard evidence. Snopes.com is way out of their league when it comes to things like this, although Snopes was the only group that managed to figure out where Dreamer first appeared. Hint: It was Albuquerque, NM. (Not the Moon, as some have speculated.)

All I've managed to find out so far has come from hitting libraries, and a crazy used book store in Durango. Libraries, in these days of the Information Superhighway (never thought you'd hear that term again, did you?), have fallen out of fashion, but they're still the go-to place for any kind of original research. A lot of the books in the world have been digitized, their contents digested into pulpy zeroes and one, and placed on the Internet, but most of the world's books are still only available in good, old-fashioned paper. The best books are always hidden away in some backwater library, relegated to the dusty parts of the stacks that no one goes into anymore except for the kids looking for some private time.

I now have library cards at half a dozen libraries in towns around here and the enmity of a bunch of teenagers who just wanted to get laid in a library.

It took me several days of searching the Southwest Book Trader in Durango, Colorado, but I finally located a book on dreams that wasn't written by a hippie. There's not much about Dreamer directly, but apparently some of the local tribes worshipped a "handsomely outfitted" gentleman who could control dreams. He got completely out of control, and they managed to stop him or at least drive him off somehow. Unfortunately the book didn't know how. Those same tribes are usually excellent at remembering things, so someone still knows how. Even then they couldn't decide if he was a hero or a villain.

Here's what I think: Evil is that thing that we don't want to happen to us. If it happens to someone else, someone we don't agree with, though, it's justice.

I've managed to keep in touch with almost everyone in our old group.

Jacob is running a biker gang - shit, *motorcycle club,* down in Las Cruces. They've apparently been running guns up and down through Mexico, probably for Mr. Smith. Jacob's MC has grown to about ten guys, most of whom are serious about being bikers. They nearly gutted one guy out when they found out he was an accountant, but the accountant won the fight and got to stay. He must have been one tough hombre; he had to fight two other members of the MC to stay in. I think I'll look that guy up if I ever file taxes again.

Frank is up in the Pacific Northwest somewhere, breaking into random buildings for the hell of it. We email back and forth every now and then. He's bored. He's tasted too much of the exciting life to ever be happy being normal. We're planning a heist for the spring, for old time's sake.

No one's heard from Eve since she walked out the door of the Waffle House. I keep having this feeling I'll wake up one morning and she'll be sacked out on my couch, and all my beer will be gone.

I actually got a postcard from Jessica not too long ago. It was addressed to Scratty McNutty, Hesperus, CO. It's mute testimony to the size of this community that the postcard made it to me. She's living on the beach somewhere in the Baja peninsula and misses green chile cheeseburgers. The front of the postcard was a picture of her in a black bikini. Well played, Jessica. Well played.

Saxton was on the news last night spreading pictures of me all over the damned place, and accusing me of associating with some terrorist organization. I honestly don't know how he's still alive. I've shot that bastard in the face twice, and Jacob and Frank both dropped buildings on him, and yet he keeps coming back. Next time we meet, I'm taking his head home with me.

Three months have passed, and my little house outside of Hesperus is nice and cozy. Fall has turned the forest into an explosion of colors that rivals any Fourth of July display. At night I can see the stars again. I hadn't realized how much I missed the stars.

My neighbors, such as they are, don't know what I've done. I suspect they'd approve anyway. People move to places like this to get away not only from other people, but for a chance to feel like they're free of governments and rules. They want to barbeque and shoot things and not worry about consequences. I love them all.

It's a simpler life, and I really like it, but I've got a feeling I shouldn't get too used to it.

About the Author

Eric Lahti is a programmer, database engineer, and Kenpo practitioner living in Albuquerque, New Mexico. He enjoys martial arts, coding, and writing. *Henchmen* was his first novel, followed about a year later by *Arise*. His third, *The Clock Man* – a collection of stories that really aren't all that short – is scheduled for release in late 2015.

You can also visit him online at ericlahti.com

Thank you very much for reading *Henchmen*, I hope you enjoyed it.

Preview of Arise, Part 2 of the Henchmen Saga

1 | I Hate Visitors

Where were you when *it* happened?

This is the current question of the day from almost anyone you meet. No one needs to ask "when what happened?" because we all know what the asker is talking about.

It's used as an ice breaker, like asking what someone's major was or their sign is. It can be a challenge: Where were *you* when it happened? It can also be a straightforward question, a way to find out about someone.

People still remember exactly where they were, kind of like a lot of people still remember exactly where they were when they found out Elvis was dead (I was six, riding in a car with my mom and asking who is Elvis?) or when the towers came crashing down.

Your answer gives you a certain amount of street cred. If you say you were in Albuquerque, people act you're a returning war hero and ask you if you're OK. I actually met someone who was in the building when it all went down and barely escaped before the building collapsed. He was telling the story to people in some bar in Durango and was getting a lot of mileage, and drinks, out of it. I had to leave before I laughed out loud when he told everyone how he had the beast cornered and would have been able to stop the whole thing if those damned government agents hadn't screwed the whole thing up.

If you say you were in D.C., people treat you like a refugee from some genocide in Africa. If you were in Colorado, you're less of a hero, but all those southwestern states are, like, right next to each other, right? If you were in Texas you get to act like you could have stopped the whole thing with your trusty six shooter. Albuquerque gives you the best props, D.C. is a close second. You lose more and more cred the further away you were from either of those places. If you say you were in Minneapolis no one gives a rat's ass.

I was at ground zero, riding up an elevator with a demigoddess on one side and Dreamer on the other, hoping to hell I didn't get shot when the doors opened.

I don't bring this up.

Most people shed nary a tear over the death of everyone in Congress. Someone went so far, probably someone on 4chan, to put up a picture of everyone in the House dead and dismembered with the caption "You can't spell slaughter without laughter." The idea of killing Congress still brings a smile to a lot of faces, but the actuality of killing Congress still terrifies and enrages.

I still get a chuckle out of it, but I'm kind of a dick that way.

* * * *

Sometimes, I can feel Dreamer in my head. I'm beginning to wonder if it was a mistake to let him in. He's not exactly there there, but he's definitely there. That probably doesn't make much sense. Oh, well. I don't know if I can explain it more succinctly than this: I had a God in my head and my thoughts are still kind of tainted by his thoughts. My dreams are extremely vivid. For about a month after we let him out, I felt like I wasn't sleeping. It felt more like I would go to sleep and immediately wake up somewhere else as someone else.

Yeah. Pretty disorienting.

It took a while, but I finally realized I was jumping in and out of other people's dreams. Once I got that, it made more sense and I could relax into the situation. The end result was I got to get some meaningful sleep because I started shutting off my brain and treating the whole process as a movie, even if it was someone else's reality I was watching. In time, I learned to control the dream. That was always something I'd wanted to learn to do, anyway, and the results were pretty awesome. I found I could jump between people's dreams and ride along or change them to suit my own needs. It was a total rush, even if I couldn't control whose dreams I was watching.

Most of the time people's dreams are pretty bland: sitting at a desk working, fantasizing about the new secretary, driving a fast car, whatever. Every now and then I'd hit a nightmare. There are people out there who can dream up some pretty tweaked shit. I once came across someone who spent the night dreaming about dismembering prostitutes while she (the dreamer, not the prostitute) was dressed in an SS uniform. I slipped into someone dreaming in North Korea and woke up devastated. This kid was dreaming of finding ways to rat out his fellow prisoners so he could eat some more food. You know you're fucked when you're dreaming about getting other people killed so you can eat a bit more gruel. We should nuke that hermit kingdom and be done with it. It would be an act of pity for the people stuck living there and an act of revenge for their leaders.

Of course, there is the philosophy that holds that all reality is someone else's dream, so maybe my sleep and wake times are really just someone else's dreams.

* * * *

Hesperus, Colorado was gorgeous this winter. We got the kind of snow that buries all the evil in the world and makes you think there's nothing wrong. It was the perfect place to dream.

It's spring now, so the worst of the snow has melted off, but there's still plenty on the ground. The snow isn't so deep that you can't travel, but it's deep enough that the tourists stay away. The air is crisp and clear in the mornings. It's so quiet I can hear someone breathing from across the room so I don't even have to open my eyes to know I'm not alone and it doesn't surprise me in the slightest when a familiar voice says, "Good morning, sunshine."

"Fuck you, asshole," I reply. "I need some coffee before I deal with you."

Wilford Saxton is sitting across the room from me, holding my gun. He's wearing his traditional business casual attire: suit, no tie, semi-dress shoes. The last time I saw this man in the flesh he was lying in a pool of someone else's blood with a whole whack of tiny arrows in his head. That was the second time I'd shot him in the face. It was also the second time someone had dropped a building on him. Yet, here he is, not a scar on him. Not a hair out of place or a wrinkle in sight, either.

"What makes you think I'm not here to kill you or arrest you?" he asks.

"If you wanted me dead, you would've shot me while I was still sleeping. If you were going to arrest me, you wouldn't wait patiently for me to wake up. You're alone in here and not wearing your ID badge. You want something. Let me get some coffee and we'll talk." I tell him.

"Well, well, well," he says and then sighs. "You're still a regular Sherlock Holmes, aren't you?"

"Can you go somewhere else? Really, anywhere would do."

I slide out of my nice warm bed. It's not freezing all the time anymore, but it's still damned chilly in the mornings. When my feet hit the tile floor it's like sticking them in a freezer. Damn. I need to invest in heated floors one of these days.

"So, Captain Willard, why aren't you dead?" I ask.

"How many times do I have to tell you? I'm not a captain and my name's not Willard."

I sigh and look around for some socks and a warmer shirt. I find some socks that don't match – left is red, right is gray - and a sweatshirt with a three-eyed smiley face and "Mutants for a Nuclear America" written on it.

"That looks like a hell of a party you had last night." Saxton says.

"What party?" I ask.

"Really, Steven, I'm not an idiot. You're a neat-freak and there are beer cans all over the floor in your living room."

"You're the neat freak. I'm organized." I say. "What beer cans?"

"The ones all over the floor downstairs. I always thought you were one of those snooty bastards who only drank small batch beers made by hippies. I may have to adjust my opinion of you up a few notches. That was no small amount of MGD you put down last night. What was it, almost a case?"

For the record, life is too short to drink mass produced beer. It doesn't necessarily need to be made by hippies, but good beer needs to be made by people who care about beer. I don't think Miller Genuine Draft counts, and I've never cared for or bought the stuff.

Also for the record, Wilford Saxton is an ass.

"Can I have my gun back?" I ask him.

He tosses it to me and I check and make sure it's still loaded. My little buddy the .45 Detonics Combat Master still has rounds.

"What's going on, Steven?" He can sense that I'm nervous and he's got his own gun out now. We may not always get along, and I did once swear to take his head, but we worked together for a long time and have learned to read other. To be fair, I was peckish when I swore to cut off his head and I get pretty grumpy when I get hungry. Also to be fair, I'm going to take his head.

"I don't know, but I do know I don't drink Miller. Someone else is in here." I tell him.

When I hear the toilet down the hall flush and the sink come on I relax a bit. People may be crazy and violent, but they usually don't waste time flushing the toilet and washing their hands when they break into your house to kill you.

A seven foot tall woman saunters down the hall and stops to stare at us. She's wearing a pair of men's sweats that barely make it to her calves and a Ministry T-Shirt. The opposite pair of my socks cover her feet; red on the right, gray on the left.

"Two questions: why are you guys holding guns and where's the coffee?"

Eve's eyes are red rimmed and her hair is mussed up. Apparently a case of MGD has the same effect on demi goddesses that it does on everyone else. It may taste like ass going down, but the hangover is spectacular.

"Hi, Eve," I say, lowering my gun. "You remember Wilford Saxton, you slammed his face into jail cell and I shot him in the head. We dropped a couple of buildings on him."

Eve peers at Saxton and recognition slowly penetrates her stupor. "Oh. Hi," she says and punches him.